Growing Acclaim
for
Going Green,
prequel to
Greener

Heather S. Ransom

"Ransom's appealing futuristic parable dives deep into issues of class privilege, inequality, and genetic modification. Sounds heavy, but she lightens the mood with clever tech and a sweet, star-crossed teen romance."

-Karen Eisenbrey,
author of *Daughter of Magic*

"*Going Green* is a confident, richly conceived and immensely readable debut where unlikely hope grows like grass punching through the cracks of an oppressive system. ...Ransom is a welcome new voice, one that rings true and clear with impressive scope and unexpected emotion."

-Dale E. Basye,
author of the *Circles of Heck* series

Greener

Heather S. Ransom

Published in the United States by
Not a Pipe Publishing, Independence, Oregon.
www.NotAPipePublishing.com
Cover Art by Randy Kintz and Marcus Odom
Cover Design by Kevin Snyder

Trade Paperback Edition

ISBN-13: 978-1-948120-18-0

Dedication

For my sister, Katie.
I won't cry because your story is over,
only because each page was so beautifully written.

Greener

Chapter 1

I'd never get used to seeing dead bodies. Glancing back down at the news tablet embedded in a study table at the University of SciCity, I reread the article title – "Black Market Operations Take Lives of Two More Teens." The accompanying picture, projected above the table in three-dimensional form, allowed me to see it from every direction.

They were just kids. Shuddering, I focused on the small piece in my ear, thinking, `Connect to digital news`, so I could listen to the story.

Two teenage girls, both fifteen, three years under the legal age for applying for Green Citizenship. Their bodies dumped in a deserted warehouse outside of SciCity. Their skin blackened and marbled with green, but not the healthy glow of Green citizens. Something unnatural.

I swallowed hard, looking again at the picture. Faces bloated, eyes bulging, tongues protruding, lips swollen, skin cracked. I felt nauseous.

Turning away, I shook my head. Some sick egomaniac taking advantage of more teens. At least a dozen kids had shown up the same way over the last couple of months after turning to unlicensed "doctors" for Green Enhancement surgery.

Touching the table top, I adjusted the picture and scrolled through the article, bringing up current related stories as well. This wasn't just happening here in New America. Youth in Eurasia were buying into the phony medical procedures as well.

Swiping back to my original article, I scrolled through the text with the picture still hovering above it. *Where were these girls' families? How had this happened? Why hadn't someone protected them?*

I closed my eyes and thought about the talk I'd heard around campus lately among some of the Greens. That these "incidents" were just kids from non-Green families who didn't really understand the process. Bad genetics – it would "clean out the gene pool." Clenching my jaw, I remembered several of those conversations ending in heated arguments.

These were humans dying here, and regardless of the color of their skin, they were just kids. Girls with hopes and dreams.

I was about to close the app when something further down the page caught my eye. The girls were "daughters of local farmers outside of SciCity," and that something "really had to be done to help the children of non-Green citizens learn to accept their place and role in our society." That "not everyone was meant to be Green." I shook my head. Not everyone was meant to be Green, but not for the reasons implied. There was a whole other life out there, one that didn't require you to be Green to be successful, accepted, loved – happy.

I smiled as I thought about my time on the Stayton farm. It seemed like a lifetime ago.

Suddenly, my smile dropped as I took a sharp breath. My heart stopped. In fact, the whole world around me stopped.

Play last section, I directed my iBud, not believing what my eyes were reading. Then I replayed it four more times, my hands covering my nose and my mouth.

"No," I whispered, my hands dropping to my lap.

"No." This time a little louder. I could hear my voice, but it didn't sound like me.

"No!" I jerked up, almost stumbling over the bench behind me.

This had to be wrong. The article had to be wrong. It couldn't have been her. Someone had to have made a mistake

But deep inside, I knew they hadn't. I had that awful feeling in the pit of my stomach, the one I always got when I knew something bad had happened that could never be fixed.

Chapter 2

"Not Ana," I said, tears now streaming down my cheeks. Then I turned and ran toward the door.

I didn't remember reaching my car or even getting on the highway. Heading for the Stayton farm, I wasn't sure what I was going to say when I got there.

I stared at the road ahead of me, not really focusing on anything. The tears stopped, and I felt numb.

Eight months, I thought. *I haven't been back in over eight months.* How different my life had been then, before I was Green. I'd been naïve – hopeful – ignorant. It had been beautiful. And devastating.

Memories flooded back, pictures flashing through my mind.

Gabe, so smart but annoying, until I'd fallen in love with him.

Nana Jane, the grandma I'd never had who taught me to love cooking and to slow down to appreciate the little things around me.

Andrew, a father who loved his family, opened his home to a city girl who didn't even know just how lost and unhappy she was.

Ben, the little brother with his deep, serious eyes and quiet soul.

And Ana. She'd taught me about being a real sister. Sassy, spunky, and so desperate, so passionate about wanting to go Green. *Oh, Ana.* Now she'd never have the chance.

"Why?" I yelled, my voice booming through the silent car. I couldn't wrap my mind around it. She only had a few more years to wait. I'd told her I'd make sure she was scholarshipped if it was something she still really wanted when she turned eighteen. *Why did she do it? Why would she have been so stupid?*

Maybe if I'd come back to the farm, if I'd stayed in touch with her, if I'd invited her to the city over the summer like I'd told her I would – if – if –

But I couldn't have gone back, even though I'd wanted to.

Once again, the thoughts tumbled through my mind. Moments racing, memories colliding, all leading to the unforeseeable events that forced me back to the city. Finding out that Gabe's best friend, Gunner, was a rebel. Learning that what I thought I knew about the rebels was seriously flawed, as well as what I thought I knew about the corporations, the security enforcers, the city. And then the explosion at the farm, knowing that going back there would put everyone in danger again.

My eyes had been opened. Life was not simple. Not black and white. The choices weren't easy, but they were necessary.

I'd understood that. But Ana hadn't. She'd thought I'd chosen the city over the farm, the Green life over her family. I'd tried to explain.

But maybe I hadn't tried hard enough. She was only fifteen. Only fifteen. Maybe if I had done something more, she'd still be – be – alive. Fresh tears streamed down my cheeks.

I should have brought her to the city to stay with me for the summer, I thought. But just as quickly, I recognized that hadn't really been a possibility. Back in the city, my family had needed me. I didn't know what we'd have done if we'd lost Livvy to the mutated virus after she'd been infected. I'd had to do everything I could to make sure my sister would survive. It was the Staytons who had showed me that – that family had to come first. It had been a long, slow process, and Livvy still wasn't well. It wouldn't have been a good place for a young, vibrant teen, looking for a fun-filled, exciting summer adventure.

And any of my time not spent with Livvy was spent trying to gather facts, to discover who was lying and why, to piece together what I could find about a major cover-up concerning the deaths of two people that I had witnessed. I hadn't been sure who to trust, who was involved – the security enforcers, the government, the rebels, the big genetic engineering corporations – maybe a combination of all of them. I used my new intern position at AHGA to search for answers in a way that wouldn't draw too much attention to me. I never could have gotten Ana involved in the work I was still doing.

I didn't know how to explain to her that our beautiful, wonderful city was no longer simple. That we couldn't look at people as Greens or non-Greens anymore. That there were good and bad people, brilliant and ignorant minds, kind and malicious intentions from both Green citizens and those who had chosen not to go Green. Assumptions based on skin color were misleading. Ana was so fixated with the idea that "going Green" would make her life everything she wanted. Just like I had been. I didn't know how to explain everything I'd learned. And experienced. And felt.

Or maybe I just didn't take the time. Another sob. More tears burned my eyes.

I wanted to think that by leaving her alone, leaving all of them alone on the Stayton farm, that I was helping them. Keeping them safe. Protecting them. But now – Ana –

Was there something I could have done? Something I should have done?

The questions continued as I pulled up to the farm. It looked just like I remembered it, except the soft yellow house was now an earthy tan, probably to cover the blast marks that had scarred the wood around the front door after the explosion.

I got out and walked toward the front porch. As I reached the steps, the front door opened.

Gabe. I saw surprise flash across his face, then it went neutral. He didn't step out or even say a word. He just stood there. I could feel the tears welling up in my eyes again.

"Gabe, I, umm ... I wanted–"

He cut me off. "I don't care what you want. You're not welcome here, Calyssa."

Then he slammed the door shut.

Chapter 3

I stood there in shock, frozen on the steps. I'd known Gabe would be upset, but – why had he slammed the door on me? I'd cared about Ana, too.

A few seconds later, the front door opened again. Nana Jane. Her face was pink and splotchy. Her puffy eyes no longer held that magical twinkle that I'd loved so much. She stepped onto the porch and held out her arms to me.

I ran up the last two steps and threw myself at her. We clung to each other and cried. I'm not sure how long we stayed like that. Just holding each other.

Feeling a tug on my jacket, I looked down.

"Hello, Ben," I said softly, tears still rolling down my cheeks. Nana Jane stepped back, and I bent over to be eye level with him.

"Hello, Calyssa," he whispered. "Ana went to live with our mom and the angels." Then he dropped his chin, looking away from me.

"I know, Ben, and I'm so sorry." I placed my hand on his shoulder, and he leaned against me. Slowly, I slid my hand down his arm and gave him a little squeeze. Ben didn't like to be touched. But once, he had hugged me. He didn't hug me today, but he didn't pull away either. I gently ran my fingers through his soft, brown hair.

He stepped away and went back into the house without another word. Nana Jane and I watched as the front door closed. She looked at me, starting to say something, but stopped.

I turned back toward the stairs. "I don't have to go in the house. Gabe's inside. I already saw him. I don't think he wants me here." More tears.

Nana reached out, placing her hand on my arm. "We're all hurting, and we each have to handle it in our own way. Gabe feels responsible. It isn't going to be easy. Not for a long time. But we're family. We'll make it through this. And that includes you, Calyssa."

Pulling me toward her, she touched the side of my face, and I fell into her arms again.

"I am so, so sorry, Nana Jane. So sorry." I sobbed into her shoulder.

"So am I, Sweetie." Then she stepped back and wiped at the tears on her cheeks. "Let's go inside and warm up. Andrew should be back in a few minutes. He got called out to the barn, but I know he'd like to see you."

I looked warily toward the front door. Part of me understood the pain that came with loss. I was still overwhelmed at times thinking about losing my mom even though it happened years ago. But part of me was ticked off that he would just shut me out. I loved Ana, too. Even though Gabe and I were no longer together, that didn't just erase the time I had spent here with his family and the memories we'd shared.

Nana Jane took my hand and led me through the door. The rush of the heat combined with the familiar smells caused me to pause just inside. I closed my eyes and remembered a different time – Ana's laugh, the touch of her hand on my shoulder, the sound of her violin and my cello as we'd played together for the family. Our family. For that one week, they'd been my family, too.

I had to reach out to steady myself against the wall. It was overwhelming. I kept expecting Ana to walk around the corner any second, saying, "Seriously, it's just a joke. I'm fine. Let's go ride the horses. Quick, before Nana wants us to help in the kitchen." Then she'd smile that mischievous grin, and we'd dart out of the house to the barn.

But there was just silence. I followed Nana into the family room and we sat down, me on the couch, her on her old-fashioned, wooden rocking chair.

"We've missed you, Calyssa. It's been, what, six or seven months since we've seen you?"

"Eight, actually," I said, sniffling.

"How's your sister doing?"

"Livvy's better. Not great, but better than the last time I was here. They still can't seem to figure out exactly what is happening to her cells, but at least it seems to be slowing down. With so many Greens being infected over the past few months, Father has designated it as a top priority for AHGA. They're doing everything they can to stop the virus."

"It's good to hear that she's doing better. We've all been worried about you."

"I'm really sorry, Nana. That I haven't been back. I feel awful. I kept thinking about coming by, but then I'd remember what happened last time I was here."

She hesitated. "The explosion scared all of us. I can see how that would frighten you, make you worry that it might happen again. We never did figure it out. Security enforcers blamed the rebels, the rebels blamed the security enforcers. It was a real mess. And with Andrew in the hospital, it was pretty chaotic for a few months." Nana's small, weathered hands sat wringing in her lap, twisting and turning as she spoke.

Looking at her, I realized she was nervous.

What? Why?

And then it dawned on me: she'd thought I hadn't been back to the farm for all these months because I blamed them for the explosion because it happened here on their farm. Which couldn't be further from the truth.

Moving to the edge of the couch, I leaned forward. "Nana, I should have told you this before. I know the explosion wasn't your fault. It had nothing to do with any of you. It was because of me. That's why I haven't come back, or called, or tried to contact you. I probably shouldn't even be here today. I've been afraid that something bad would happen to all of you because of me. I'm so sorry that I brought 'Green issues' into your home. Andrew and Ben being injured, the damage to your house, the mess with the authorities ... it's all my fault. I'm so sorry." Tears. Again.

"Hello, Calyssa." A deep voice.

Walking over and sitting next to me, Andrew continued, "Honey, we don't hold you responsible for what happened here, so you can't blame yourself either. Things happen in life. Good and bad. All we can do is choose how we'll react to them. You didn't choose for the explosion to happen at our house, did you?"

I quickly shook my head, not willing to trust my voice, afraid I might start sobbing again.

"Well then, all we can do is move on the best we can. A new door, some new paint, a few repairs to the front porch, and the house is fine. I'm happy you've come back to see us."

They were so amazing. I knew that what had happened here was my fault. Both Father and Jaxx, the head of security at AHGA, had told me as much. But the Staytons still cared about me.

"You know, Andrew, I still regret it sometimes. That I didn't just stay here with you all. What you share is incredible. Your life, your family, your ..." I looked away. I didn't know how to tell him that what I had experienced here was perfect. Until I had made a mess of their lives.

Placing his hand on my arm, Andrew said, "My father used to say to me, 'It's always greener on the other side of the fence.' I don't think I understood what that truly meant until I was an adult. Every family has its own strengths ...

and faults." Then he looked up at the picture of Ana on the mantle. I felt my heart break for him. His only daughter was gone.

"I'm so sorry about Ana. I know that doesn't help. It doesn't change anything or make it any better, but I want you to know how sorry I am."

His frown deepened, and he nodded slowly, his eyes downcast. When he looked up, they held tears. "Thank you. I know you loved her, too."

I leaned over, reaching my arms around him. He hugged me back, our sorrow enveloping us together.

When I sat back, his face looked worn. "We've all lost loved ones, haven't we? It never gets any easier. At least we know that Ana is with her mom. And your mom. We'll see them one day again."

"Really? So typical." Gabe stood at the entrance to the room, rage seeping out of him. His body rigid, fists clenched, scowl embedded, he continued in his harsh tone, "You got to say your piece so you can feel better about yourself. Take your lies and fake tears. We don't need them or want them. Now get out of our house."

Chapter 4

"Gabe!" Nana Jane and Andrew snapped in unison, both standing up.

"That's enough," Andrew continued gruffly. "You will not be rude in my house. Calyssa is—"

"Don't you say she's our family. Or even a guest in our house." Gabe's eyes were wild, the volume of his voice continuing to rise as he spoke. "We all know Ana worshipped her. 'Lyssa this' and 'Lyssa that.' Always talking about them being Green together and what it would be like."

"Gabe, I said that's enough." Andrew interjected. His voice was low, but I could tell he meant business.

"No, Dad. I won't stop. Not when what I'm saying is true. Ana worshipped her and then Calyssa walked out on her. Left her. Crushed her—"

"Stop, Gabe." This time it was Nana Jane who interrupted him.

What had he meant? Crushed her? I'd crushed Ana?

"Gabe, I loved Ana! You know that! She was like a sister to me!" I stood, yelling, surprising myself and startling everyone else as well.

"You're full of crap, Calyssa! The only person you truly love is you! Just because you say you love someone doesn't make it true. Actions speak louder than words, and despite your words you haven't been anywhere around for the last eight months!" Gabe lunged across the room, and Andrew stepped in front of him just before he reached me.

"I said enough, Son." His voice was softer this time and he placed his hand on Gabe's shoulder. Gabe shrugged it off and stepped to the side.

"Maybe, just once, could you show a little emotion, Dad? Get mad about something? Like your only daughter dying trying to become like her?" Gabe shook his hand accusingly toward me. "Ana wanted to be like her more than she wanted to be with us, Dad. Even if it meant killing herself."

In an instant, Nana Jane was in front of Gabe, and then in the next, she slapped him across the face.

Reaching for his cheek, he stepped away, a look of shock in his eyes.

Tears trailed down Nana's cheeks, but her voice was like steel. "I never want to hear those words come out of your mouth again. Your sister did not know what she was doing. She was only fifteen."

Andrew placed his hand on Nana's arm as Gabe continued to back away from them. "Jane, it's okay. He's hurting, too, and he's not thinking about what he's saying."

"Gabe, I ... Gabe ..." I didn't know what to say to make any of this better.

"Forget it, Calyssa. You got what you wanted. The Staytons love you. Everything is great here at the farm. Life is merry as usual. Does your conscience feel better now? Can you finally get the hell out of our house and go back to your own?" One last hatred-filled glare, then Gabe turned and left the room. A few seconds later, a door slammed.

I stood there in shock. Was Gabe right? Had Ana done what she had *because* of me? Because she wanted to be like me so much she felt she had no other choice? I felt the room closing in on me. I couldn't breathe. My heart was beating so hard my chest hurt.

"Calyssa?" Andrew was trying to steady me.

When I turned and looked into his eyes, I saw my answer. The immense pain. The uncontrollable grief. And somewhere deep in those dark brown eyes, I saw it. That little bit of blame. Because he knew that at least part of what Gabe was saying was true. He had let me into their home. Let me become a part of their family. Let Ana love me. And, maybe he could have stopped it. But he hadn't. And now she was dead.

I stepped away from him. Walking toward the door, I said, "I have to ... go ... I have to get back home ... I'm sorry to have bothered all of you ... truly sorry ... I ... I ... I'm so sorry."

"Calyssa, you don't have to go." Nana Jane's voice.

"Calyssa." Andrew's voice.

But I didn't turn around, and they didn't follow me.

I didn't stop until I made it to my car. Placing my hand on the roof to steady myself, I sucked in a breath and let out a sob.

"I meant what I said." I turned to see Gabe standing at the side of the house. "You don't have to care about me. I don't care that you threw away what we had like it was nothing. Like I was nothing to you. But to do it to her ..." He shook his head, looking disappointed and disgusted at the same time. "That was low, even for you, Calyssa."

"Gabe, I never meant to hurt her ... I loved her ... I ..."

Gabe walked up to me in three quick steps. Nose to nose.

"Stop. Lying."

"Gabe, I'm not. Oh, Gabe, I—"

He grabbed me by the shoulders and roughly shook me, just once. I immediately threw up my arms, breaking his hold on me and stepping away from him. My head spinning.

"Don't you dare touch me!" I yelled, taking one more step back. "Not ever again! Do you understand me!" It wasn't a question. He had no right. I was hurting, too. I loved her, too.

Gabe just let out a curt laugh. "Finally. You got the message. You're not welcome here. You don't get to hurt anyone else in my family. Leave, Calyssa. And don't ever look back because no one will be waiting here for you."

I looked at him, not wanting to believe my ears, not wanting to trust my eyes, definitely not wanting to feel the rip through my heart, the one that still hadn't healed completely from the first time I left him.

How could he be so cruel? How could he have changed so much in eight months? He was the most incredible, loving person that I'd ever known in my life. How could he be so different now?

Thoughts raced through my head, but my body began to move on its own. I felt my mouth move, heard my voice say, "Door open," sensed my body sliding into the driver's seat, finger touching the ignition panel, and felt the car begin to move. All like someone else was controlling it. It wasn't me. It couldn't have been. I was still trying to make sense of everything that had happened.

Gabe stood there as I drove away. I could see him in my mirror, not moving, arms across his chest. Then I turned the corner and he was gone.

After a couple of minutes, I let the car roll to a stop. I just sat there. In the car. In the middle of the road.

What had happened? I felt as if my whole world had changed in the last hour. I'd had to leave the Staytons before, but I'd always thought I'd be back. That they'd accept me with the same love and kindness as before. That someday, when things were better, that Gabe would hold me in his arms again and tell me he loved me. That he'd never stopped loving me. Just like I'd never stopped loving him.

But there was no love in his eyes now. We would never be together again. He held me responsible for his sister's death. He hated me.

I never meant for anything bad to happen to Ana. I'd only wanted the best for her. If only Gabe had listened to me – if only he'd heard what I had to say – if only he'd–

A horn blasted from behind, startling me out of my trance. Whipping my head around, I saw a truck sitting right behind my back bumper. Gabe!

Chapter 5

But it wasn't Gabe's truck. A man stuck his head out the window and motioned for me to go. It seemed that just moments later, I arrived home. Then I was in my bedroom. On my bed, eyes closed. Lulu, my pet mini-cow, curled up next to me, and I ran my hands through her silky, pink hair. And then, for a long time, I cried.

Waking up the next morning, I felt like I was coming out of a fog. My eyes hurt, my head ached, and my heart felt shredded. If I stayed in bed, I'd just feel crappy all day. I knew I had to compartmentalize and tuck away everything that had happened yesterday. I wasn't ready to deal with it yet. I knew I was putting it off, but the memories were too raw, and thinking about them just made me want to cry again.

But crying wouldn't bring Ana back. It wouldn't change what happened at the Staytons' yesterday. And it wouldn't change how Gabe felt about me now. I needed to focus on things I could change, that would make a difference, that mattered.

Slowly climbing out of bed, I walked over to my mirror and sat down in front of the desk under it. I spoke to the digital enhancer beside the mirror, "Calyssa, Diary Log Entry One." A yellow light flashed in the corner, a prompt that a security code had to be entered for the loop to play. "One-eight, three-four, five." My age when all of this started, mom's age when she died, my age when mom died. Numbers I wouldn't forget.

Instantly, another me appeared in the mirror. The other me didn't have puffy eyes or a splotchy reddish-green face, but there was a definite look of edginess to her. I'd made this recording about four months ago when I'd decided I needed to keep a private log of what I had found out, and of what I was planning to do. I'd started it as a reminder for myself, since I didn't have anyone to talk to about it. A record in case something happened to me.

The recorded image started by clearing her throat. Well, my throat. "My name is Calyssa Grace Brentwood. Recently, I came into possession of a series of digital images. Ones that I thought had been destroyed. That I had been led to believe had been destroyed. I don't know who destroyed the original set, but I now know that a duplicate set was accidentally made, and I believe that I am the only person who knows this set exists.

"Although the whole set is significant, one of the images is particularly important. It proves a major cover-up by SciCity's Security Enforcers in two deaths." I watched as the me in the mirror paused and took a memory bracelet out of my pocket. Holding it up to be recorded by the digital enhancer, I'd accessed a specific link and quickly selected one specific image. It projected up from the bracelet as a holographic image.

This image, made famous by local media, showed two crumpled, bloodied bodies, a man and a woman, lying on the ground, the man clutching a shiny, metallic object in his hand. It was the object in his hand that differed in my image from the one shown by the media.

In the media's version, a small, silver gun shone brightly in the hand of the man that lay dead. That image supported the security enforcers' version of the events: the man had fired on them and they had been forced to return fire to protect themselves, killing both the man and a woman with him in the exchange of gunfire.

My version of the image, however, didn't support those facts. The recorded me continued, "This is the real image taken from the field where Jesse Fitting and Elaina Johnston were brutally killed in cold blood by security enforcers. The other image, the one that has been broadcast over and over by the media stations, has been tampered with. Jesse did not have a gun on him that day, at least not in his hand. As you can see from this image, he was holding a 'Lost Star,' used by the Fitting brothers' group to identify their fanatic rebel followers.

"I know this because I was the person who took this picture. With my memory bracelet. I personally watched it happen. Then, somehow, it ended up in the hands of security keepers, only to be tampered with, to support their version of what happened." My eyes in the recording looked away from the mirror. I remembered what I had been thinking then: *Should I say who was with me that day? Who also witnessed these deaths? The one person who could back up my story?*

But even now, I knew I'd made the right decision, not to put Gabe's name in my log entry. Even though I was so angry with him, so hurt by him, I knew I couldn't endanger the Staytons by naming Gabe. I still loved them, even if I didn't love him anymore.

Did I really not love him now? I searched through the pain, the aching in my heart as I saw his face in my mind. I didn't think so. Not after yesterday.

I watched as the recorded me turned back to fully face the mirror, jaw set, brows slightly furrowed. "Now I must decide what to do with this information. I no longer know who is lying and who is telling the truth. I don't trust the security keepers or the rebels. I'm not sure I even trust my own father, the CEO of Advanced Human Genetics Assessments.

"I also don't know how the government of SciCity and the big corporations, including AHGA, fit into all of this. But I believe they do. Somehow. My goal is to get to the bottom of all of it. To expose the lies of the fanatics on both sides.

"I believe that every life on this planet, Green or non-Green, is important. I've made my decision. I will do what I pledged when I was enhanced. I will find a way to help my community and change the world. I'm not sure how yet, but I will expose the truth." My image froze in the mirror, then faded.

Four months ago. Sometimes it seemed like years ago. Other times, it felt like yesterday. I'd been naïve. I'd believed that one picture would change the world. Looking back now, I knew I should have done things differently.

About a week after I had begun the log entries, I started researching how to expose cover-ups and lies. I cruised the global digital network, running multiple scans and searches on recent exposés from around the world. Everyone was "catching images" these days – socialites being bad, politicians being worse, crimes in progress – then trying to get famous, showing the world what had happened by posting it, so anyone could view it over and over again. Everyone was busy watching, but no one was stepping in to stop the things being recorded. They just let them happen, and then said, "Oh, look. That was awful. Those are really bad people."

But what about the people doing the recording? In my mind, they were part of the problem because they weren't choosing to do anything about it. They could have stepped in, possibly even stopped what happened,but then, it wouldn't have been big news. And big news was always exciting.

I started cruising some online forums, thinking I was being careful, wary of anyone too interested, worried that the person on the other end of the conversation might be a security enforcer informant. I ended up connecting with a guy, Buck, who told me he worked for an underground media circuit. He told me his group leaked evidence to traditional media sources to expose secrets that the government didn't want the average person to know about. I told him I had something important the world needed to know about. He said he was interested.

Buck sent me links to lots of stories he attributed to his group's "leaks," including a major party leader on the south coast who had to resign after connections were proven between his family and a rebel group that blew up a courthouse, killing over a dozen people. We continued our discussions over several weeks, either online or by iBud. I wanted to meet in person, but Buck said that wouldn't be safe for either of us.

Eventually, I told him about the image of Jesse Fitting with the star in his hand. He was obviously excited. He told me he could get it on all the major networks, that it would go viral on digital media, that it would be seen in every home around the world. This was what I'd been waiting for. This was my chance to show the world that not everything was as it seemed, that checks and balances had to be put into place, that we had to hold all people accountable for their actions.

I told him I was ready. I was willing to be interviewed, to tell the world what had actually happened. And I sent him the picture.

The next day it showed up. On a sensationalistic digital media talk show. With a host that more people laughed at than believed. But the picture did catch on. For a while. I waited for Buck to let me know he'd set up interviews for me to talk, but I didn't hear from him.

A few legitimate news stations picked up the image, but it was quickly rebutted by the Chief of SciCity's Security Enforcers. He personally came on several shows to talk about image tampering and how the rebels were so desperate to try to make the "good guys" look "bad" that they would do just about anything to swing public opinion. He continued with the importance of Green citizens staying diligent and educated on political issues, so they could look out for the best interests of SciCity.

I was furious. I called Buck. No answer. I left messages. No answer. I couldn't believe he was blowing me off. He had given my image to some scandalous journalist who had used it to try to boost ratings, not to someone who was serious about exposing the truth. And now, everyone thought the image was a fake. Created by the rebels to advance their propaganda. No one was going to believe it was my story,or worse, they'd try to connect me to the rebels and label me as an obsessed follower of the Fittings.

I never heard from Buck again. Soon after the image was released, his iBud locator was disconnected. I was sure he was trying to avoid me. A few more weeks and I gave up trying to get a hold of him. About that same time, the picture lost momentum. It became "old news," and the world moved on.

But I didn't. I knew that I had to be smarter now. I had to work harder to find and share information with others who truly wanted to make a difference. My goals hadn't changed. But my game plan had.

Chapter 6

I looked into the mirror one more time. I was happy with the person I had become. I had started classes at SciCity University in the fall and began my internship at AHGA. Both places allowed me to explore, learn, and observe.

At AHGA, my position as an intern in the Community Benefits Outreach Program gave me plenty of opportunities to work on whatever I wanted. I was supposed to be researching new tech needed by schools, compiling reports about what I'd found, and submitting them to the department head. It was a job I could do in my sleep, so it left me with a ton of free time.

I noticed that when I was quiet, when I listened attentively but looked like I was doing something else, I was virtually invisible to those around me. People would say things, things they didn't realize I'd overheard, that I was sure they didn't want me to know, like I wasn't even there. That was their mistake and my advantage. Someone at AHGA had stolen my pictures and given them to the security enforcers. Maybe the person who turned them over knew what they would be used for. Maybe not. But either way, I was going to find out who it was.

I got up from my desk. I couldn't stay home and cry all day. I needed to get back on track. To think about something besides – Ana. Forcing myself to focus on the day in front of me, I mentally tucked away all my memories of the Staytons. I had to fill my time, to keep busy, so I wouldn't remember.

I jumped in for a quick shower cycle with autodry, then applied subtle makeup, and pulled my hair half up, but with enough down that it could still hide my face if I needed it to. A black, knee-length skirt and a light peach, button-up-the-front shirt that accentuated my soft green skin and dark green hair. I needed to look pretty but not stunning, smart but not overly intellectual, pleasant but not exciting. I needed to blend in and become a part of the background. I had always been good at being that nice girl that nobody really remembered. And now, it was paying off.

Grabbing the books for my afternoon classes, I headed to my car. Off to "listen" at AHGA.

I passed Livvy lying on the couch, all bundled up in a flannel blanket.

"Bye, Sis," I said as I walked by, waving in her direction.

She smiled softly but didn't say anything, her eyes closing as I passed. Five months home and she still didn't look very good. Thin, more yellow than green, and she always seemed just a little bit out of it. But at least she was still here. Still with us.

Unlike Ana.

Feeling the threat of tears, I shook my head as if the shake could literally send the thoughts flying out of my mind. I needed to focus. To listen. To do something that would make a difference.

I used the drive to work to review what I had learned over the past few weeks, and to keep thoughts of Ana out of my head. I focused on "eugenics resurgence," a casual comment I'd heard in a passing conversation, one that had struck me as odd, so I'd made a note of it. My new iBud 25 had a note-taking app that allowed me to record thoughts, like call messages from friends, so I could access them later. It was a convenient way to remember something without anyone knowing I'd noted it.

That day had started out just like any other. I'd had to run some paperwork to another floor. When the elevator doors opened, I recognized a research scientist from the Human Biotech division who was visiting with a doctor from the Green Enhancement unit. I stepped on the elevator. They both smiled and nodded. I smiled back and then put my hand to my ear, a universal sign indicating I was engaged in an iBud conversation. They turned back to each other and continued talking in low voices.

"...the eugenics resurgence. A new IRB has been assembled, including some high-ranking security enforcer, but I still don't think we're ready for dissemination..." They exited the elevator at the next floor together, continuing their discussion.

31

Eugenics resurgence? A new IRB board? High ranking security enforcer? Dissemination? I noted the conversation on my iBud app with a reminder to do some research of my own. I remembered learning something about eugenics at school, about programs to develop humans based on specific genetic choices, or something along those lines, but nothing more.

I knew what an IRB was – an institutional review board, an impartial board that scrutinizes human trials for the safety of those involved. But usually they didn't include security enforcers – in fact, I didn't remember ever hearing of any IRB's that had included enforcers, high ranking or not, at AHGA. And I definitely hadn't heard anything about a new board forming. Then the door opened at my floor, and I went back to work.

About a week later, in the staff room, I'd found a digital tablet sitting on a table in the corner near the express lights. Picking it up, I'd expected a security screen to pop up asking for a fingerprint to access files, but instead a memo appeared on the screen. Whoever had been on it last must have just left and the security screen hadn't timed in yet.

I'd glanced through the memo, looking for a name to return the tablet to. Then I'd noticed the clearance level noted at the top. "Classified – Red." That meant this was a document that wasn't meant to be seen by 99% of the people who worked here. Including me.

Knowing that whoever left this would probably be back as soon as he or she discovered it had been left, I'd quickly scanned the entire document. I wasn't sure why it was classified. It didn't seem to contain any startling information. Just some current rates on Green Enhancements at the facility along with organelle acceptance verification numbers. Near the end, it mentioned an upcoming meeting for the "Viridis Eugenics Project." It stated that "V" would be in attendance.

I hadn't heard of this project, but that wasn't unusual. There were probably a couple hundred projects going on at any one time at AHGA – it was one of the most prominent human research and advancement facilities in New America.

I'd also never heard of this "V" person, but I'd assumed he was somebody important since it was noted that he'd be attending the meeting. I didn't know everyone that worked here, but I'd never heard Father or Livvy talk about a "V." The name had never been mentioned by anyone that I could remember, and I hadn't seen anything in all the files I had been through.

That had struck me as weird. Weird enough that I'd made a note on my iBud app to research any staff member at AHGA with a first or last name starting with V. I'd glanced back down at the screen and saw that the memo screen had timed out and the security access screen was on.

"What are you doing with my tablet?"

I'd jumped at the sound of the voice. A tall, muscular woman stood at the door of the room. She'd looked anxious, glancing over her shoulder before she'd marched across the room and ripped the tablet out of my hands.

"I ... uh ... I was about to bring this to the front desk. I found it sitting over there by the express lights." I'd pointed to the corner. Like she needed to know where the express lights were.

She'd turned the tablet over in her hands. Then she'd just stood there glaring at me.

"Sorry," I'd said, stepping back from her. "The security screen was up, and I wasn't sure who it belonged to."

She'd looked back at the screen again, closed her eyes for a second, then looked back up at me. "It's okay, and I didn't mean to come off so angry. It's just been an intense week. Losing this would have made my life ... difficult." She'd sighed. "Thanks for grabbing it for me..." she'd said looking at my name badge, "...Calyssa." Intern's name badges only had first names. Which was good for me – the fewer people who realized I was a Brentwood, the better.

"That's okay, Dr. Morlan," I'd said, noting her name as well. I'd added her name to my notes, too. "I know how crazy things can be around here."

She'd given me a half-hearted smile, then turned and left the room.

My search of the staff directory turned up thirty-nine people with a first or last name that started with V. Seventeen women and twenty-two men. There were six I had met. A few more that I knew in passing. Six were doctors and nine were researchers. The rest were associate staff members – secretaries, assistants, cleaning crew, lab techs, that sort of thing. Probably not people who would be attending a meeting that had to do with Green Enhancement statistics.

I had looked up info on each of the fifteen, but nothing popped out at me. They all had been with the company for at least five years and seemed to be respected in their departments. I had filed the information away and moved on.

But then, two days ago, I'd gone to see Father in his office on the main floor. His door was slightly ajar, and I could hear a heated discussion taking place. Not shouts, but unquestionably tense.

"I don't know why," a voice was saying, "but obviously it's not an option."

"I don't know if I like what you're implying." Father sounded upset.

"I'm not the one implying anything, but V is insistent, and I have to give the new IRB something. General Sanson is being ... challenging," the other person responded.

If I hadn't seen "V" referred to in the memo, I probably wouldn't have caught it. I probably would have thought the person said "he" or "she" and would have dismissed it. Father was always upset about something at work.

And, who was General Sanson? The name was familiar, but I couldn't place it. Probably a security enforcer. Was he the member of the new IRB? I'd searched, but I hadn't found anything about a new IRB.

Reviewing the conversation once more, I knew I'd obviously missed something. I decided this was going to be the focus for my morning. I'd do another search for IRBs, using the pretext that some of the advanced tech classes at the schools were interested in new biotech we'd developed recently or were in the process of developing – some of those required IRB approval. I only had a couple of hours today, and then I'd have to head to the U. But maybe I'd find something useful.

I pulled into the parking lot designated for staff, nodding to the security officers as I passed their monitoring station. One of them nodded back, noting my arrival on his tablet.

Inside, I took the elevator down three levels, and headed to my work station. Originally constructed as a visitor center for the dam it was built next to, AHGA had been expanded over the years, tunneling much further back into the mountain behind it, and down more than thirty stories. The deepest levels were highly classified areas, allowing only those with top security clearance. I had only been allowed down there after Livvy had contracted the PKPH virus and the doctors were trying to save her.

I worked for the first half hour on a report that needed to be finished up from yesterday. Then I dove into the IRB search. But, after two hours, the results were the same as before. No new IRBs had been formed. All current projects were utilizing existing IRBs. Another dead end.

"Hey, Lyssa. Would you mind doing a favor for me before going to the U today?" A short, stocky man with a tight crew cut stood by my desk.

"Sure thing, Karsten. I was just finishing. What's up?" I smiled at him. Karsten was the marketing guru in our department who worked on publicity for AHGA. He was the one who made sure that AHGA looked good to the public when it came to our charitable donations to schools in SciCity and the outlying areas. He'd been friendly from the start, and he always seemed to have a positive attitude.

Maybe it was because I was a Brentwood, but he seemed genuine, and I liked him.

"I need this flash pack dropped off at a digital media station downtown. It's the one near First National Bank. Channel 447. Do you know where it is?"

"Sure. No problem. I'll take off in a few minutes and drop it off before I head to class."

"Thanks. Saves me a trip downtown." Karsten handed me the flash pack and I tucked it into my jacket pocket.

A few minutes later, I was in my car. It took me longer than I'd planned to get there. And then I couldn't find parking. After finishing Karsten's errand, I started walking back to my car. It was cold out, but the sun shone brightly in the afternoon sky. At least it wasn't snowing today.

I connected to my iBud and realized that I was running late. I tried to pick up the pace, but the sidewalk was slick and the heels on my boots made walking quickly potentially dangerous. I tried to focus on where I was stepping, but just then something caught my eye.

Chapter 7

I almost missed it. I don't know what caused me to look in the direction of the café in the first place. Something made me look over the two children, scooping up snow and tossing it at each other. Past the group of little old ladies, hats bouncing as they agreed with each other over their warmed nutrient drinks. To a small table in the far corner of an outside patio. I tightened my scarf as I glanced over there one more time.

And then I stopped so abruptly that the man walking behind me bumped into me, almost knocking me to the ground. We both danced a little, working to keep our balance, grabbing at each other, trying to make sure that the other didn't fall.

I immediately apologized, and he grumbled something in response then kept going. I turned to look back at the café patio. What had I seen? I scanned the area again and my eyes stopped once more at the same small table. A young couple sat there. All bundled up.

Even from a distance, something about them seemed familiar. He faced me, a non-Green wearing a heavy gray coat, pulled up high around his neck, his blonde curls poking over the collar. His light gray beanie matched the pattern in his coat, and his dark sunglasses gave him a sporty look. Her back was to me and she was dressed in all black – a long, heavy winter coat, a thick scarf around her neck, a stylish winter hat, boots with heels, and gloves covering fingers that moved through the air as she spoke. He laughed at something she said, taking her gloved hand in his bare one, stroking the fingers, then bringing them up to his mouth for a kiss.

She laughed again, tossing her head back, then immediately reached for her hat as it started to slide off her head. Her hair had been pulled up inside the hat, and as she readjusted it, a few blonde wisps fell out, spilling down over her scarf and onto her black coat.

No, I thought, *not blonde*. More yellowish, more – like – like – Livvy's!

I found myself walking toward them to get a better look. I knew it wasn't Livvy. It couldn't be Livvy. Livvy was home. Livvy was still weak, still struggling to get back to her old self, still … still …

What in the world? The closer I got, the more the color looked *exactly* like Livvy's, that odd yellowish color it had now turned. Now she was stable, but not well enough to be sitting outside in the winter cold – downtown with a man, visiting, laughing, flirting–

A soft, wet clump of snow hit the side of my face, startling me back to my surroundings.

"Sorry," one of the children sang out, then they both giggled and ran off down the sidewalk. I shook my head, wiping at my face with one of my gloved hands.

The old lady with the biggest hat stood up and yelled after the kids, "Manners, children! Manners!" She shook a finger at them, and they laughed even louder as they skipped down the block, bumping into each other, kicking up snow as they went. She looked at me and shook her head disapprovingly.

"I'm okay," I mouthed to her, smiling to let her know that no real damage had been done.

Then I looked back to the table. The couple was gone.

I walked closer to the patio, scanning the area to see if I could figure out where they went. Crossing the street, heading toward a park, I saw the man in the gray coat and beanie, hands now jammed into his pockets, walking briskly away from the café. I didn't see the woman anywhere.

As he stopped at an intersection, waiting for the light to change, he took off his glasses, rubbed the bridge of his nose, and then looked up in my direction.

Gunner.

What was Gunner doing in the city? The last time I'd seen him, he'd been in a rebel camp's makeshift hospital bed with a hole in his lung. That was when Gabe and I had gone to make sure he wouldn't die. When I had gone to the Stayton farm for spring break. It seemed like a lifetime ago.

I picked up my pace walking toward him, but then the light changed, and I had to jump back up on the curb to avoid being crushed by a bright red XR-17 Maserati that slammed on its horn and swerved, missing me by only inches. I shook my head, looking back in the direction where I had just seen Gunner. Now, there was a mass of people crossing the street, but he was nowhere in sight.

That was definitely Gunner. But was that Livvy? With Gunner? What? No way. Livvy was home, probably napping, still wrapped up in a blanket on the couch watching a digital movie, or if she was feeling up to it, working on something on the computer for AHGA.

She hadn't been out of the house in months. Not since she came home from AHGA, not since she contracted the PKPH virus. She wasn't well enough to be out.

Is she? I thought about that. She had been looking better. I mean, not completely Green again, but a little stronger. No, what was I thinking? But that hair. I'd swear that was her hair.

That was it. I walked straight to my car and headed back to the house. I had to know. Was my imagination playing games with me, or was my sister far better than she was letting anyone know? And if she was better, why was she keeping it a secret?

Chapter 8

Twenty minutes later, I pulled up to our house. All the way home, I'd kept turning it over and over in my mind. It looked like Livvy's hair – but it couldn't be Livvy. Livvy was still so weak. But I'd never seen that hair color anywhere else. Wouldn't I have known if Livvy was well?

Walking up to the door, the house looked empty. No express lights shining through the windows, no movements or shadows, no sounds. I stepped up to the eye scanner and held my breath as the door slid silently open. Stepping in, I stopped and listened. I was about to walk down the hall to Livvy's room when I heard a sound from the kitchen. It was Lena's day off, so it had to be Livvy.

I instantly headed in that direction. Most of me hoped that I'd find a pajama-clad, clumsy, slow-moving Livvy, fumbling around for a snack, since she had to eat now to supplement her failing chloroplasts. But a small part of me was hoping that Livvy would be there in her black outfit, hair messed up from the hat she'd worn outside, cheeks rosy from the cold of the winter day. That would mean she was better. But it would also mean she'd been lying to me. And to Father.

Turning the corner into the kitchen, I looked past the large island between us, and saw Livvy standing at the sink, staring out the window with her back to me. Her odd yellow hair hung delicately over a flannel blanket wrapped around her shoulders. I released the breath I had been holding. Pajama-clad Livvy. I was relieved and disappointed at the same time.

"Hey, Livvy," I said softly.

"What the—" she said sharply as she whipped around, losing hold of the glass in her hand, flinging it into the side of the island where it shattered into a thousand pieces. The blanket dropped. And there stood rosy cheeked, black-winter-clad Livvy.

"Lyssa, what are you doing home? Aren't you supposed to be at class for a few more hours? Did something happen? Why are you here?" The questions shot out as her eyes darted to the digital clock on the wall. Then she immediately bent over and started picking up pieces of glass.

I just stood there. My mind raced.

She was better.

She'd kept it a secret.

She was meeting with Gunner.

Gunner was a rebel.

After a few seconds, when I was still standing there motionless, speechless, Livvy slowly stood up and looked at me.

"Lyssa, I ... I ... need to tell you a few things."

That was an understatement.

"Lyssa–" she started again, but this time I cut her off.

"Livvy, I saw you. Downtown. With ... a man ... a..." I hesitated.

"With Gunner," she said.

I leaned back against the wall. This was more than my mind was willing to comprehend. Those crazy thought circles spiraled again. Livvy was obviously better – Livvy knew Gunner – Gunner was a rebel – did Livvy know Gunner was a rebel?

Livvy let out an unexpected laugh. "Oh, Lyssa, I wish you could see the look on your face right now." She leaned over to start picking up glass again. "We knew we'd have to tell you at some point." She glanced back up at me. "Actually, I'm relieved you know. It'll be easier now."

Okay, I'd had a chance to process all of this, and I was a little ticked off.

"Seriously? That's all you've got to say? You're relieved? Really? How long have you been lying to me? To Father? Pretending you're sick! Pretending you're weak and helpless! Fooling us into doing everything for you. Worrying about you. Babying you. That's it, isn't it? Back to the same old selfish Livvy of the past. Fantastic. Manipulating all of us so you can stay home all day, letting us do all the work. Unbelievable." I shook my head as I spat out the words. She was better. So why was I so angry?

Livvy just stared at me from her crouching position on the floor, one hand full of broken glass pieces, the other paused over one last piece she was about to pick up.

"You done, Little Sis?" she asked, one eyebrow raised.

"What?" It came out with more outrage than question. I glared down at her.

Grabbing the last broken piece, she stood up, tossed the glass she held into the autorecycler, and picked up the suction-bot from the corner and placed it on the floor over the remaining glass splinters. Then, she walked over and hugged me.

I stiffened. I wanted to walk away. I wanted to yell at her. I wanted to slap her. But then she squeezed a little tighter, and I gave in. I always gave in when it came to Livvy. And I hugged her back.

"I am happy you're better. You are obviously better, right?" She stepped back and nodded her head. "But what ... how ... when ...?" Back to unformulated questions.

Livvy laughed again, picked up her blanket from the floor, took my hand, and led us out of the kitchen to the family room. "Her room" as she called it since coming home from AHGA, where she liked to snuggle down on the couch in front of a toasty, simulated fire.

We sat down together at opposite ends of the couch, facing each other, and she tossed one end of the blanket to me. We both pulled it up over us, the flannel warming our legs.

"Okay, here goes. Gunner and I practiced how I would tell you, but it was a lot easier when he was pretending to be you." She smirked.

"Livvy, I know Gunner. I—"

"I know, Lyssa. I know about everything. Let me talk you through it. Just listen."

That was fine by me. I was so astonished that I didn't think I could have said anything at that point if I'd wanted to.

"I actually met Gunner about two months ago." My mouth dropped open.

"Don't say anything. Just listen," Livvy's eyes pleaded with me as she spoke.

I closed my mouth and nodded.

She continued, "Let me back it up a bit more. Right after you went to college, I started feeling a little better. Not great, but enough that I could be up and awake for more than just a few hours at a time. My test results from AGHA weren't coming back any different, so I didn't want to get anyone's hopes up, but the better I felt, the more I started wanting to get connected with my old friends again. Just to see what everyone was up to. What had been happening outside of this house." She paused, looking toward the fire.

"It wasn't like I wanted anything from them. I just wanted someone to talk to. You and Father were gone all day. Lena was in and out, mostly gone during the day, unless she was cleaning. I was lonely."

"You should have said something, Livvy, you should have—" She cut me off with a wave of her hand.

"You were busy. Everyone was busy. A couple of my friends replied to my messages, but once we video chatted, I could tell they weren't interested in being friends anymore. I mean, look at me. I'm certainly not Green but

I'm not a non-Green either. I'm some weird oddity in the middle. Zypher let it slip that 'some people' thought it was odd that I survived after contracting PKPH and Azra didn't. I tried to explain that no one knew why, that the scientists hadn't figured it out, that they still didn't even know why the virus was attacking the modified chloroplasts in humans instead of those in plants, but he just looked at me like I was lying." She shook her head, tears beginning to well in her eyes.

"Livvy..." I started again. She shot me a warning look and I stopped.

Wiping her eyes with the back of her hand, she went on. "After the initial video visits – after they got to check out the freak, the girl with chloroplasts who had to eat again – everyone stopped returning my calls. I realized just how alone I really was.

"My *friends*, the people I had poured all my time and energy into before the virus, they weren't really my friends. I didn't have anything to offer them anymore. No more hookups, no more backstage passes, no more business connections. I realized I was a nobody. I didn't matter anymore.

"That was the day I decided to kill myself."

Chapter 9

I couldn't breathe. Livvy had thought about killing herself? How could I have not known? Why didn't I see any signs? How could she have been in so much pain and I didn't even notice? I started to get up to move closer to her, but she shook her head.

"I started cruising the online sim rooms, to find people to talk with, to figure out what would be the best way to do it. You know I'm not very tough, not that good with pain. There are lots of people out there with ideas. It's actually really scary, the things people come up with to end it all. The offers that are out there. People that will 'help' you do it.

"Somehow, I ended up talking with a guy, NexGen77. He wasn't like a lot of the creepers. When he talked about how bad things were, he never talked about ending it, he just talked about living with the sadness. Like I was.

"At first, we just chatted about the weather, about things going on in SciCity, you know, just everyday stuff. But then he asked where I worked, and why I was online at all different times, pretty much available whenever he came on. I don't know why, but I told him about working at AHGA, about Father, about you … and about the virus."

My mouth dropped open again.

"Don't even say it, Lyssa. I know it wasn't smart. That he could have been some crazy stalker or fanatic rebel that was out to kill Green citizens' families. But he was so kind and understanding. He told me that it wasn't fair, the way I was being treated by my so-called 'friends,' and that he thought I was pretty incredible. He made me feel good."

She smiled with a faraway look in her, like she was remembering something special.

I gave her a few seconds, then asked, "Did he tell you about himself?"

Her eyes focused on me again. "Yeah, he said his parents had died when he was younger, and that he lived with another guy and worked on and off in SciCity as a tech analyst. I talked about working at AHGA. He said he had done some temp work there in the past, and that maybe we had even met, and we just didn't realize it. That was when he asked to video chat.

"I was really nervous about that. I mean, I'd told him that I had been really sick, but I hadn't actually told him what I looked like. I was scared he'd be done with me. Like everyone else. But he told me I wasn't being fair, that he didn't care about how I looked, that he just wanted to see me smile when I laughed ... because the sound of my laugh always made him feel better no matter how bad his day was.

"So, I decided I would. That was the first day that I got up and really tried getting around again. It took me a while and I was winded pretty quickly, but I found that I actually felt better moving around again, having a purpose. I tried makeup, but it all looked weird because my skin is such an awkward color. So, I scrapped the majority of it, just a little eye makeup, and I brushed out my hair. When I looked in the mirror, I was okay with what I saw. I wasn't beautiful anymore, but I wasn't horrid. At least, I'd hoped NexGen77 wouldn't see me that way."

"Livvy, I think you're still beautiful."

"You're my sister. You have to say that." She flipped a dismissive hand in my direction and went on. "That afternoon I was shaking as I logged on for our video chat. I felt sick to my stomach, I had a headache, and I canceled the chat twice before the link went through. But the third time, he logged on before I could disconnect, and there he was on my screen. Blonde curly hair, boyishly handsome, tanned skin, and not Green. That surprised me. It must have shown on my face because the first thing he said was, 'Not what you expected, huh?' and then he laughed. His eyes twinkled when he laughed, and that made me feel better.

"Then we just started talking like we always did, about our day, about things going on, just the usual stuff. He never once mentioned how odd I looked. After about forty-five minutes, I finally said, 'I guess I'm probably not what you expected either, am I?' Then he just stared at me for like ten to fifteen seconds. It was so awkward. Right when I thought I couldn't take it anymore, he said, 'You're right, you're shorter than I expected.' And then we both laughed."

"Was he—" I started to ask, but Livvy shot me a look and I stopped mid-question. There were so many things I wanted to ask, but Livvy wasn't finished.

"After a few more video chats, he told me he wanted to meet in person. I told him I wasn't sure. I mean, leaving the house? Looking like this? I wasn't sure I was ready to have people gawking at me.

"And, I hadn't told you and Father about how I was feeling. But then I thought, 'What if I could pull myself back together, and then surprise the two of you? Wouldn't that be a real reason to celebrate?' And if I couldn't do it, I thought it would be better if you didn't know, so I wouldn't disappoint you. Either of you.

"NexGen77 kept at it. He was persistent about meeting me. He suggested that we could meet in less populated areas, stay outside, walk around, like in one of the parks in SciCity. That I could bundle up so most of my skin and hair wouldn't show if I was worried about it. And, he said that he thought it would be good for me to get out in the fresh air and work on building my muscles back up. He had lots of convincing ideas."

I'm sure he did, I thought. *We're so lucky he didn't take you away and cut you up into tiny pieces or sell you off to some crazed pervert or …*

"So we set it up for the next day at 2pm in the Maze of Fountains Park, just past that big parking structure for all the law offices downtown. The fountains are never on once the weather cools off, so you can walk through all the mazes and talk privately. It's really peaceful.

"He was already there by the time I arrived. I drove slow, nervous because it had been so long. But I was fine. I walked up to him, and he held out his hand, saying, 'Hi, Livvy. I'm Gunner. It's great to meet you.'

"I was shocked that he knew who I was, and he must have read it on my face because then he hooked his arm through mine and started walking me toward one of the mazes. He told me he'd done research on me based on what he knew: that my dad owned AHGA, that I had contracted the PKPH virus, that I had been enrolled at the U and working at AHGA. He said it wasn't hard to put together.

"I watched him as he talked. He's always so animated, so alive, so ... everything I felt I had been missing out on since I had been sick. Being with him gave me energy. His attitude was contagious. He made me feel that anything was possible again.

"For the next two weeks, we met every day at the same park. And we walked a little further each day. I felt stronger and stronger. Then one day, he asked me if I wanted to get lunch. I was uncomfortable about being in a restaurant, but he said he knew of the perfect little café that had outdoor seating year-round so I could keep on my winter attire, even during the meal.

"It was at lunch at that café, the same one we met at today, that Gunner told me about what he really does. About his rebel group. About how they're fighting against corrupt security enforcers and dangerous corporations. At first, I defended AHGA, but the more Gunner talked to me, the more I began to see the truth in his words. I mean, I've worked there for over two years, Lyssa, and I've seen and heard some things. Most of it I just dismissed as propaganda or as disgruntled employees, but hearing it from Gunner, some things started to make sense."

"Okay, wait a minute," I interrupted, and this time I didn't stop. "You just took his word for it that 'bad' things were happening at AHGA? Doesn't that seem a bit naïve, Livvy?"

"It would have except Gunner had file names for the things he was telling me. I didn't believe him at first either, but when I got home, I logged on to the AHGA server and went browsing through the files he'd mentioned. The information was easy to locate, to verify. Things like land that AHGA purchased way under value due to previous 'accidents' on the location so nobody could hold up the sale."

I swallowed hard as I thought about Leah and her kids, a family that lived in the same rebel camp as Gunner. Leah had been told that her husband had been "murdered by rebels" and she had lost her house and a son to a fire set by that same "rebel group." The same group that later took her in, along with all six of her remaining children, and gave them a home, meals, comfort, friendship.

Livvy was staring into the simulated fire again. The reflection glowed in her eyes. "Each time we met, Gunner gave me more information, more files to check into. And each time, the facts matched up with what he said. I mean, not everything was there. AHGA officials are too smart to keep records that would directly implicate them, but there are just way too many coincidences. Way too many things that make sense when the gaps are filled in with Gunner's information."

I sat up straighter. "Does Father know? Have you told him about what you've found? Have you shown him the files?"

Livvy turned back to me, hesitating.

"You haven't told him?" Even as I asked, I knew what Livvy's answer would be. Because I had asked myself the same question. "You're not sure if he's involved, are you?" I sat quietly, hoping she'd tell me she had proof he wasn't.

"It's not that simple, Lyssa. I've been through hundreds of documents, memos, land acquisitions, banking statements, security enforcer reports ... but I just don't know. Not for sure. Each time I think he's involved, I find something that doesn't seem to fit, that makes it look like he doesn't really know about what's happened. And when I start to believe that he's not connected with any of this, then I'll find something that doesn't look good for him, something that implies he's in on it. I really don't know. I mean ... he's our dad. I can't believe he would be involved in anything terrible. But then, until a few months ago, I believed that AHGA was all about making the world a better place."

Livvy paused and rubbed her face with both hands. "I don't want him to be involved in any of this, but I keep thinking, 'He's Dad. It's his company. He knows it in and out — nothing happens without his knowledge, his approval.' Right?" She leaned toward me a bit, frowning, her forehead creased. "What do you think, Lyssa? Do you think he could do it? Be involved in killing people, stealing their land, just to advance the company?"

My mind was racing. And, my heart felt like it was trying to keep up with my mind. I blew out a deep breath. "I'm ... I ... well, I think..."

Then the door sensor went off. Someone was standing at the front door.

Chapter 10

Livvy and I both automatically turned toward the sound and then quickly looked back at each other. I jumped up and started out of the room.

"Wrap up in that blanket and curl up on the couch. Pretend like you're asleep," I said, then adding as I glanced back over my shoulder at her, "like you usually do when I come home." If she caught my sarcasm, she didn't say anything. She rolled herself up in the flannel blanket with only a bit of her face showing, then lay down on the couch with her back to the fire.

I activated the security monitor next to the door that allowed me to see who was standing outside. Jaxx. Great, just the guy I wanted to chit-chat with. Not. Ever. Rather than opening the front door for him, I pressed a button that allowed him to hear me. "Good afternoon, Mr. Jaxx. Is there something I can help you with?"

He looked directly up into the camera. No smile. "Hello, Miss Brentwood. Can I come in? Your father sent me to check on your sister."

What? Father sent Jaxx over to check on Livvy during the day? Did she know? More importantly, did this happen often? Did this mean he was suspicious about her and Gunner? The thought made me a little nauseous. Whether or not Father was involved with anything scandalous at AHGA, I was willing to bet money that Jaxx had his hand in it. As head of security, nothing slipped by his scrutiny. I don't think the man ever slept. Just watched video feeds whenever he wasn't "checking in" on someone or something.

"Livvy's fine," I said, pressing the button again. "Just sleeping. No reason to wake her."

"Please, Miss Brentwood, open the door. I would rather we speak inside. Unless there's some reason you don't want me to come in." Same old Jaxx. Twisting things around. He was excellent at manipulating people to get what he wanted. "Miss Brentwood, is there an issue? Should I call the security enforcers? Are you unable to let me in?"

Fine. *Jerk.* I hit the button to open the door and pasted on a plastic smile.

"Of course not, Mr. Jaxx. Please come in. Sorry about that glitch with the door. Doesn't always open right away. So weird. Tech, it can be crazy, you know." Plastic smile securely stuck in place.

"I'll have someone check into it right away, Miss Brentwood. Wouldn't want anything to happen to you two girls when you're here alone." No smile on his face.

Seriously. I couldn't stand this guy.

"By the way, Miss Brentwood, why are you home right now? Shouldn't you be in class at the university for another couple of hours? I believe you're currently missing a World Ethics seminar with Professor Layton, aren't you." Not a question. He obviously already knew that answer.

"I didn't realize that you actually knew my college schedule, Mr. Jaxx." I just stared at him.

"Of course, I do, Miss Brentwood. Since that 'incident' at the Stayton farm over spring break, I've kept much closer tabs on everyone in the family, per your father's request." He never broke eye contact. I don't even think he'd blinked since he came in the door.

"It's wonderful to know we have someone as diligent as you looking out for us." I tried to keep my voice sweet, but sarcasm was beginning to seep through.

"Again, may I ask why you're not at school? The transponder on your car alerted me that you were 'off schedule' today." I felt my eyebrows shoot up. He was tracking my car? He just totally moved up to a whole new level of creepiness.

"I wasn't feeling well this afternoon, so I decided to come home early. I'm current in all my classes." Why did I tell him that? I was an adult. I didn't need his permission to come back to *my* house.

"Should I call your father or perhaps your family physician? Feeling so ill that you cannot stay and continue your studies must be serious."

I immediately shook my head. "No, thank you. Just a headache. I thought a little rest would help. I'm feeling much better already."

"Well, that's good to hear. I wouldn't want to have to report any major issues to your father. And your sister, Naleeva? She's here?" He didn't wait for an answer, just started walking around, poking his head into rooms.

Total jerk. He had to throw a few veiled threats in to make sure I was staying in line. Just like when he took me from the farm. When he'd given me the talk about choices and consequences, and basically told me he'd ruin the Staytons' lives if he had to in order to keep my family "safe."

"Yeah, Livvy's right here in the family room, sleeping." I stepped around him and headed toward the room without even looking back to see if he was following. Livvy was curled up in a nice tight ball, wrapped up in the blanket, breathing rhythmically, maybe even a little too heavily. I looked at Jaxx, pointed to Livvy, placed a finger on my lips, then turned and walked out of the room. Jaxx followed.

I walked straight back to the front door and pressed the button to open it. "Thanks for stopping by, Mr. Jaxx. I'm sure you have plenty to do for AHGA besides just checking on Livvy and me. We wouldn't want to keep you from your duties." Plastic smile in place again.

Jaxx hesitated for a moment. Like he was going to say something. But he must have changed his mind because he just walked toward the door.

Pausing at the door frame, he looked back at me. "Remember that I am here for your protection, Miss Brentwood. For your own good. And for your sister's. Please be safe." Then he turned and left.

I shuddered. I didn't think that Jaxx and I had the same definition of what was "for my own good."

Making sure the door was locked, I headed back to the family room. Livvy and I had to talk more about her conversations with Gunner. What exactly did she know? She'd said she'd been through hundreds of documents now. Why? What was she looking for? What had she already found?

Livvy was still lying on the couch. But her breathing was softer, and her body more relaxed. I touched her shoulder, and she murmured something, but she never opened her eyes. She was actually asleep now.

Looking at her face, the worry lines that had been so prevalent in our earlier discussion had disappeared. She looked peaceful. I wanted to wake her up to talk more, but I decided to let her sleep. She may have been feeling better, but I didn't think she was totally well. Father still ran weekly tests on her, and he hadn't said a thing about her results showing improvement. That just made this even more confusing.

My iBud sounded and I connected.

Lyssa, it's Ayva. You are coming to class today, right? I've got the most awesome hook up, but you can't tell anyone. I'm only telling you. Nobody else. But not over iBud. I have to see you today. She paused, just long enough for me to jump in.

Well, I was thinking I might skip today. Something's come up with my sister and... I thought back to her, glancing back at Livvy one more time.

No way! Not today. This is something you have to get in on right away, Lys. Come on, please?

I considered heading over to the University. World Ethics would be out before I could make it back, but the other class I had today, Fundamentals of Persuasive Public Speaking, was the one Ayva and I had together, and I could still make it if I left right away.

One more look in Livvy's direction. If I stayed here, I'd just sit staring at Livvy until she woke up so we could talk more. I didn't think I'd be able to get anything else done. I figured I might as well kill the hours in class. It would help take my mind off my conversation with Livvy. Then, when I got home, we would finish our talk.

Lyssa, are you still there? Lyssa? Lys?

Oh yeah, sorry. Just figuring out if I can make it work. I think I can. What's all this about anyway? Ayva always had something going on. She knew where all the best parties were, what the next big trends would be, all the "right place, right time" stuff. She was a lot of fun, but she could be exhausting.

I told you, not over iBud. But don't make any plans after class. I'm getting you in on something big. I'm talking totally elite status. You might think it's a little risky, but it'll be worth it, I promise.

It's risky? I thought back. I don't know, Ayva...

Don't flake on me, Lyssa. Just get to class. I'll explain everything there.

Then she disconnected.

Chapter 11

I headed toward the University, wondering what had Ayva so excited. She always had something new to tell me, but this must have been different. She usually didn't message me to make sure I would be at class.

Ayvalisa Banebriar was one of the first friends I had made in college. Like me, she had a late birthday and was a new Green when classes started. Also like me, Ayva had always known she would be Green as soon as she was old enough to be enhanced. Her parents were both Green and came from Green families. Her dad was a lawyer who worked for a firm that focused on international law, so he was often out of the country. Her mom didn't work, but she was always busy with one charity group or another. Ayva was an only child, so she grew up doing pretty much whatever she wanted.

At first, I'd thought I didn't care for her. She was opinionated, loud, and spent money like there was no tomorrow. But we'd been paired together for our first persuasive speech, debating against two other girls in the class over whether businesses in SciCity should be allowed to choose if they wanted to be "Green only" establishments. In a blind draw, the other team drew the supporting position. I was relieved to be on the opposition team. But I didn't think Ayva would be thrilled.

However, she surprised me by diving right in. She arrived the next day with a massive number of digital files from across New America as well as other countries that opposed the idea of segregated establishments. I told her I was impressed, and that I was happy she supported our position.

"Oh, I actually think we should allow businesses to choose who they want as patrons, but I'm probably the most competitive person you'll ever meet. There's no way I'm letting those two gaudy girls beat us. I'm sure they'll just pay someone to write their speech – Amelie's dad is a politician, so she's got speech writers at her fingertips. And Nova's mom is some big publicist. They're both telling everyone they've got this one nailed down.

"But screw that. If there's one thing I've known how to do since I was in diapers, it's argue a point that seems to be a lost cause. Runs in the genes, I guess. My dad's never lost a case that's gone to court."

She looked me over once, then went back to perusing the files.

"So, don't worry. I'll get us a good – no, make that excellent – grade. Trust me."

I'm pretty sure I just stood there with my mouth open. Yep, I definitely had that "average-girl" look down pat.

"Listen, Ayvalisa–"

"It's just Ayva. Thanks," she interrupted without even looking up.

"Okay. Listen, Ayva." I paused until she looked back up at me.

Once I had her attention, I continued. "You may have the files, but I have personal, first-hand experience with some of this Green versus non-Green stuff. I know some very intelligent and important non-Green citizens who work hard to make our community a better place. Their contributions have had dramatic, significant effects on our world as we know it today. You need to understand–"

She cut me off before I could say more. "This is awesome. You're truly passionate about this issue. Fantastic! That will give us an edge that we can utilize. You should've seen your face just now – it's impressive the way you can just turn that on. You didn't need a warm-up or anything." She just sat there staring at me.

Okay. Awkward.

"Ayva, I'm not sure this is..."

"Yes, it will. Or, it is. A good idea and will work out. I know I can come off a little overbearing, or aggressive, or zealous, or ... whatever you want to call it, but I like you. I've listened to you in class. You don't say a lot, but when you talk, you make sense. That's more than I can say for about ninety-five percent of our class. I'm a planner –

ducks-in-a-row type of girl – and then I'm a doer." She was nodding her head now, like she was wholeheartedly agreeing with what she was saying.

I just stared at her, then I closed my eyes and took a deep breath.

When I opened them, Ayva was smiling. "So, it's agreed then. We're good. We'll rock this speech and put Team Glitterati in the gutter!"

I couldn't help but smile, too. Ayva's enthusiasm was contagious.

And Ayva was true to her word. She worked harder than anyone I'd ever met, gathering facts, reports, news articles, case judgements, whatever she could get her hands on. We had two weeks to prep for the speech, and she demanded we meet every night.

The first couple nights we worked on campus. Then we went to my house. I was a little worried about Livvy, but Ayva was surprisingly accepting. Every time she came over, she went out of her way to stop in and visit with Livvy for a bit. Ayva acted as if there wasn't anything wrong with her. And Livvy seemed to enjoy talking to Ayva.

The day before we were scheduled to present in class, Ayva invited me over to her house.

"I have a surprise for you," she told me when I arrived. And, then, without waiting for me to ask what it was, she said, "My dad just got back into town, and he said we can practice in front of him. Then he can give us pointers on anything he'd change if it was his closing argument."

My stomach immediately knotted up. Really? In front of her dad? I was still a little nervous about the speech in front of the class, but now, in front of an international lawyer?

I must have looked panicked because Ayva grabbed my hand, and without another word, she pulled me down a hall to a large room filled with books. The old kind. Thousands of them sitting on shelves all the way around the room. I was so intrigued with the books that I didn't even notice the man sitting behind the desk.

"Dad, this is Lyssa Brentwood, the one I'm working with on the speech. Lyssa, this is my dad, Audrick Banebriar."

"Good evening, Mr. Banebriar," I said, reaching out to shake his hand.

"I like this one," he said to Ayva as he reached out to take my hand. "She calls me 'Mister.'" Then he laughed a deep, hearty laugh.

Ayva shook her head. "Funny, Dad. You have to focus. We'll need to run this through several times to make adjustments after your comments. Lyssa and I each have only five minutes to speak and it's important that we get this right."

Ayva's dad just laughed again and looked at me. "Audrick's fine by the way – the 'mister' part just makes me feel old. Welcome to our house, Lyssa. Can we get you anything before we get started? Sometimes Ayvalisa forgets her manners."

Ayva looked at me impatiently. "I'm fine," I said, laying my jacket over a chair.

"Great. Then let's just get at it." Ayva handed me a digital tablet with notes, and then took a second one out of her bag. "You sit over there, Dad. Lyssa and I will position ourselves over here. Then we'll do it just like we've practiced. Right, Lyssa?"

Audrick laughed again. "I've learned it's better not to sass her when she's like this."

I laughed and nodded my head.

Ayva rolled her eyes. "Can we begin?"

Audrick and I laughed one more time, then we all settled into our roles. The night went well. Audrick had some helpful ideas, and Ayva and I adjusted as necessary. When we finished, Ayva's mom, Shassa, brought in nutrient drinks and we visited for a while.

"Well, I can't imagine you two young ladies not persuading your teacher and your class tomorrow. You have a very compelling presentation. I'm glad I didn't have to go up against you. If I had, I might have lost that case. And, my favorite golf club would be a very different place." He chuckled.

I looked back and forth between him and Ayva. "You were actually on this case?"

He nodded, "Not this exact case, but one very similar. Bryce Valley Country Club vs. the American Association of University Non-Greens. The AAUN wanted BVCC to have to start taking non-Green citizens as members if they met all criteria other than being genetically enhanced. It happened a little over a year ago and was a passionately argued case.

"Although I usually only deal with international law, I'm a member at BVCC and was asked to step in. The team representing AAUN was good, but I was better, and the ruling currently stands in SciCity that private businesses can set membership requirements that include genetic enhancement. But it was close. I'm sure the non-Greens will find a way to bring it before the courts again."

I didn't know why it surprised me – Ayva's dad supported the separation of Greens and non-Greens. "Don't you think that kind of discrimination, based simply on skin color, is an outdated way of thinking?" I asked. From the look on Audrick's face, I knew I'd crossed a line in their house.

Ayva's mom let out a small, but audible gasp, and then she quickly excused herself from the room. Ayva looked back and forth between her dad and me, saying nothing. Audrick looked at me, but he was no longer smiling.

"There's more here than a simple issue of skin color. This is not a topic that I expect you girls to fully understand although you are in college and I would hope that your education includes the studies that led up to the Green Enhancements along with the screening that happens. The color of our skin is just a side-effect of the process. We have undergone a medical enhancement that allows us to do more, to be more, both physically and mentally. It's very complicated, but at its core, the procedure enhances us as humans. In simple terms, it makes us better.

"I'm not judging those that are non-Green; I'm simply stating a fact. Medically, scientifically, we are better. Our bodies are more efficient. So are our minds. Being enhanced at a cellular level gives us that advantage. Non-Greens, at least those who are qualified to apply for the Enhancement, are making a choice to accept their current level of the human state. That is their choice, for whatever reason. I would never support taking that choice from them, but by choosing to not be enhanced, they are accepting a lesser life, in both mental and physical aspects. And then, of course, those who could not meet the screening committee's requirements to be enhanced are functioning at a level even below that. It's an incredible responsibility to choose to be enhanced. We must lead our society, our world.

"And, thinking about it now, I'm surprised that I even need to have this discussion with you, Lyssa. You are the daughter of Kassius Brentwood, as in the AHGA Brentwoods, aren't you?"

I felt a small trickle of sweat slip down the back of my neck.

Chapter 12

"Of course, she is, Dad. And, of course, she already knows everything you've just said and more. I mean, really, she practically grew up in a genetic engineering facility. Right, Lyssa? We're in college, remember? We're supposed to be challenging our parents. We're supposed to be frustrating and demanding and full of ourselves. Just like you were. Right, Dad? Don't say you weren't, I've heard the stories from Grandma and Grandad." Ayva smirked.

I watched as Audrick's frown disappeared, caught up in his daughter's whirlwind, attention-grabbing performance to change the subject.

"I'm going to have to get after them again. They're not supposed to be telling you anything. Especially not about your dear, old dad." Audrick glanced out the door to where Ayva's mom had disappeared. "I wonder if your mom is grabbing us some water. I think I'll go check. You want some?" he asked us.

"Sure, Dad. Thanks." As Audrick left the room, Ayva took the chance to quickly gather up her stuff. I did the same. I wasn't sure what she was thinking, but I felt like it was a good time for me to leave. I didn't want to cause issues between Ayva and her dad, but I definitely didn't agree with what he was saying.

I felt like he was twisting the facts just enough to make them support his stance. I could have twisted them in the opposite direction to prove him wrong, but I didn't think I was going to change his mind here tonight. His feelings of elitism didn't develop randomly one day. He clearly, truly believed everything he had just said to me. And he was a well-respected, well-known, upstanding man in SciCity.

I followed a still-silent Ayva out of the room to the front door. When it slid open I stepped out, but then I stopped and turned back. "Umm ... Ayva ... I hope I didn't ... I'm sorry if I ... but..."

A huge smile broke out across her face. "Don't apologize. It's not often that I get to see someone stand up to him. Most people just compliment him and agree with everything he says. I love it that you questioned him. And that he felt he had to defend his stance. You were awesome."

She leaned out and gave me a hug. "We're going to be unstoppable. Prepare for the toppling of Team Glitterati! See you tomorrow, Lyssa."

And, she was right. Amelie and Nova had no chance against us. Not only was our presentation better, but we killed them in the question and answer session. By the end, we were answering questions directed to them, but turning them in our favor. And, I thought that quite a few people in our class were really considering our side of the issue, not just as a persuasive speech, but as an actual issue in our city.

Later that night, when we went out to a nutrient drink cafe to celebrate, Ayva told me that she still wasn't totally on my side with a "no segregation requirement" for private clubs in SciCity, but she did think that regular businesses should have to allow everyone, even those without genetic enhancement, to patronize their establishments.

"You're making a believer out of me, Lyssa. I think I need to meet some of these non-Greens who have impressed you so much. They must be pretty cool people."

"They are." A couple of seconds of silence ticked by.

"Oh. My. Word. One of them is a totally hot, non-Green guy, isn't it?"

I tried not to smile.

"Don't you dare deny it! Seriously. Why am I just learning about this now? We've been friends, like ... forever."

"For like two weeks," I said. "And I don't even know if can count those first few days. I hadn't decided if I liked you yet. And he's just a ... well ... I haven't seen him in a while."

Ayva feigned pain. "So hurtful. And, besides, who cares about last week? We're going to have so much fun this year. And, I'm going to meet this mystery guy."

I laughed again, we said our goodbyes, and I went home.

Since then, Ayva and I had spent time together almost every day. Both in and out of class. Fortunately, I never had to speak on a topic against her, which was a good thing, because Ayva really was an excellent speaker. Even though it wasn't a competition, it always was to her.

As I pulled up to the university parking area, I wondered again what had Ayva so excited. It was obviously something that made her nervous enough to not want to iBud message about it. Which was weird, because both of our iBuds had an extra security app installed, the one owner brain wave transmission software upgrade. I hadn't heard of anyone that had successfully hacked it.

Walking into our classroom, I saw Ayva at the back talking to several other students. As soon as she saw me, she headed in my direction. Her eyes darted around the room as she rubbed her hands together, and when she got close to me, she bumped into a chair, tipping it over. Ayva was not clumsy – she was – nervous? What was going on?

"I'm so relieved you're here. I thought you might not show. It's going to be so cool. I can't wait." All her nervous ticks seemed to vanish as she spoke. She squeezed my arm, and leaning toward me, she whispered, "After class, we're going to meet up with–"

"Good afternoon, Ladies and Gentlemen. Please be seated and we'll begin." It was Dr. Penning, our course instructor. Ayva smiled, eyebrows up, and mouthed, "As soon as class is over."

I started to say something, but Dr. Penning shot a look in our direction. Class seemed to drag on forever. Dr. Penning was usually interesting, but I had a hard time following her tonight. She was leading a discussion reviewing the organizational pattern of speeches, focused on Monroe's Motivated Sequence, noting it was developed well over a hundred years ago, but still applied today. She brought up examples from our previous speeches, asking what had inspired people in our class to take action. Several students brought up that first speech that Ayva and I presented.

"...and do you feel you satisfied step five – action and actualization? Do you feel you left your audience with specific things they could personally do to solve the problem?" Dr. Penning was staring in my direction as she completed her question.

Crap, I thought, scrambling to remember what I knew about Monroe's fifth step and how it related to the speech we had given. Ayva was smiling at me and nodding. Everyone in the class was looking at me. A few more seconds ticked by.

I cleared my throat and began, "I ... I do, Dr. Penning. I believe we satisfied the fifth step. Ayva and I gave our classmates options that would allow them a sense of ownership of our solution. We were careful not to give too many expectations, so it wouldn't seem overwhelming. I feel our suggestion of creating a campus committee that could review all businesses and clubs on campus to ensure an open enrollment and participation policy for all university students, Green and non-Green alike, was well accepted. An actual committee has been formed, headed by one of our own classmates, Cruz Boyer, and I know that several students from this class have joined the committee.

Cruz, can you tell us more about what the committee is doing?"

All heads, including Penning's, turned toward Cruz, a short, dark, young Green with intense eyes. And I released a breath I had been holding. Ayva looked back and gave me a quick thumbs up, mouthing a "wow" before she turned back to Cruz. Cruz spoke for a few more minutes and then Dr. Penning released the class, reminding us that final speeches of our choice would be coming up soon.

As I gathered my things, Ayva appeared next to me. "Impressive, Lyssa. Way to divert attention to Cruz so he could make us look good. We have to be at the top of Penning's most valuable list."

"I don't think she has a most valuable list. She just gives us a grade and passes us on to the next class." I rubbed my forehead, feeling a little tired of the "forever-running-competition" in Ayva's mind.

Ayva's brows furrowed as she tilted her head slightly. "What's up, Lyssa? This doesn't sound like you."

"It's just been a hard couple of days," I replied, thinking about Ana and Gabe, about Livvy and Gunner, about my life right now. But I didn't tell her about any of it – I wasn't really sure why. Maybe, it was because I felt that down deep she viewed the world like her dad. I closed my eyes and rubbed my forehead one more time. "I think I'm just tired. I should probably head home." I threw my bag over my shoulder and took a step toward the door.

"Oh, no. That is so not happening right now. Trust me. You'll thank me later." Then she hooked her arm through mine and ushered me quickly out the door.

That was that. Ayva had made up her mind and we were going to do "it." Whatever "it" was. I hoped it wasn't actually dangerous because I was too worn out to care. And that, I knew, was a risky position to be in.

Chapter 13

Ayva ushered me out the door to her car. I tried a few times to ask her where we were going. She just smiled and said to trust her. Cranking the music up, she jammed out, leaving the campus behind. About ten minutes later, we arrived at a large, modern-looking house. There were several cars parked out front.

"I'm not in the mood for a party, Ayva," I said as she pulled into the driveway.

Ayva parked the car, then sat silent for a few seconds. When she turned toward me, I could see excitement in her eyes.

"Have you ever thought about what you want out of life? I mean, not like things you can buy, but like the things that really matter? Like living longer ... being healthy ...

feeling good all the time ... like you can make every minute count?" She stared at me.

"Well, uh, yeah, I guess. I mean doesn't everyone want to be happy and healthy?" What was she getting at?

"I don't just mean 'happy and healthy.' I'm talking next generation wants and needs. I'm talking the future ... I'm talking Greener, Lyssa."

I felt a little shocked. I'd heard about "Greener" experiments – mostly black-market procedures that tried to utilize the properties of chlorophyll to increase Greens' ability to produce energy from light. Occasionally, something came up about it at AHGA, but as far as I knew, no one had found a way to make Green citizens "Greener."

There were no shortcuts. All Greens had to spend adequate time under express lights to fully utilize the benefits of the chloroplasts in their bodies. Different types of lights, along with nutrient drinks, were about the extent that current science had to offer to boost Green citizens' health. We already experienced many benefits just by having chloroplasts in our cells – they controlled hunger (since adequate food was always being made through photosynthesis), they stimulated quicker healing (so we were rarely sick), they fought genetic abnormalities (like cancers), they produced advanced antioxidants (which slowed the aging process), and they even basically eliminated body odor. I wasn't sure what more Ayva thought we needed.

"Being Greener is a myth, Ayva. Everyone knows that. It's just crazies out there trying to make money off naïve citizens who think they can cheat science. You know that." My turn to stare at her.

"What if I told you it's not a myth *anymore*? What if I told you cutting edge science is happening right here in SciCity? That we can get in on it now? It's just for the elite, Lyssa, just those of us who really understand about wanting more ... wanting to be more. It's—"

I cut her off. "Who's doing this cutting-edge science? I haven't heard anything about it at AHGA. Wait a minute, don't tell me you've bought into some quack's bogus super-caplets that will instantly make you a bigger-better-faster-stronger version of yourself." I searched her face. "I know you're smarter than that, Ayva."

She just laughed. "There aren't any 'quacks' here. Come inside with me. Meet the people I've gotten to know. Hear what they have to say. I think you'll be impressed. Oh, and by the way, you might as well turn off your iBud. They've got anti-transmit tech here. Can't let any of the secrets out." She gave me a wink, then got out of the car and started to walk toward the house. Just like that. She didn't even wait for me to respond.

Seriously. So like Ayva. I wasn't sure what to do – I trusted her, but I didn't have a good feeling about this. Then again, as I watched her walking away from the car, I also realized I didn't want to be sitting out here alone.

I can go inside and listen, I thought. *I don't have to do anything I'm not comfortable with. If it seems too weird, I'll just talk Ayva into leaving.* I instinctively reached up and touched my ear while thinking, **iBud off**. *Better to do it now than have it start to squeal from the anti-transmit tech.*

That always gave me a headache. The newest software update was supposed to include a sensor that would automatically shut down the iBud in anti-transmit tech range, but it was still a little glitchy.

Catching up with her at the front door, I noticed Ayva had pulled a small plastic card from her purse. She held it up to the scanner and the door slid open. Glancing in, it looked quiet. I didn't see anyone.

"Come on." Ayva headed through the door and down a hall. She obviously knew where she was going. This was not her first time here, I realized.

We came to another door with a scanner. This time she leaned in for a simultaneous retinal scan and palm scan. Really? This was some expensive tech. I felt a knot growing in my stomach.

The door slid open, exposing a dimly lit set of stairs. I heard faint voices as we descended, but I couldn't tell exactly where they were coming from or what they were saying.

At the bottom of the stairs, Ayva led the way down the hall to another door. The voices were slightly louder here, but I still couldn't make out anything clearly.

"Ayva, I—"

But she shushed me, then leaned forward, typing in a code, and spoke into a panel. "Ayvalisa Banebriar." Another layer of security? A few seconds ticked by, and then the door slid open.

Voices immediately spilled out into the hall where we stood. I followed Ayva into a huge, brightly lit room. There were people everywhere, over fifty, I guessed. Quite a few were in a sitting area with multiple couches and a dozen or so big, soft chairs. Others congregated around an island, standing or sitting on stools. A few were talking near a wall almost completely covered with paintings, some realistic, others abstract. No one seemed to notice our arrival.

As Ayva slipped off her jacket, a girl appeared, seemingly out of nowhere. She reached for Ayva's jacket and gave her a hug. I crossed my arms, hugging my jacket to me. I wanted to be ready to leave as soon as possible.

"Ayva, Luv, so ecstatic that you could make it tonight. And you must be Lyssa," she said, stepping around Ayva and hugging me as well. "We've so been looking forward to meeting you, Dear."

Okay, this is awkward. I stepped back from her embrace. She looked a few years older than us, maybe, with waist-long hair done in perfect multi-tone green curls. Her one-piece black bodysuit covered her completely except for her hands and neck, and in her black stiletto boots, she towered a good six inches over Ayva and me. I'd always considered myself a little taller than average, but she was definitely over six feet. Everything about her long hair, long legs, and long arms made me feel small.

She was engaged in a lively conversation with Ayva, but I wasn't listening to what she was saying. Her long eyelashes batted as she pursed her lips from time to time. All of her movements were graceful and swooping. She had large eyes that were an interesting shade of green, a light sea foam, so light that I couldn't help but stare. And in contrast, her vibrant green skin almost seemed to glow. It was a truly unusual combination – something I'd never seen before – until another girl that looked *exactly* like her came through a door across the room and headed straight toward us.

Same eyes, same skin, same black suit and heels, but this one had short, spiky hair that stood straight up. She walked directly to us, nodding, and although her movements were graceful as well, rather than seeming elegant and rhythmic, she gave off an impression of power and crispness. Crossing the room, she seemed even taller than the first girl, but when she stood next to her carbon copy, they were identical in height.

"Ladies, I'm glad you could join us this evening. Calyssa Brentwood, yes?" she asked, nodding again, but this time in my direction. She continued, obviously not expecting an answer. "I'm Ellorna, and this is my sister Dreeah. Most of our friends simply call us El and Dee. Please feel free to do so."

I nodded, holding out my hand. "Nice to meet you, El." Her handshake was firm and quick.

"We've already met, Sweet Sis," Dee said to El, but that didn't stop her from hugging me again.

El turned back to Ayva. "You cut it pretty close. A few more minutes and you wouldn't have made it into this session." She was frowning. It looked like she did that a lot.

"Sorry," Ayva said quickly. "Lyssa and I came straight from the U. We–"

El cut her off with a wave of her hand. "Just make sure you're cognizant of the time." Then she turned and headed toward the group at the island.

Dee laughed. "She can be so abrupt, but don't mind her, Luvs. We really are excited that you're here." Then she excused herself, wandering toward the group admiring the paintings.

"Aren't the Twins awesome?" Ayva was smiling, looking back and forth between the two of them.

Awesome. Not the word I'd choose. Odd, maybe. One syrupy and gooey, and the other machine-like and efficient. I got the impression that their looks were their only similarity.

"We'll start as soon as Maddax is here." Ayva leaned around me to get a better look at the couch area.

I stepped back in her view, directly in front of her. "Ayva, I'm not sure about this, and I'm not really feeling comfortable here. Maybe we should just go." I glanced back toward the door we'd come in.

"Don't be ridiculous. You're going to love this." She grabbed my hand, heading toward the couch area. Leaning in close, her voice dropped to a whisper, "Don't refer to any non-Green topics here, okay? This is a Green only thing. An elite Green only thing. Just listen tonight. It's so enlightening."

What? What was she saying? I wanted to roll my eyes and walk out. *This better not be a non-Green bashing session.* I wasn't in the mood. I stopped and glanced back toward the door again.

Ayva laughed and punched me lightly in the shoulder. "Stop it. Lighten up. You'll have fun, I promise." Then she pulled me toward the couches.

"There he is, Maddax. He's the other lead in all this – the Twins' older brother. Come on," she said, tugging on me more, "I'll introduce you to him."

As we walked across the couch area toward a group standing by the wall, I felt the knot growing in my stomach. Something about all of this was not okay. Looking around the room, I was just getting ready to try one more time to convince Ayva that we needed to leave, when I heard a deep voice say, "Ayva, and you must be Lyssa."

Looking toward the voice, I immediately had to adjust my eyes up. In front of me, standing next to El, but a good six inches taller than her, stood the most incredibly handsome Green guy I'd ever seen.

Chapter 14

Maddax stepped forward, holding out his hand. I just stood there, unable to look away from his face. He had the same vibrant, glowing skin, as well as the same amazing sea foam green eyes as his sisters, but his eyes had flecks of darker greens in them as well. His face was an interesting combination of smooth textures and rugged lines. He wore his wavy hair all one length, and it hung slightly below his chin. As he looked down at me, it slid forward, dropping over his eyes. Very nonchalantly, he tossed it back with his other hand, never once breaking eye contact.

"Lyssa, seriously." Ayva nudged my arm.

I immediately took his hand and gave it a quick shake. "Oh, sorry, I ... uh ... I'm Lyssa." Duh. He obviously already knew that. I wanted to smack myself in the head.

He just laughed, a deep, warm laugh; and somehow, it didn't make me feel ridiculous. So, I laughed, too.

"Thanks for verifying." He continued to smile, his eyes still not breaking contact with mine. "Can I take your jacket? We've got a place to put personal items while you're here."

"Sure," I said, sliding off my jacket and handing it to him. Had I really wanted to leave? I was beginning to think I could really like it here.

"Hang here for a second. I'll be right back and then I'll give you a personal tour of the facility." I turned and watched him walk away. Same effortless grace as his sisters.

"He's totally into you, Lyssa. You are so lucky. He's got to be the hottest guy in here, and he's like ... twenty-five, I think." Ayva was talking in a low voice and she had a hold of my arm again.

Her voice brought me back to reality. I had been seriously staring. What was I thinking? I felt myself beginning to blush. "No, he's just being nice. I'm new and he probably shows everyone around. And he knew your name, too, Ayva."

"He didn't offer to personally show me around the first time I came here," she said, grinning. "And he didn't know my name *before* I introduced myself to him."

"Stop. You're being silly." But, I couldn't quite hide my smile. I looked back to the direction where Maddax had disappeared. Why was I feeling like this? I didn't even know this guy. The last time I felt like this it had been with – Gabe. I felt a pang of guilt, thinking of him. Then it quickly turned to anger. My last conversation with him at the farm briefly flashed through my mind.

"Whoa, everything okay?"

I turned to say something to Ayva but caught sight of Maddax out of the corner of my eye. And, once again, I found I couldn't look away. He seemed to be staring at me, too.

El grabbed his arm and whispered something to him. His eyes flashed dark as he leaned back, saying something in her ear. She glared at him, then turned and walked the other direction. And then, his smile was back in place with his sparkling eyes focused once again on me.

"Ladies, sorry for the delay. How about that tour I promised?" He stepped between us, placing his arms around our waists, and began walking toward a door on the other side of the room.

Ayva spun out of his grasp, saying she just saw someone she absolutely had to talk to, then she winked at me and took off back toward the couches. And, suddenly, I felt awkward. But then, Maddax took my hand, and said, "Come on, we'll be back in a few. Before everything starts. Don't worry." And he winked at me. Then I blushed. Again.

Maddax led me through the door into a smaller room with three desks and lots of tech. Media tablets, digital monitors, scanners, and several types of machines that I didn't recognize. "This is our office. It's where El and Dee and I put our minds together to make the magic happen. And this," he said, walking through another door, "is where the magic actually happens."

I looked around the second room, even more amazed. It was like I had stepped into a full research lab at AHGA. They had every piece of equipment that I had seen before and more. Not only were there the common items like beakers, test tubes, tongs, funnels, ring stands and rubber hoses, but there was also equipment used for molecular biology and genetic engineering like thermocyclers, UV cross linkers, and gene pulse electroporators (which I only knew about because I had to help a lab tech clean up a mess a few weeks ago while he'd tried to impress me with his equipment knowledge.) And, there was a huge amount of equipment that I didn't recognize.

"It's pretty cool, huh?" Maddax was staring at me again. I was starting to like that.

"What's all this for?" I asked, walking around the room.

"Well, El and Dee have always been advanced for their age. I'm five years older than they are, but they were only one year behind me in school. And, I'm no Drone myself." He laughed. I winced, just a little. I really hoped he wasn't a non-Green basher.

He continued, "At twenty, I was in my third year at the U, and the twins had just started. They were only fifteen but had taken a year off school to travel the world before joining me at college. It was a tough scene for them. They were smarter than most of their peers, but socially, they weren't ready to be there. I suggested to our parents that they buy a house, close to the campus, where the twins and I could live together, and work on our own 'science projects' in our down time. Our dad was content to get us out of his hair – he never really did connect with any of us – so he was more than comfortable to dish out money for whatever we wanted. Mom 'just wanted us to be happy.' We told her *this* would make us happy." He waved his arms around the room.

"It's taken several years to accumulate all of it, but I'd put us up against any lab on campus, or even in the city ... even AHGA, wouldn't you say?" He cocked his head to the side, looking at me with those beautiful, soft green eyes.

"It is amazing," I said looking around again. "Do you use all of this?"

"Well, the three of us have degrees in chemical engineering. Dee also has a degree in chemical biology, El has one in synthetic chemistry, and I got my second one in physical chemistry. El recently added another in genetic engineering and decided to go back this year to get one in structural engineering, too, although I don't really know why. And Dee is considering something in neuroscience. We'll see.

"When we started out buying equipment, we focused on things that all of us could use, then as we diversified, we each wanted lab equipment specific to what we were studying. We told Mom, she told Dad, and just like that, it showed up. It was always easier for them to show their love with money." He looked around the room. "They sure do love us a lot, don't they?" He laughed, but it didn't sound sincere this time.

"Hey, don't looked stressed, Lyssa. The twins and I have always been happy together. And we can figure out just about anything when we set our minds to it."

"So, what do you do, or make, in here?" I still couldn't quite figure all this out. If they were so brilliant, why weren't they working for one of the big research corporations? If they were that good, they could write their own ticket for anything they wanted.

"You're wondering why we're here in this little building instead out there in the 'real world,' aren't you?"

I glanced away, feeling guilty that he'd read my thoughts.

"I'll just explain it like this – out there, we'd have to report to people that aren't as smart as we are. We'd have to follow all *their* rules and regulations, watch out for all *their* red tape, report in and change anything that *they* didn't like. But in here, we're our own masters. If we want to try it, we do it. No questions, no paperwork, no *no's* from anybody.

"Our only rule is that when one of us works on something, the other two support it, build on it, take it as far as it can go. And we've gone some incredible places. Like what you'll see tonight." He winked and took my hand. "Let's join the others – it's all about to start."

I probably should have been scared, but holding Maddax's hand, I simply felt – what had Dee said? Oh, yeah – ecstatic.

Chapter 15

Everyone was gathered in the couch area. We walked in still holding hands, and I saw Ayva give one of her not-so-discreet "thumbs-up" motions. As we approached, it got quiet. El and Dee stood up, and Maddax motioned me to the chair that El had just left. Each of the girls stood on one side of their brother. They really were a stunning trio. Dee with her mile-wide smile, El with her piercing eyes, and Maddax with his — perfection. I didn't know how else to describe him. Perfect seemed to sum it up nicely.

"So, let's take care of business first. Ladies and gentlemen, if you'd be kind enough to pull out your currency cards, the girls will do a quick tap for the fee and we'll be on with it." Fee? What? What were we paying for? I looked around to find Ayva.

Maddax smiled at me. "First time is on the house. How many first-timers here tonight?" Four other people raised their hands. At least I wasn't the only newbie.

El and Dee made their way quickly around the room. No one disagreed. Or even asked how much they were paying. In just a couple of minutes, it was done.

The lights dimmed, and people seemed to settle back into their seats. Some closed their eyes, others leaned over onto their neighbor's shoulders. What was going on? These people looked like they were settling in to take a nap. I looked around again for Ayva. I could see her at the far end of a couch, eyes closed, smile on her face. She looked like she might have dozed off.

Soft music came on. No voices, just instrumental. Nothing I'd ever heard before.

Okay, this is getting a little weird. Maybe– My thoughts were interrupted by Dee's voice.

"Breath in and out normally. Use this time to visualize yourself as you know you are meant to be. Allow yourself to see what you can become. Recognize that this is your time. We will lead the next generation. We will break out of the Green mold cast by our parents. Although it was our beginning, it is not enough for us. For those of us genetically destined to be more, we will become more."

Her voice was smooth, calming. It instilled trust. I wanted to instinctively believe everything that she said, but something was nagging at the back of mind. Something that wouldn't let go.

What had she meant by "genetically destined"? Going Green was a procedure that allowed us to focus our time and energy on helping our community, on making our world a better place. And even if someone didn't have the money, anyone who really wanted it, who worked hard, who studied hard, could get a scholarship to go Green. But we couldn't pass our chloroplasts on to our children, just like our parents couldn't pass their chloroplasts on to us.

About that time, I noticed a fine mist filling the room. It was light and had a pleasant, almost fruity smell. I looked around. No one else was moving. No one else seemed concerned. Even Maddax just stood there. His eyes closed.

What was I breathing? Why wasn't I getting up? Why wasn't I running out? Why ... why was I concerned? I realized I actually felt happy – relaxed – comfortable. And over the next few minutes, while the music played softly in the background, I think I might have dozed off. Because when a bell chimed, I jumped, and my eyes flew open. A new, upbeat song filled the air, one that I recognized from the popular group G-Cubed.

Everyone was getting up. Laughter filled the air. People were hugging and dancing. The room felt instantly full of energy. And I was totally revitalized!

I joined in, hugging everyone around me. Even people I didn't know. I just felt so good – I wanted to share that with everyone here. Suddenly, Maddax appeared beside me. He leaned toward me, and I dove into his arms. We hugged for what seemed like minutes, although I'm sure it didn't actually last that long. Then we broke apart and started dancing.

Maddax was a phenomenal dancer. The way his body moved, rhythmically, gracefully, perfectly. It was like we were made to dance together. His touch sent sparks of electricity through my skin. His eyes never left mine. Everyone else seemed to disappear.

I'm not sure how long we danced like that, but I never got tired. And I never wanted to leave, or stop, or do anything else. I just knew that I wanted to be there with him, touching him, and having him touch me.

When the music changed to a softer version of some older song, Maddax grabbed my hand and led me back to the room he had shown me earlier. He took a couple of bottles of water from a refrigerated wall unit. And I suddenly noticed that I was incredibly thirsty. I drank the whole bottle, and Maddax laughed as he passed me another.

"I forgot to tell you that Nocking can make you really thirsty. Or maybe it was all the dancing." He drank a second bottle as well.

"What's ... 'Nocking'?" I asked in between gulps of water. It was icy cold, and I just couldn't get enough of it.

"Nocking – it's what you just experienced. I purposefully don't explain it ahead of time to newcomers because I truly believe you must experience it to understand it. It feels amazing, doesn't it?"

"It does," I said, pulling my hair back away from my face. "Nocking. It has something to do with that mist that filled the room, doesn't it?"

He nodded. "The mist contained a new enhancement drug that the twins and I developed. We call it 'Nock.' That stands for nitrogen-oxygen-carbon-plus a 'kick,' which is a new form of liquid chlorophyll that Dee's been playing around with." I could tell Maddax was studying me, to see if I understood what he was saying.

"So, you've created a new drug, that makes you feel really great, and it enhances the chloroplasts in our cells?" I was trying to stay positive while piecing together what he was saying, but warning bells were going off in my head. I had just been drugged. I knew that I felt awesome, but still, they had drugged me without my permission, without my knowledge. Was it even tested? Was it safe? Was I going to be okay? My concern was mounting as the drug began to wear off.

"Lyssa, look at me." Maddax reached out and took both of my hands. I looked at him and tried to smile, but I felt uneasy. "Lyssa, focus on me. The first time it begins to wear off, you feel a little ... unbalanced. But it'll subside quickly. Trust me. Just focus on me."

Those beautiful green eyes. I stared into them and found that he was right. I was beginning to relax again. Maddax wouldn't do anything to hurt me. He had gone through the treatment, too, along with Dee and El.

"What does Nock do?"

"It's the perfect cocktail of nitrogen, carbon dioxide, and chlorophyll for our cells. It enhances chloroplast production, which in turns gives us more energy. And, a beautiful side effect," he said leading me across the room to where a mirror hung on the wall. "Look."

I turned and studied my image in the mirror. My skin had the same glow that Maddax's skin had, not as vibrant, but I definitely noticed a difference.

"After a few more sessions, your skin will be even more beautiful. You'll see, over the course of the next couple weeks as you continue enhancing, you'll turn more Green. We simply refer to it as the 'Greener Effect.' It's stunning to watch. I didn't think it would be possible to make you more beautiful, Lyssa, but I think I was wrong.

"My enhancements will go beyond making you the 'perfect you.' They'll take you to the next level. And you'll notice an increase in energy and productive work time. You'll feel less stressed, more intelligent, and ... happy."

I was trying to listen, but I was still stuck on the part about him thinking that I was beautiful.

"What do you think, Lyssa? About Nock? About how you feel? What's going on in that beautiful mind of yours?" He smiled as he brushed a piece of hair from my face and tucked it behind my ear.

I blushed. He made me feel so – so – perfect. It just kept coming back to that.

"I think it's incredible, Maddax. I mean, I still feel great, and the treatment was done, like what ... at least a half hour ago?"

Maddax laughed again. "You mean four hours ago. It's 1 am, Lyssa."

Surprise must have registered on my face, because Maddax laughed once more. "I know. Time flies on Nock. Or maybe it's just time spent with you."

I'm sure I turned a whole new shade of reddish-green as I glanced away from him. I couldn't believe that he was into me. I looked back, and he was still staring at me.

"If Nock is this good, why isn't it out on the market?"

"Well," Maddax hesitated, "Nock isn't for everyone. At first, we hoped it would be. That it would be the next step in enhancement for all Green citizens. But it doesn't work for everyone."

I felt one of my eyebrows shoot up, the way it automatically does when I felt like something wasn't making sense.

"But no worries, Lyssa. We've done lots of testing now, and we've only had minimal issues. After researching those who've had problems, we've found that it often comes from inconsistent family heredity. You know, those scholarshipped to go Green rather than those born into it."

"But no one is born Green."

"Technically, you're correct. But we've found that people who have a family history of going Green have cells more accepting of the Greener Effect. Those who have been scholarshipped often don't have the same cellular capacity ... but, that's work talk. I don't want to bore you, and I don't want to spend what time we have left tonight talking about the science behind Nock."

Then, he leaned forward and kissed me.

Kissing Maddax was like nothing I'd ever experienced. I mean, I hadn't kissed a lot of guys, but I did have some experience. Maddax made me feel more alive than I'd ever felt. Special. Beautiful. Important.

Then the door to the room opened, and El walked in.

Chapter 16

I jumped back from Maddax, but he held firm to my waist, not letting me separate completely from him.

"What is it, El?" he asked, his voice slightly perturbed.

El looked from him to me, then at the ground. She shifted her weight and then looked back up at him.

"El, you're making Lyssa uncomfortable. What is it?"

What? Me? "Oh, no, Maddax, I'm fine. In fact, I should probably be finding Ayva. We should be getting home." Home. After 1am. I hoped Father didn't have security enforcers out looking for me. Or Jaxx. I shuddered at the thought.

Maddax released me, shooting a glare at El. She didn't say a word, but she didn't break from his glare either. She just glared right back at him, matching him in intensity.

"My jacket?" I asked Maddax.

The glare disappeared, and the smile returned. "One moment. I'll grab it for you." He shot one more look at El and disappeared through a back door.

"How are you feeling, Calyssa?" El's piercing stare was now directed at me.

"Great." I smiled at her, but her expression didn't change.

"Any dizziness? Light headedness? Nausea? Temporal throbbing? Unidentified clicking sounds? Warm sensations in any part of your body? Itchiness? Muscle cramping? Neck pain?" As she fired off the questions, I shook my head, trying to stay caught up with what she was saying. Why was she asking me these things? She walked across the room, stood directly in front of me, and stared into my eyes. Uncomfortably close. I could feel her breath on my face. Then, just as quickly, she stepped back.

"Here's your jacket, Lyssa," Maddax said as he walked back into the room. He looked between El and me. "El, you weren't being rude, were you?" he asked sharply, turning in his sister's direction.

"No," I answered quickly. "We were just talking about how great Nock makes you feel." I smiled at El, but her face remained unchanged.

Maddax looked from me to El and back to me. He didn't look like he believed what I'd said. But he simply handed me my jacket, then leaned in and gave me a soft kiss on the cheek. "Let me walk you out." He hooked his arm through mine and we walked past El. She watched us but didn't follow.

Back in the main room, I saw Ayva sitting on the couch with a guy. Her legs were up over his lap, and she was playing with his hair while they spoke.

"I'd wondered where you two had run off to. I was about to come looking for you." Right. By the looks of things, Ayva obviously hadn't been planning on going anywhere. "Lyssa, this is Taydon Longshire. Tay, this is my best friend, Lyssa. And, of course, you know Maddax."

Tay immediately stood up, almost knocking Ayva off the couch. They both giggled.

"Yes, Taydon and I know each other. Remember, I issue the invites." Maddax continued to smile, but his voice seemed a touch less friendly.

Dee's sing-song voice called out from across the room, "Oh, Luvlies, don't forget to pick up your parting gift. A little something to give you a boost until our next meeting. Same time, same place, next week. And don't forget – we don't Nock and tell. Our invite list stays exclusive, and you don't want to find yourself off the list, do you?" Murmurs through the crowd. Lots of shaking heads.

I looked questioningly at Maddax. "We've had to add new levels of security. It's for everyone's protection."

"I was actually wondering about the parting gift." I smiled sheepishly as Maddax tucked another stray hair behind my ear.

"Oh, that's included in the weekly fee. It's a modified inhaler that administers a micro-dose of Nock. The inhaler is programmed to your genetic specifications for security measures – you blow into it once, and it collects particles of saliva and DNA. From then on, you simply place it in your mouth, inhale, and you get a small dose of Nock delivered throughout your respiratory system. It won't work for anyone else, so you don't have to worry about somebody using it.

"You should use it once a day. Each inhaler holds seven doses. But no more than one per day. That's enough to continue to boost your system until you come back for another full enhancement treatment." He reached into his pocket and pulled out a small L-shaped device about the size of my little finger and handed it to me. "Keep it somewhere safe. And, be sure to use it each day. I suggest in the morning before you leave your house." I nodded and slipped it into my jacket pocket.

"... but why? I don't get it. I'm willing to pay extra. Whatever it takes." A rising voice caught our attention. Maddax and I both turned to see a big, muscular guy in a serious conversation with Dee.

"Now, Luv, you know the rules. One per person."

"Come on, Dee. I'm a big guy. I need more than that. You know it."

Dee just shook her head and started to turn away. The guy reached out and grabbed her wrist, whipping her around so hard she nearly lost her balance.

"What the—" She hadn't even finished her sentence when Maddax and El both appeared by her side. Maddax smoothly grabbed the guy's other arm and twisted it up behind his back, and El pressed her hand against the guy's neck. He immediately relaxed, letting go of Dee and leaning back heavily on Maddax. I wondered if she'd used some sort of a micro-infuser on him.

Dee shook her arm scowling, rubbing her wrist. But then, as if remembering where she was, her smile appeared back in place. "Everything's fine. Remmy just forgot the rules momentarily. But all's right again. Isn't it, Remmy, Dear?" The big guy smiled lazily and nodded his head.

Maddax and El escorted him toward two other guys. "Maddax, so sorry. It won't happen again. You know Remmy loves Dee. He just ..."

Maddax's eyes looked like ice when he turned to the guy talking. "Just get him out of here. Now. Before I change my mind about what to do with him. And if he ever lays a hand on my sister again ..." He let his voice trail off as he shoved the now docile guy into the other two. His tone and his actions startled me. He didn't just look or sound angry. It was meaner. Cruel, even. I shuddered.

I didn't like that side of him. Maybe he wasn't really the guy he seemed to be. How could someone be so kind one minute but so cold the next? Like he had a switch he could flip.

El touched his arm, then placed her hand on his neck. They stared at each other for a moment, and just like that, the switch flipped again. Then Maddax walked back over to Ayva, Tay, and me, like nothing had happened. He leaned over, kissed me quickly on the lips, winked, and headed over to another group putting on their coats.

I hadn't moved since he had left to go to Dee's rescue, and I still felt stuck in place. What had just happened?

"You should be going. We'll see you next week." El was standing next to me, motioning toward the door.

"Yeah, we need to get home. Want to walk us out, Tay?" Ayva had grabbed my hand and was pulling me toward the door. Tay followed us out, backtracking through the security until we were outside the house.

"Whoa. I've never seen him like that before, but I guess that's why they call him the Mad Man. I've heard some crazy stories about him. Like the time when—"

Ayva cut Tay off with a wave of her hand. "Those are just stories. He was just defending his sister. That guy was hurting her. I didn't see you rushing over to help Dee."

"Well, I was going to ... if it all hadn't happened so fast ... I was just about to..."

Ayva laughed. "Don't worry, Tay. We won't tell anyone, will we, Lyssa?" Then Ayva leaned over and kissed him.

And – awkward. They just kept kissing. Really? I was coming out of my Maddax-enhanced stupor and I was beginning to feel a little irritated. Out in the fresh air, I felt like I could think more clearly.

I had left school over five hours ago to go to some "event" that I didn't even want to go to. Once I got there, my "best friend" (first time ever I could remember Ayva referring to me that way) took off and left me alone. I was drugged with some new experimental enhancement compound, then basically threw myself at a guy. Well, he was a super-hot guy. And, a super-smart guy. And, he did really seem to be into me. But still. What the heck? I wanted to get out of here. I needed to think, and I wanted to do it away from here.

I cleared my throat. No response from the Ayva-Tay mass. I sighed loudly, a couple of times. Still no response.

Finally, I brushed past them and leaned heavily against Ayva's car. Well, maybe I actually kind of slammed into it because the car alarm began to screech. Ayva and Tay jumped apart, both giggling again, as Ayva clicked off the alarm.

Really? They sounded like little kids. I felt annoyed. "Can we go, please?" I tried to sound nice, but it didn't come out that way.

"Her first time, huh?" Tay looked at me. "Next time, the transition will be smoother. Just make sure to take your booster all week. That'll help." He leaned over and kissed Ayva once more. "See ya soon, gorgeous." Then he turned and walked toward a car parked down the driveway.

"What'd he mean by a smoother transition?" I said as I got into the car.

"It's hard to explain, Lyssa. I felt kind of cranky after my first session, too. I mean after I left. You know, easily irritated. Annoyed. Not necessarily at anything in particular. Just, well, I don't know ... like you're feeling now." She glanced over at me. I rolled my eyes.

"But it gets easier each time. And Tay's right. Take your booster each day. You'll be amazed at how you feel." I could hear her smiling in the dark even though I couldn't see her expression.

"Right. Thanks for letting me know I was going to get drugged tonight." It came out harsher than I intended, but Ayva didn't seem to notice.

"Not drugged. Enhanced. Not just everybody gets an invite you know. Maddax personally asked me to bring you."

What? Maddax knew who I was before tonight? How? Why? "He asked you to bring me?"

"Yeah, well, I wasn't supposed to say that, but I guess it really doesn't matter. I mean, the only way to get in is to be invited by Maddax or the twins. Everyone else can make suggestions, but they're the only ones who can give an official invite to bring someone new in."

I wasn't sure if I should have felt flattered or creeped out.

"Did you tell Maddax about me?" I turned to look at Ayva. I could only make out her profile in the dim light of the car.

"Um, no, I don't think so. No, now that I think about it, he asked me about knowing you. I was kind of surprised at first, but then I thought that maybe you two had met somewhere along the way at some sort of science research thing, like at AHGA, or something. Maybe you met, and you just don't remember. You're always saying that new people are in and out of AHGA all the time."

"No, I'd remember him." That I was sure of. I had never met Maddax before tonight.

"How many times have you come to these things, Ayva?"

"This is my ... third session."

"You've been doing this for three weeks? The enhancements? The boosters in-between? Do you really know anything about it? Have you done any research at all? How do you know it's safe? Maddax told me that there's been some *issues*. How–"

"Lyssa, stop. I feel great. I look great. Let it go. Maddax, El, and Dee are geniuses. Let them worry about the science stuff. You'll feel better about all of it in the morning. Just sit back and relax. Enjoy the ride." Then she turned the music up and hummed along with the song that was playing.

About twenty minutes later she pulled up in front of my car back at the U. I got out without saying anything. Ayva just smiled and waved as she drove away.

I jumped into my car. The whole drive home I thought about what had happened tonight. About Nock. About the Greener Effect. About Maddax.

On the surface, it felt wonderful. But a closer look made me uncomfortable. I worked at AHGA. I grew up with scientific testing talk in my house.

I had a sample in my jacket pocket. I knew that I should give it to Father. To make sure it was safe. If it really was as good as everyone said, I was sure AHGA could probably improve on it, make it better for all Greens to use.

Stepping up for an eye scan to open the front door, I was surprised when it slid open before the scan even began to engage.

And I was even more surprised to see Father standing in the doorway.

Well, I thought, *great way to round out the night.* This wasn't going to be good. Father looked angry. And then it got worse.

I noticed Jaxx standing directly behind him.

Chapter 17

"Father ... I—"

He cut me off. "Do you realize what time it is?"

"I—"

"Or how many people have been out looking for you?"

"I—"

"What in the hell have you been doing? Where have you been? Who have you been with? Are you out of your mind? Jaxx traced your car to the University, but you weren't there. We've been sitting here waiting for a ransom demand. Wondering if someone had taken you. If you were dead." He glared hard at me.

"Father, I—"

"You what? You'd better have an excellent explanation. And it had better not be something to do with that Stayton boy. I know you've been back out to his farm recently." He glanced sideways at Jaxx, who simply nodded once.

Okay. That was too much. I realized it had been irresponsible to stay out this late, but honestly, I was an adult now. I was in college, not high school. Jaxx had obviously been tracking me more than I knew. And to throw in something about Gabe after what had happened at the farm – all that "crankiness" that Ayva talked about seemed to kick in full force.

I looked back and forth between the two of them, then walked right between them, brusquely bumping into both as I moved through the door and down the hall toward my bedroom.

"Young Lady, you get back here right now!" Father demanded.

I didn't even pause.

"Calyssa, I'm serious. Get back here. We're going to discuss this right now."

As I walked into my room, I turned back to look at him. "No. We're not." Then I closed my door and locked it.

Immediately I heard loud footsteps coming down the hall.

"Music. G-Cubed. *Instantaneous*. Level 10." My room filled with the same pop music that I'd heard earlier tonight at Maddax's house. It was loud, loud enough that I barely heard the pounding on my door. But I didn't care. Not tonight. Too much had happened in the last two days.

Lulu sat up, looking at me from her small bed in the corner of my room, and batted her long eyelashes. Then she laid her head down and closed her eyes. Good. I wasn't in a cuddling mood right now anyway.

I focused on the song. As I listened to the words that drowned out Father's demands, I realized that the singer, Hunter Green, was telling a story about seeing a girl and knowing they were meant to be together before he'd even met her.

The heart knows what the mind can't feel,
In a single moment, I'm a thief ready to steal.
Like an addict that needs his fix,
Just seeing you, I can't resist
Because I know
You're my instantaneous.
You catch me staring but I can't look away
I don't know your name or even what to say.
Like the moon pulls on the ocean waves
I'm in over my head but I'm not afraid
Because I know
You're my instantaneous.

As I listened to the words, Maddax kept popping into my mind, and each time the chorus came around, I felt as though the song had been written just for me, for right now, for my life.

It's unavoidable, uncontrollable
Being lost in your smile.
It's magnetic, shockingly electric
Just being near you a short while.

Quicker than a moment
It's instantaneous.
You're my instantaneous.

Was Maddax my "instantaneous"? Everything about him seemed perfect. His looks. His passion. His touch. His kiss. He wasn't anything like Gabe, but maybe that was just what I needed.

But what about Nock? What about the testing? What about– I silenced the little nagging voice in the back of mind. I was tired. And tonight, I just wanted to sleep. As I scooted under the covers and closed my eyes, I listened to the last verse.

Reaching out to perfection, I can't let you slip by,
I'll turn every stone, touch every star in the sky,
You make me want to become the man I should be,
Your fairy tale prince who gets down on one knee,
Because I know
You're my instantaneous.

And I dreamt of Maddax.

I woke up a couple of hours later. Still dark outside. *Instantaneous* still playing.

"Music off." My room went silent. No sound of Father. The house was quiet. I walked to the kitchen to get a glass of water, and noticed a soft light coming from the family room. Livvy. "You're up," I said, walking in and seeing her sitting on the couch with multiple tech devices in front of her.

"Yeah, my sleep patterns have been off since I came home from AHGA." She looked up at me. "You really ticked off Dad and Jaxx tonight. Anything you want to talk about?" She smiled.

"Not right now." I rolled my eyes.

"Then, I suppose we should finish our conversation. Dad's totally out. I checked on him a few minutes ago."

"Are you sure? I don't want him overhearing us."

"Seriously, Lys. I think he was exhausted from the hours of pacing and yelling, waiting for you to get home."

I winced. Deciding to change the subject, I said, "Did you know Jaxx has been keeping tabs on us? He's been tracking my car."

"I know. He stops in here just about every day to 'check in' on me. He put a tracker on my car, too, but I saw him do it on our video surveillance. I've gotten pretty good at using it since I've been home so much. He put it under the driver side fender in the front. I always pop it off now before I go anywhere, leaving it in the garage so it looks like my car is home."

"Isn't that risky?" I thought about her meetings with Gunner. "What if he shows up when you're not here?"

"I've told Father I feel best in the morning and that I like to nap in the afternoon, so Jaxx usually checks on me before lunch. Seems to have worked well enough up to now. Today was the first day he's shown up in the afternoon, but it was probably because he was tracking your car and you're not usually here at that time."

"Still..." I said.

"And, at least Father hasn't given him his own code yet. Someone does have to let him in."

"As far as you know." I felt sure that Jaxx could get in if he really wanted to. Involuntary shudder. Up to ultimate creeper status.

Livvy just shrugged her shoulders and looked back down at the computer in front of her. I noticed she had four monitors set up with files open on each. She kept flipping through folders on her computer, then flipping the files to different monitors with a flick of her fingers. I watched for a few seconds but didn't see a pattern to what she was doing.

"Livvy." No response.

"Livvy." Still no response.

"Seriously, Livvy. Come on. We need to talk about you and Gunner and what you're doing. Now."

Livvy sighed and closed her eyes. When she opened them, she stared at me for several long seconds.

It was then that I noticed her eyes were a gold color. They were beautiful, not a strange yellowy-green like the rest of her, but soft, almost amber. Besides the odd yellow of her hair and the strange tone of her skin, she was still stunning. Just like before. And looking past the color, I could see that she did look stronger, healthier, just – not Green.

"Long story short, Gunner and I have become close. I care about him. And his friends."

My eyebrows went up.

"And, yes, I've been to his camp and met them."

I was pretty sure my eyebrows were now touching my hairline. Livvy had been to Gunner's camp? The rebel camp? When? How? Why? Questions raced through my mind with no logical answers in sight.

Livvy chuckled. "Perplexed is not a good look for you, Lyssa." The she got serious again. "Listen, I've been careful, but I needed to know what Gunner was fighting for – who he was fighting for. Talking with the people there. Listening to their stories. They're ... they're..." Her voice trailed off.

"I know." My voice was a whisper.

"Yeah, you've been there. You've seen it. But Gunner lives there. Day in and day out. And more people join them all the time. It's getting really bad for people who aren't Green and don't want to fall in line with expectations for non-Greens."

"Livvy, I–"

"Let me finish, Lyssa. We've grown up in a totally different world from them. We've never needed anything. And whatever we wanted, we got. Well, especially me. I felt I deserved it. That the world wouldn't be where it is today without the Brentwoods, so everybody basically owed us. Owed me. I can't believe how selfish I was." She paused.

I remained silent.

"Don't jump in and stop me or anything."

"Don't worry. I won't. You were selfish. And annoying. And don't forget rude."

She laughed. "You always have been honest when I've asked for your opinion. I know I didn't do it often." Then in a gentler voice, "I always thought you were a little too soft, a little too caring, a little too ... like Mom.

"And I was like Dad. Wanted to be just like him. Rich, powerful, and running AHGA by his side by the time I was in my mid-twenties. Crazy how much can change in a year."

I couldn't believe the Livvy I was listening to. When had she grown up? When had she looked outside her own little world and thought there was more? Where had I been? Why hadn't I noticed the change in her?

"... so we kept meeting and talking. And the more we talked, the more I realized I had to be a part of the change, that I couldn't just stand by and watch unfair things happen anymore. I had to know how much AHGA is involved. How much Dad is involved."

I could see the pain in her eyes. She loved him, but she didn't worship him the way she used to. She didn't know if she really knew who he was. I wasn't sure either. I didn't have any answers for her.

"Livvy, let me tell you what happened over spring break. What really happened."

And so, over the next hour, I told her. About how I ended up at the farm, about the Staytons, about going to the rebel camp to see Gunner, about witnessing the murders, and about falling in love with Gabe. I told her about the explosion, my return to her at AHGA, Father and Jaxx's accusations, and telling Gabe it was over.

Livvy sat silently through the whole story. As I finished, I watched tears roll down her cheeks. She got up and silently walked over to me. And she hugged me.

That's when my tears started to fall. I thought I was done crying about all that. But sharing it with Livvy, made it fresh again. Maybe it was because it was the first time I had shared all of it with anyone.

"I love you, Lyssa," she whispered in my ear. That just made me cry harder. I realized for the first time that she really did. Not because she had to. But because I was her sister, and that mattered to her.

"Where is this Gabe guy now? I'd really like to meet him. Gunner has mentioned him, but he doesn't talk about him much."

I sighed and leaned back, wiping the last few tears from my cheeks. And I told her about Ana's death, my trip back to the Stayton farm, and Gabe's reaction. "It was like losing him all over again, Livvy."

"I'm so sorry, Lyssa. He doesn't deserve you. You must know that. You were protecting him and his family, and there was no way you could have known about his sister." She leaned forward and put a hand on my shoulder. "I know how much it hurts to lose people you care about. People who you thought would always be there for you. But, like Gunner says, true friends don't just sit with you in the sun. They run with you in the rain." She smiled.

And I realized she did that every time she talked about him. About Gunner.

"You love him, don't you?"

"Gunner?"

"Yeah. It's the way your eyes light up when you talk about him. How you smile when you say his name. It's cute."

She smiled even bigger. "I do love him. I love him for being there for me. For showing me there's more to life than being Green. For caring about me. For helping me learn to love myself again."

"Oh, boy. What would Father say? His oldest in love with a rebel. He'd flip out for sure."

Livvy looked at me funny, her head tilting to the side. She didn't say anything for several seconds.

"What?"

"You really don't know, do you?"

"Know what?"

"I love Gunner, but I'm not in love with Gunner. Gunner loves Kye, Livvy. They've been together for over a year now."

Chapter 18

"Gunner and Kye? Together? What..." Kye had been the one to sneak onto the farm last spring break when Gunner had been critically injured and was asking for Gabe. He'd risked a lot to bring Gabe and me to Gunner at the rebel camp.

"You can be so oblivious, Lyssa. You were there. In their camp. You even slept in their tent. Their tent. As in theirs together. Didn't you notice the pictures they had up? Or how much they cared about each other?"

"I saw their pictures ... they looked like great friends. I mean ... thinking back on it, Gunner did talk about how important Kye was to him..."

"It doesn't even matter. I'm only telling you so you don't get it stuck in your mind that Gunner and I have something going on. We don't. He's like a brother to me. So, I do love him, just not as a boyfriend. I don't think I'm girlfriend material right now anyway. Best to focus on things I have some control over." She looked back down at her computer.

Okay. So, Gunner and Kye. I wondered if Gabe knew – he hadn't said anything to me. But he must have known. Gunner was his best friend growing up. He probably thought I knew.

I remembered all the time I had spent mentally matchmaking Gunner with my friends. Livvy was right. I could be oblivious to what was going on around me. At least back then. I felt like I was more observant now. Or at least I hoped I was.

"So, what are you looking for tonight?" I asked as Livvy went back to flicking files to the various monitors.

"I'm just logging new purchases of land made by AHGA in the last couple of weeks. They're significantly higher than in the past couple of months, and I'm not sure why. I mean, the company is always expanding, and they sell as much as they buy, but recently it seems different. I just can't quite put my finger on it. Something's off here." She continued to study the screens.

"Tell me what you're seeing. Maybe I can help." Although looking at the mess of what must have been several hundred files between the four screens, I wasn't sure I understood what I was looking at. This was way over my head.

"It's just that they're buying property in weird locations now. Some are really far away, like hundreds of miles from our closest facilities. I've been researching what else is in the area, like other genetic engineering companies, to see if maybe someone is thinking about a takeover, but I'm not finding anything. I'm just not making any connections." After a few more flicks, she turned off the monitors and her computer.

"Lyssa, I need to ask you for something. I don't know the best way to do it, and I'm not even sure what you'll think of me if I ask, but I have to anyway." Her face looked pinched, somewhere between discomfort and actual pain.

"What? You need an anti-diarrhea infuser?" I laughed as I said it, but Livvy's face didn't change.

"I'm not joking, Lyssa."

"Oh." She was actually serious. I sat up a little straighter.

"I need to ask you for a favor. I need your help. Well, we need your help. Gunner and me. I wouldn't ask if it wasn't important. I wouldn't get you involved if I thought there was any other way." She was speaking faster with each sentence.

"What? Of course, I'll help you."

Relief flashed across her face, but it was immediately followed again by worry. "You shouldn't say yes until you know what I'm asking."

Okay. This was definitely serious.

She licked her lips and glanced around the room, then down at her computer again. Brushing something off her leg, she reached back and rubbed her neck with one hand.

I found myself leaning toward her as the seconds ticked by. "What is it, Livvy? You're stressing me out."

She looked into my eyes, took a deep breath, then said, "I need you to find something for me in the mainframe at

AHGA. I can't seem to get to it from home. It's significant information the rebels need. But it means putting yourself in a position to basically spy on AHGA. And I know your work is really important to you. I wouldn't ask you to take the risk if I could think of any other way. But I've tried everything I can think of." Then she bit her lip again.

And I burst out laughing.

Livvy's mouth dropped open. She started to get up. "This isn't funny, Lyssa. Not at all."

"Wait, Livvy. Don't get up. Don't leave. I'm not laughing at what you're asking. Well, I guess I kind of am. But it's not what you think."

Livvy sat back, but crossed her arms, frowning.

"Come on, Livvy. Don't be mad at me. What I meant is that I'm already looking into things at AHGA. That's what I've spent the last four months doing. Trying to find out what's really going on there. Or if there is anything not ... quite right ... happening."

Livvy's arms dropped and she shook her head. "What?"

Then it was my turn to take a deep breath. And I told her about realizing I still had the pictures of the murder in the field, ones that she gave to me when she found my old memory bracelet. I told her about Buck and his betrayal. About learning from my mistakes, and about using my job as a cover to gather more information. Trying to find out how deeply AGHA was involved.

"I've kept video logs of everything I've learned. I'm not sure what's significant and what's not, but I know that AHGA has been involved in some shady dealings with some of the SciCity Security Enforcers and a few government officials."

"Can I watch your logs, Lyssa? You may have stumbled on to something important and not even known it." Livvy started to get up again off the couch.

"Right now?" I asked, suddenly feeling uneasy. Why was I feeling weird? This was Livvy, my sister. But that was just it. This was Livvy — and the old Livvy was always looking for an angle. But she was different now, right? I thought so, but my stomach still felt like small butterflies were swooping around, desperately trying to find a way to escape.

"You got something better to do?" She smiled at me and reached out her hand. After a second, I took it and we went to my room. I sat down at my mirror and activated the digital enhancer, softly stating the security code while Livvy was busy pulling an extra chair over from across the room. Something still felt awkward, but I tried to ignore it.

I pulled up the first entry I had made and watched it again with Livvy. She sat totally still, completely silent. Maybe she was making mental notes on her iBud, maybe she was just really focusing on what I had to say, but she didn't say a single word until the entry was over.

"Whoa, Lyssa. I think you're actually a rebel at heart, too." She was smiling.

"I'm not a rebel, Livvy. I just think people have the right to know what's really going on around them. Not some mocked-up version that the government thinks is politically convenient, or some jazzed up form of the truth flaunted by the big corporations. Or some fanatical twist on actual events spewed by crazy rebels to support their side of the story. Just the plain, simple truth."

"I don't know if the truth can ever be simple. I mean, there's always more than one side to any story." Livvy glanced back toward the digital enhancer. "Can I watch them all, Lyssa? I'd really like to. If it's okay with you."

"I ... um ... sure. I guess you might be able to make some connections with everything you know. Something that I missed. But, like I said before, I don't know if there's really anything useful in there."

"Let me be the judge of that." And then to the enhancer, "Play next log entry."

I continued to sit next to her as the logs played. After about an hour, I moved to the bed, sitting on the end of it, then lying back, and eventually pulling my pillow under my head.

Then it was morning. Light spilled through the windows. The digital enhancer was silent. And Livvy was gone.

Chapter 19

At least it was Saturday. I curled back up under the covers, thinking that going back to sleep sounded like a great idea. But my mind wouldn't stop racing. Last night kept replaying in my head. Sighing, I gave in and got up.

I found Livvy in the kitchen having breakfast with Lena. Sweet, warm scents filled the air, and for just a second, I thought I was back on the Stayton farm cooking with Nana Jane. But just as quickly, I knew I wasn't. That seemed like a lifetime ago now. A life where Ana was alive, and Gabe loved me. A life where I wasn't Green yet.

"You okay, Lys? You don't look so good this morning." Livvy sat holding her lightly toasted bagel just below her mouth.

I shook my head to clear my thoughts, then yawned and stretched, trying to look relaxed. "Long night." I tried smiling, but it felt forced, and I didn't think Livvy or Lena were buying it.

"I was telling Livvy that your father had to go in for work today. There was another rebel attack last night. This one was in the city. They blew up one of the medical buildings downtown." Lena took her plate from the counter and walked toward the sink. "It was one of the new clinics that posted it would only treat Green citizens and their families. I guess someone wasn't very happy about that." Then she quickly added, "I mean, that's every business owner's right, to choose their customers, but I'm not sure it's smart right now to do it so publicly."

Eyebrows up, I shot a look at Livvy, mouthing, "Did you know about this?"

Silently, she mouthed back, "No," fervently shaking her head.

Lena turned back toward us and we both froze.

"Your father's worried that the rebels may be targeting Green-only businesses in SciCity now. He said he'll be out all day, and home late tonight. He told me to take the day off since you'd be here with Livvy. Is that okay with you, Lyssa?" she asked, glancing from me to the clock on the wall and then back to me again. She seemed uncomfortable – I couldn't quite put my finger on it, but something was off.

"It's no problem, Lena. I'm fine, even if Lyssa has other things she needs to do. Enjoy yourself. Got anything fun planned for today?" Livvy seemed to be picking up on Lena's vibe, too. I could tell she was studying her.

"Oh, no real plans," Lena said, smiling. "Just going to do a little work around my house. Maybe go out a bit in my garden." She walked over to a small cupboard in the corner, reached in, and took out her coat and purse.

I started to get up. "Do you want me to help you? I mean, I've got no plans today – I'd be willing to come over to your house and do some work in your garden."

Lena looked at me, and an odd expression flashed briefly across her face, so quickly that if I hadn't been watching her so closely, I would have missed it.

"No, Honey. You just relax today. But thank you for the offer. You two girls enjoy a little time with each other." Then she winked and headed out the back door.

"What was that all about?" I looked at Livvy, trying to replay the exchange over in my mind. "Is it just me, or was Lena acting kinda strange?" I looked back toward the door. Livvy hadn't stopped staring at it.

"Livvy? Livvy? Livvy ..."

Her head snapped back toward me. "Huh. That was weird. Lena seemed in a rush to get out of here, like as soon as you were up, she was ready to go ..." Her words dropped off and she looked back toward the door again.

"Maybe she already had something planned. Or maybe she was relieved to get the day off." I could tell that I was trying to find an excuse for her. But why?

Livvy shook her head once more. "I don't know. But that was weird about the Green citizens and customers thing. I don't think I've ever heard Lena talk about anything political. Ever. I mean, she's not Green, but I think of her as

126

part of our family. Maybe the rebel stuff has her worried about us."

We both just stared at the door for a few more seconds.

"Speaking of rebel stuff, Lyssa, I need to talk to you more about the favor I brought up last night."

No more time to think about what was up with Lena. Maybe Livvy was right, that she was worried about us. Or maybe it was nothing. Maybe Livvy and I were reading more into it than what was really there.

"Did you watch all the log entries?" I figured she had, but suddenly I felt nervous. What was Livvy going to ask me to do? Would I be able to do it? What information did she need that she couldn't get to?

She nodded her head, then got up and walked out of the kitchen.

Okay.

I followed her into the family room where her computer and screens were still set up.

She sat down on the couch in her usual spot and tucked her legs up so she could rest a digital tablet on her lap, and began clicking away at the keys. I sat down in my new "usual" spot on the opposite end of the couch. Seconds ticked by. Livvy remained silent.

After what seemed like an eternity, she looked up. "Like I said, this isn't easy. I hate asking you but–"

I interrupted. "We already talked about this, Livvy. Just ask me."

She winced a little. "Sorry, Lys. I'm just–"

"Ask, Livvy."

She took her fingers off the keyboard. "Okay, so here goes. I need you to go down to level twenty-four to the Data Loading and Storage Center. It takes up most of that floor. Mostly it's just analysts. The hard drives there are independent of the company's main server. They hold important AHGA documents. Things like original patents, company contracts, building plans, corporate memos about land deals and takeovers, and GMO research projects. Important company stuff that AHGA doesn't want other corporations to have access to." Livvy paused.

"I don't know if I can access that level. My access pass only clears me for levels one through eight. That's way past my clearance." My stomach was starting to feel a bit queasy. "Let's just imagine that, miraculously, somehow, I was able to get to that level, and past all the employees who are actually supposed to be there. What do you want me to do?"

Livvy hesitated. Again. My stomach was feeling like it was doing little flips now.

"You'll get off the elevator and turn right. Three doors down on the left is a door marked '24771.' At least I think it's marked. It is on the map I found. But even if it's not, it's the third door on the left after turning right from the elevator—"

"Livvy."

"Right. Sorry. You'll need a code to get into the room. I can get that for you. Once you're in, you'll go to the fifth station on the left side. There should be a digital air screen. You'll be able to access it with a spoken code. It's not a voice identifier as far as I can tell, you just have to use the correct code. Once it's activated, a screen will be projected in front of you. Flip through to the correct file, then load it on a boosted micro drive that I'll have given you, and then you're out of there. Should be easy." Livvy swallowed and cleared her throat, nodding her head.

Easy. Right. Nothing about that plan sounded easy.

"Assuming that, somehow, I can do everything you just said, which I don't even understand most of, but just say that I do and I'm successful, what is the file that I'm getting for you? What's so important?"

"I haven't been able to access the file myself. I only know what I've been told. It's a file containing documents that prove that someone in AHGA management worked with SciCity officials to evict two small businesses in southeast SciCity so it could become the location of the city's New Growth Housing Center. Both businesses, a small corner market and kids' second-hand clothing store, had non-Green owners. The center was never actually built because of some regulations that were enacted, and then the land was sold to AHGA at a fraction of what it was worth.

"It's actual proof, Lys. It gives names, dates, specific plans and instructions of what had to be done. And a timeline of what AHGA needed in order to have a new building up before one of our competitors. And before either of the small businesses could do anything."

"Do you think Father knew about it?" My stomach was churning now. I felt like I might puke.

"I don't know. I hope not." Livvy didn't look very confident.

My mind was racing. If what Livvy said was true, it was proof. Real proof of the games being played, of the lies being fed to the people of SciCity. It was another chance for me to expose the truth – to make right what I had screwed up last time.

"Livvy, are you sure, really sure, that's what in the file? With that bomb going off this morning ..." I stopped. I knew I didn't have to finish.

"I've checked with Gunner – a quick iBud conversation right after Lena left. That wasn't us, Lyssa. I promise. Gunner was as surprised as we were. He's looking into it. There are a lot of rebel factions out there. But that's not what we're trying to do. We want to show what's really going on so Greens are held accountable for their actions. And to remind them they can't just take whatever they want from non-Greens. That we're all citizens of the same city."

I rubbed my forehead. Livvy and I wanted the same thing. And this was a way to get it started. Accountability. Responsibility. Acceptance. Mutual respect.

"But how? How can I get that file?" The more I thought about it, the more impossible it seemed.

And for the first time since we started talking, Livvy smiled. Not a sweet smile, but the old "mischievous-Livvy" smile.

"This is where it gets fun."

Chapter 20

Except it wasn't fun. Well, maybe it was for Livvy. It was a lot of tech stuff – hacking systems, placing virtual triggers inside programs inside other programs, turning monitor cameras off at the right time, even utilizing a second micro drive that would automatically copy a drive it was placed next to – it sounded like Livvy had put a ton of thought into this.

"How long have you known about this file?" I asked as she was mid-sentence, explaining something about a sensor on a door.

"What? Oh, a few weeks, I guess."

"So, for a few weeks you and Gunner have been trying to decide how to tell me about all of this? So, I could help you?" I felt the anger in my voice, but I wasn't really sure why. I mean, wasn't I just feeling excited that Livvy was better and that we were getting closer?

Livvy tilted her head to the side and just sat there, looking at me. Staring at me. Not saying a thing. Well, two could play that game. I kept my lips pressed together. I wasn't going to say anything else.

That lasted for about twenty seconds. "Really, Livvy? Nothing to say now?"

She bit her lower lip, looking away. "You have a right to be mad at me, Lyssa. Maybe I'm pushing too hard, too fast, but we need that information. I won't ask you to do it if you don't want to."

I sat silent. Why was I questioning doing this? I had been spying on AHGA, too, collecting information, trying to put things together ... all the same things Livvy had been doing.

Turning back toward me, Livvy leaned over and took my hands in hers. "I know you want to be a part of something bigger than yourself. Something that matters. This is your chance. Our chance. To make a difference. To play a part that matters. Really matters."

"Yeah, but—"

"We're not the crazy ones, Lyssa. We're not the ones trying to wipe out everything that's genetically modified, but there does have to be a balance. The modifying, just to show that you can, has to stop. The taking from others, just because you can, has to end. Green or non-Green, it shouldn't matter. Everyone has the right to be happy and healthy and loved."

"Livvy, that's what I've always wanted. From the beginning. From the time when I found that I still had copies of the images in the field. I want people to be held accountable for their actions regardless of who they are. The fanatics on both sides."

"We want the same thing, Lys. Can't you see that? This is our chance to work together. To make the changes we both know are right. I love you, Lys. Help me." Her voice was so sincere, her eyes so pleading, that I felt tears begin to well in my eyes.

Livvy loved me. And she needed me. Now, more than ever. It didn't matter if I was afraid. We could do this. Together. Livvy and me.

"Okay," I whispered, then she threw her arms around me and hugged me.

"You won't regret it. I promise." Livvy squeezed me once more before leaning back.

I hoped with all my heart she was right.

We spent the rest of the morning talking about how things would work. Livvy decided that we would get the file on Tuesday because codes changed every Monday, and she wanted to double check that she had everything perfect before she sent me in. She drilled me over and over on the steps in each part of her plan. I listened, repeated, messed up, listened more, repeated more, and after what seemed like hours, we finally took a break.

"I think you're getting it, Lys. I'm so proud of you."

"I'd take that as a compliment if I didn't think there was some sarcasm behind it. You had to spend half a day to make sure I can carry out a five-minute plan." I rubbed the back of my neck, scowling.

"Lighten up, Sis. You're doing good." She smiled as she headed toward the kitchen. "I need to eat something. You know, the whole non-functioning chloroplasts thing. Want to make me something cool like you used to do when we first got home from AHGA?"

I got up, following her. I did cook for her when I first got back from the farm, when she had just come home. When had I stopped doing that? I had loved cooking for her, making things I had learned from Nana Jane at the farm. Like cookies. With Ana.

I felt my eyes start to fill with tears again. Ana had hated cooking; she'd thought the kitchen was the worst place to get stuck in the house. She'd rather muck out a stall than bake cookies.

Now she'd never do either one. Ever again.

"Lys? You okay?" Livvy was standing directly in front of me, brows furrowed, concern in her eyes.

"Yeah. I'm fine. I'd love to make you something. Or how about I teach you how to make something new?" I couldn't think about Ana. Every time I did, all I wanted to do was cry. But that wouldn't help anyone. I forced a smile and grabbed Livvy's hand. "Let's go see if we have the stuff to make cookies."

We didn't end up having everything we needed to make cookies, but I was able to scrape enough together to make pancakes with razzlemelon berry syrup. They smelled delicious.

Livvy offered me a bite, but I stuck to my nutrient drink. The drink didn't really smell like anything, but I knew it wouldn't upset my stomach either. Weirdly enough, after the Enhancement was fully complete, I never got hungry. I'd tried eating a few bites of things at first, stuff I had made for Livvy, recipes that I'd loved at the farm, but it always made me feel sick. Father said it was part of the effects of the Enhancement procedure, not to worry about it, and to quit trying to take things into my body that it didn't need anymore. I was disappointed, but it wasn't worth feeling totally nauseous afterward, so I'd stopped trying.

But I still loved the smells.

Livvy only had a few bites of pancake left on an almost completely clean plate. Two breakfasts in one day, but she didn't seem to mind. I obviously hadn't lost my touch in the kitchen. I needed to cook for her more often. We both enjoyed it. Then I noticed that she had stopped eating and was staring intently at her fork.

"What? Something wrong?" She didn't say anything, so I reached over and plucked the fork from her hand.

"Huh? Oh, sorry. It was an iBud call." She looked up at me. "It was Gunner. He wants to meet me. Now."

From the tone of her voice, I knew it wasn't good.

Chapter 21

Livvy immediately stood up and took her dishes to the sink. She seemed to be looking everywhere but at me.

"What'd Gunner want? You don't seem very happy about his call."

She still hadn't looked at me. What was up with that?

"Livvy?"

Still no response. She just stood there, staring into the sink.

"Livvy?"

I got up and walked over to where she was standing. Gently touching her arm, I turned her toward me. "Livvy, are you okay? What did Gunner say to you? Are you in trouble? Is he in trouble?" My mind started to spin as I immediately jumped to the worst: Gunner had been caught, or injured, or had told someone about her and now she was in trouble or —

She finally looked at me. "No, I'm ... fine, Lys. I've just got ... a lot to think about right now. You know, making sure everything is going to work out on Tuesday. And, you know, the other stuff I still need to get done for Gunner. And the group. And, really, it's no big deal. You look completely stressed out right now. You should see yourself."

She let out a little laugh. But it was a high, nervous-type laugh, not a laugh-at-your-little-sister-because-you-stressed-her-out-for-nothing laugh. I'd heard that laugh plenty of times from Livvy. But Livvy never seemed nervous. At least not the old Livvy. I wasn't sure about this new Livvy. I didn't think I really knew her now.

"Really, Lys, I'm fine. Gunner just needs to see me. We need to talk about some things with some other people. Really. I'm fine." She was beginning to sound more confident now, but there was still a trace of something there. I almost believed her. I wanted to believe her.

"How about if I go with you? I don't have any plans today. We sent Lena off. We told her we were hanging out together today. And I'd love to see Gunner again. Actually talk to him this time. Just give me a minute to change my clothes." I got up and started to head out of the room.

"No. You can stay here. You don't need to go with me. I'm fine to go alone. Stay home. Relax." She was talking fast. Okay, now she was really weirding me out. She obviously didn't want me to go with her, but why?

I stopped and looked at her for several seconds. She just stared back at me.

"You're being straight up with me, right? We can count on each other, right? Because I'm about to put myself in a really bad place for you in a couple of days because you asked me to. Because we're on the same side. We're working together, right?"

Livvy sighed. Like she used to do when she had to explain something to me that she didn't want to. An old-Livvy sigh. And that irked me.

"Whatever." I started to turn to go again. Maybe I had it wrong. Maybe Livvy hadn't really changed. Maybe it was the same-old-thing. Her getting what she wanted from me because she always talked me into it. Maybe—

"Lyssa, stop. Don't walk out like this. Please." Her eyes had that pleading look again. But this time there was worry there, too.

"Then talk to me. We're both adults now. You don't get to pick and choose when you get to treat me like an adult." I crossed my arms in front of me.

"Okay. I'm going to be straight with you." She hesitated.

"I have to go meet with Gunner. He's taking me to meet someone important. I don't know who it is. I swear. He wouldn't say over iBud, but he said to meet him in thirty minutes at our usual place at the park. And, he said I had to come alone, Lys. And to make sure I wasn't followed or being tracked. I trust Gunner. You have to trust me that I'm making the right decision here. Please."

"But—"

"No buts. Weren't you just the one talking about trust?"

"Livvy, I don't—"

"I don't have time to argue with you, Lys. I told you what I know. You have to understand that this isn't that unusual for me. You're just usually not here to see it."

She was right. In the last twenty-four hours, a lot had changed in my life, including what I had thought I'd known about my "sick" sister. I blew out a deep breath.

"Okay. Go. But be careful."

Livvy practically ran over and threw her arms around me.

"Thanks, Sis. I'll message you as soon as I can." Then she was headed down the hall. A few seconds later, I heard the door to the garage open and close. And then the house was silent.

I wandered back to my bedroom and lay down on my bed. Lulu looked up, then ambled out of the room.

"Now what?" I said aloud.

I rolled over and glanced at the small nightstand next to me. The small, dark, L-shaped tube was sitting there. That made me think of Maddax. And that made me smile.

"Oh, what the hell," I said, looking up at my ceiling. "I think I deserve a little 'happy' right now."

Then I picked up the cylinder, placed in it my mouth, and took a deep breath.

Chapter 22

Lying back on my pillow, I closed my eyes and almost instantly began to feel more relaxed. I moved my fingers over my sheets and noticed how smooth they felt. Like I was feeling them for the first time. Cool, crisp, silky. I'd never noticed that before.

Slowly, I opened my eyes. Colors in my room seemed more vibrant. Deeper reds. Cooler blues. Warmer greens. Brighter yellows. And the rays of sunshine that peeked around the edges of my blinds were dazzling. It was as if the light itself danced on the air. I watched it moving, gently swirling, gracefully falling, then softly lifting once more as it spilled on to the floor.

"Blinds up," I commanded, and like a dam bursting, light flooded into my room, bathing me with warmth and a sense of well-being. And suddenly, I felt truly, deeply happy. Completely fulfilled. Every molecule in my body felt satisfied. No, more than just satisfied – elated – joyous even.

I leaned forward and soaked in the sun. Its heat slid across my skin, igniting my whole body. I knew it wasn't possible to feel my kidneys filtering my blood, or my lungs moving oxygen from my bronchi to my alveoli, but I swear I felt my chloroplasts, ecstatically photosynthesizing, capturing every ounce of energy from the sunshine engulfing me and producing exactly what my body needed.

It felt so – perfect.

Maddax was right, I thought. *Nock really does make me feel more … more of everything.*

My eyes swept over my slender green arm, my delicate green hand. They were beautiful. I felt – beautiful.

And then I wanted to play. I walked to the corner of my room and picked up my cello. This was what I knew, what I loved. From the time I was old enough to hold a bow, I'd loved playing music. Everything about it made sense in my mind. Its language was as natural to me as breathing.

The music inside me began to simmer, as if the heat from the sunlight was whipping it into a frenzy.

"Audio record," I murmured as I pulled back my bow. The heat turned to a boil, and as I touched the strings, it erupted into a flurry of motion. It swelled through me into my instrument, and we became one. It was as if I was no longer in control, as if my cello commanded my arms, my fingers, my thoughts.

Notes became fire. Crackling, sizzling, snapping, popping. My hands flew. My fingers danced. I was a fire walker. A fire breather. I was heat. I was light.

Music seared through the air, blazing in brilliance. Smoky flats. Flashing sharps. From pizzicato to staccato, I plucked the strings and the bow pranced in a whirlwind of relentless sparks that pulsed and swirled until my entire room was ablaze. Unwavering and unremitting, the score continued. No shadows. Nowhere to hide.

And then the raging tempo softened. No less complex, but less visceral, more sophisticated, more elegant. A mesmerizing melody began to take shape. The once brilliant fire receded to embers, suppressed but not controlled, still reminiscent of the piercing invigoration of heat, but now saturated with enveloping warmth.

The unison of the notes became more fluid, as if the cinders of the melody searched for the echoes of the harmony in flickering intervals of the fleeting bass. And the heat became hypnotic, a silken, rich fuel, powerful yet tranquil.

In the calm, I finally saw her. Swaying at the edge of the last of the light. Eyes closed. Hair lifted gently by the updraft of the heat all around her. Beautiful. Then she opened her eyes and held out her arms to me. And we danced.

My music was where I went to be with her. To feel her. These past few months it had been harder to find her here. But not now. Not today. The years since she'd left me melted away. Like they'd never happened. Like she'd stayed, and loved me, and watched me grow up.

Then the pitch changed once more, and I felt the notes drawing to a close. I wanted to fight it, but I couldn't. I wanted more time, but I felt her slipping away. As she spun through the smoldering cinders, she seemed to fade. I reached out a hand, to touch her, to hold her, to feel her one last time. She smiled, lightly kissed my cheek, and whispered, "I love you, Calyssa."

"I love you, too, Mom."

And then she gone.

I sat alone again, in silence.

Finally, I opened my eyes. My room was dark. Startled, I stood so quickly that I almost dropped my cello. After placing it gently back in its stand in the corner of my room, I walked over to the window. I could see the moon, the glow coming from other houses down the street. How long had I been playing?

"Continue audio recording?" a voice asked. I jumped.

"What? Oh. No. Stop recording."

I went back over and sat on my bed. I felt exhausted. My arms ached. I rubbed my lower back, which made my fingers hurt. Holding them in front of me, I gently pressed them together. Tender to the touch.

"Last session. What was the audio recording time?" I hadn't been sore like this after playing since that summer institute I'd attended between my sophomore and junior years in high school when they made us plays for hours to "build up our stamina."

The voice responded, "Last session, recorded today. Total recording time: five hours and twenty-six minutes."

What?

"Number of breaks in the music?"

The voice responded again, "No breaks. Continual music recorded for five hours and twenty-six minutes."

I'd never played that long in my life. I actually couldn't think of a time that I'd ever wanted to play that long. And, thinking back now, I didn't even know what I'd been playing.

"Playback, from beginning." I leaned back on my bed, gently rubbing my hands, wondering what I was about to hear.

And the music flooded back.

As it filled my room, I remembered. The notes. The twists and turns. The intense exhilaration. The glittering undulation. From the pulsating vibrato to the smooth legato, the notes created a stream of musical consciousness that I'd never experienced before. I almost couldn't believe that it was me playing.

But I knew it was because Mom had been there. We'd been together. When I'd played.

I listened, jumping to different sections. It was incredible. *The music of my soul*, I thought.

After several hours, I crawled back under the covers on my bed, feeling a little chilled. I'd been so hot before, like I was on fire, but now I was cold. And exhausted. I snuggled in and let my heavy eyelids flutter shut. The music filled my head once more. Maybe I'd find her again, in my dreams. Tired but relaxed, I drifted off.

Until a shrill tone jolted me upright in bed. An emergency call on my iBud.

Connect, I thought. I felt groggy.

Lyssa? Oh, Lyssa! It's terrible! I can't believe it! Why is this happening? Oh, Lyssa. I'm so scared. And then sobbing filled my brain.

Chapter 23

Who? What? Suddenly, I felt wide awake, and the voice finally registered in my mind.

Ayva!

Ayva, slow down, I thought back to her. **I can't understand you. Start over. What's happened?** I got out of bed and immediately started getting dressed.

It's Tay, Lyssa. He's been in an accident. He'd just dropped me off. We were messaging on our iBuds. Lyssa, they think he's going to die! The sobbing started again.

I froze. Die? Tay?

Tay? The guy you were with at Maddax's house?

I thought I made out a **Yes** in the hysterical crying.

Where are you, Ayva? Are you at home?

Again, I thought there was a **Yes**.

Stay there. I'm coming over right now.

I disconnected, grabbed my jacket, and headed out of my room. Passing Father's study, I noticed a light from under the door. Hesitating, I knew I'd better let him know I was leaving. He'd just track me anyway and come looking for me.

I knocked once and opened the door, not waiting for him to respond. I didn't have time for niceties, and I wasn't really feeling like I wanted to talk to him anyway. Father looked up. He was seated behind his desk, his hair ruffled, his tie loosened and slightly askew, his jacket laying haphazardly thrown over a small sofa next to his desk. Something was definitely up. Father was always "spot-on."

"Calyssa. I thought you were asleep." Nothing about last night. That was interesting. That's what I'd thought he'd lead with.

"I was. But I just got a message from Ayva. Her boyfriend's been in an accident. I don't know anything other than she thinks he's not going to make it. She's a mess. I could barely understand her. I'm heading over to her house. I need to be with her right now."

"All right. Drive carefully. It's late." Then he turned his attention back to the tablet on his desktop.

Really? After the reaction I got last night? The yelling and pounding on my door? I started to say something, but then thought better of it. Father was back to his usual self, probably engrossed in some AHGA project. Something more important than me.

I stepped back out and closed the door behind me. Passing the family room, I noticed Livvy asleep on the couch, her tech equipment laying all around her. I paused at the doorway. We still needed to talk about her "meeting," but she didn't call out to me, and Ayva had sounded so desperate. I hurried out to my car.

I thought about removing the tracker like Livvy had done on her trips but decided against it. Father knew I was going to Ayva's. I didn't have anything to hide.

Driving across town, I directed my iBud to search for news on car accidents tonight in Sci-City. Thirteen news stories came up, but as far as I could tell, none of them involved Tay. Rounding the corner to the street that led up to Ayva's house, I had to slam on my brakes to avoid a security enforcer's car sitting in the middle of the road. There were several more as well, a little further up. One officer held up a hand and motioned me to move forward slowly.

"Do you live on this street?" he asked curtly.

"No, but my friend does. I'm on my way to her house. She's expecting me."

"Who's your friend?"

What? Why did that matter? The officer stared intently at me.

"It's ... Ayva. Avya Banebriar." Suddenly I felt nervous. The officer kept staring at me. What was going on?

After several more seconds of uncomfortable silence, the officer, stepping back slightly, said, "You've been cleared, Calyssa Brentwood. You may proceed to the Banebriar residence." Then he took a few more steps backwards and began to wave his hand, indicating for me to move.

It took another second for it to register that he knew who I was without ever having asked my name. Only for my friend's name. A couple more seconds, and he was stepping back toward my car, frowning. I took off with a jolt, a little faster than I intended, but I didn't want to talk to him again. He probably just knew who I was because of the license plate on my car. But I had pulled up so fast, from around the corner, and it was dark—

Then I saw Tay's car. Or what I assumed must have been Tay's car. At least I thought it was a car. Hover lights had been set up all around the scene, directed at an almost unrecognizable object. The front of it was completely crushed in, shoved up against a concrete barrier. Behind the barrier had been a large metal pole with mounted security surveillance equipment. It looked like the pole had come down over the barrier and smashed in the top of the car. The entire mess only took up about half the space a car would need. A crumpled pile of metal, strewn with broken glass. It didn't look like it had ever been drivable.

Another officer waved me past the scene and pointed toward Ayva's driveway. I continued forward. Ayva was right. There was no way that anyone could have made it through that. It was a horrifying thought to imagine Tay inside.

As I got out of the car, Ayva's father met me at the door. "Ayva said you were coming. I was considering calling you myself. She's not so hysterical now. The doctor's given her something to calm her down, but now she's refusing to talk to anyone but you."

Audrick's face was strangely neutral. He didn't look upset or sad or worried, which seemed weird. His daughter's boyfriend, or guy friend, or whatever he was to Ayva, was probably dead or at least dying, but I couldn't detect any emotion.

"I'm here for her. I'd only just met Tay, but he seemed like a really nice guy."

Audrick's face darkened. "You knew Taydon Longshire?" His voice sounded harder than before.

"I'd only met him last night. When I was ... with Ayva." Oh crap. At a party. Dosing on Nock. Until one in the morning.

"Where were you two when you met him?" Audrick placed his hand on my arm and his eyes narrowed. I swallowed hard.

"Uh – we – I–"

"Oh, Lyssa! You're here!" Ayva came running out of the house. I pulled loose from Audrick's grasp and ran to meet her. She threw her arms around me, crying.

Looking around, Audrick walked up behind us, and began moving us toward the house. "Let's go inside, girls." I noticed some neighbors standing at the edge of their driveways, watching us.

Taking Ayva's hand, I led the way. Once inside, Ayva's mom, who'd obviously been crying, too, gave me a quick hug and suggested that we go to Ayva's room. Audrick gave her a stern look, but Shassa scooted us down the hall.

Once we were in Ayva's room with the door closed I asked, "Ayva? What happened?"

She looked at me then said, "Music on. Level 5."

Pop music filled the room, not so loud that we couldn't talk, but loud enough that I had to move closer to her to hear what she was saying.

"...scared, Lyssa. They're asking so many questions. I messaged Maddax and the twins right away. Dee got back to me first and said I couldn't say anything. Nothing. Not to mention anything about them. About Nock. About the parties. About any of it. She kept asking me if I understood. I told her I did. She said one of them would be contacting me again shortly, but I haven't heard anything yet."

"Why did you message Dee? What does she have to do with any of this?" I felt sick. This had something to do with Nock.

"Oh, Lys. I'm going to be in so much trouble. My dad is going to kill me if he finds out. And, Tay, oh, Tay. He's dead. They confirmed it. He was dead in the car. I overheard one of the officers say his head looked like a smashed melon – brains spilled out everywhere." Then she broke into sobbing again.

I took her in my arms and held her while she cried. I couldn't tell her it would be all right because it wouldn't. I hated when people said that after someone died. That things would "be all right." Tay was never coming back. There was nothing even vaguely close to being "all right" about that.

As her wracking sobs began to subside, I pulled us apart enough to look in her eyes. "What does Nock have to do with Tay? With the accident?"

Ayva glanced toward the door and leaned over, whispering, "I told him I didn't think it was a good idea, but he just laughed. He seemed so sure of himself. Like he knew what he was doing. But I should have stopped him. I could have stopped him, Lyssa. The accident ... it's my fault."

Chapter 24

Ayva leaned over and buried her face in her hands. She was silent now, but her shoulders were still shaking. It was like she had cried all the sound out, and all that was left was the sadness still trying to seep out of her body.

I put my hand on her back. "Ayva, you have to talk to me. Tell me what happened. I need to know. When I first got here, your dad was questioning me about Tay. About where we met. What we were doing. That sort of stuff. What have you told him already?"

Ayva sat up slowly, rubbing her eyes once more. Sniffling, she said, "I haven't really told him much of anything. Dad did most of the talking." Her voice began to firm up, not quivering so much anymore as she went on. "He always knows about my friends."

Okay. That was a little creepy. And it made me wonder how much Audrick knew about me.

"I told Mom and Dad earlier tonight that I was going to go hang out with a friend for a while. Dad started asking questions, but Mom told him to relax and let me go have some fun. That ticked him off, but he doesn't like for them to argue in front of me, so he just said to be home early tonight.

"Tay swung by and picked me up, and then we headed down to Mode Essential, you know, that new designer shop in the Jewel District?"

I simply nodded my head, and she continued, "We shopped around for a little while, but couldn't find anything super cute, so Tay suggested we go check out the new air park. We've been boarding together lately."

My eyebrows went up. I hadn't known that Ayva was in to airboarding. That didn't really seem her style.

A quick smile fleeted across her face. "I took it up in high school. Mostly because Dad didn't like it." Then the frown returned. "Tay said he had some friends that were going airboarding, so we could hang out and watch them. I didn't care where we went. I just wanted to be with him. And he was super excited about introducing me to his friends.

"We got there, and a couple of guys were showing off. Some new air currents had recently been installed, so it was intense. They were doing aciddrops and airwalks and wallrides like they were nothing. Then one guy jets right out in front of everyone else, coming out of the backside of a super burly air current, then kickflips his board, tic-tac-ing out of it to keep his balance and slides right up to where I'm standing. It was crazy."

I just looked at her. I didn't understand about 90% of what she had just said or why she was telling me. I must have looked impatient because then she said, "I'm getting there – this is important. It's what started it all." She paused, waiting for a response from me. I just nodded again so she'd go on.

"So, this guy stops about three inches from my face and says, 'Hey, Babe, want to hop on my board? I'm sure I've got a few tricks you've never seen before.' Then he grabs me around the waist, pulls me forward off the viewing platform, and the next thing I know, I feel like we're falling. Then he tugs me into him, whispering, 'Lean back and enjoy the ride.' It happened so fast, I didn't even realize what was going on."

She shook her head, frowning. "I told him to take me back, but he just laughed. I tried to move away from him, but it caused the board to rock, and for a few seconds, I thought I was going to dump. And I wasn't leashed to the board, so I would have dropped like a rock. That really scared me.

"Next thing I knew, Tay was on a board beside us. He signaled the guy I was with to take me back. The guy laughed again, and we slid up on the platform with Tay right behind us. Another guy was standing there. He took the board from Tay and immediately jumped back out onto the air current.

"Tay was totally ticked off. I thought he was going to punch the guy in the face. But then the guy said, 'Hey, Little

Cuz, you gotta lighten up. I was just showin' your girl around the course.' Then Tay laughed, too, and hugged him. Guys, seriously, right?" She almost smiled, but just as quickly it turned into a muffled sob. "I can't believe he's gone."

She started to cry again.

"Ayva, what does any of this have to do with the accident? With Nock?"

She seemed startled at the word "Nock" and glanced warily at the door.

Sniffing a couple more times, she pulled it back together, and continued. "Turns out the guy was Tay's friend from when they were little kids. The guy's name is Dashell, but everybody calls him Dash. He and Tay grew up together. He's like a big brother to Tay. Well, he was." Ayva looked like she was going to lose it again.

I put my hand on her arm. "What happened next?"

Ayva seemed to draw strength from the touch. "Well, the guys talked, catching up, I guess, for a bit, then Dash got a funny look on his face. He asked Tay if he was 'on something.' Tay laughed it off, but Dash wouldn't let it go. He said Tay looked different, something weird with his eyes. Tay said, 'Yeah, better version of the old me, huh?' But Dash grabbed his arm and got in his face. He asked him what he was on. Speed, Synaxx? He even accused him of being on ZT6. Can you believe that? Tay on ZT6? That stuff's crazy!

"Anyway, Tay shook him off and told him he was fine, that he wasn't 'on' anything, that he was just super happy right now because he'd found me. Dash didn't buy it, I'm sure, but it reminded him that I was there, I think. He told Tay that they'd talk more about it later. He didn't look happy, and everything just felt awkward. Tay said something about us having to go, and he and Dash kinda hugged, then we took off. But I could tell that it was really eating at Tay. What Dash had said."

Ayva stopped, chewing on her bottom lip. Tears were in her eyes again. I started to reach out, but she shook her head. Clearing her throat, she went on. "When we were back in the car, I asked Tay about Dash and the ZT6. He said Dash used to do some of the designer drugs, nothing major, just a little here and there. Then one night he got all jacked up at a party on ZT6 and got in a fight and something happened. Tthe other guy slipped and hit his head, or something, and ended up dying. Tay said Dash was cleared of all charges, but Dash has never touched any type of party drug again. That he's adamantly against it. And he gets worried about Tay over all kinds of little things. Tay said that sometimes the big brother act got old, but that most of the time, Dash was a cool guy to hang with.

"That was when Tay pulled his inhaler out of the middle console in his car. He said, 'Let's dose together right now. This whole thing with Dash has been a huge downer, and I could use a little pick-me-up.' I told him I'd already dosed this morning and that I didn't even have my inhaler with me. I asked him if he had already dosed today, too. He got quiet, then said, 'Yeah,' but he didn't think it was lasting as long. That he was totally fine, that the airride had used up a ton of energy, so he'd be fine with a second dose.

"I told him I thought it was a bad idea, that Maddax and the twins had said only one per day, no more. But he leaned over and kissed me, telling me that he loved how much I cared about him, and that I was so cute when I was worried. And, that he'd done it before. Double-dosed in one day." She stopped for several seconds.

"He even said I could drive his car home if that made me feel better, that I could see how he reacted, and that if he was acting weird, he'd just stay at my house for a couple of hours, and we could watch old digital flicks. He seemed so sure of himself. Like he totally knew what he was doing. Then, ... then ..." The words faded out as her bottom lip trembled.

Then in a soft voice, so soft I almost couldn't hear her, she said, "He told me he wouldn't do it if I really didn't want him to, and I just laughed and kissed him again. Then I said, 'But I'm definitely driving home.' He dosed. I drove.

"He seemed fine the whole way home. In fact, he seemed even clearer, and happier again. We talked about airboarding. Lyssa, he's so good, and he's taught me so much over the last few weeks. He says I'm a natural, even though I ride goofy – that's with my right foot forward." Ayva stopped and put her head in her hands. "I have to quit that. Talking like he's still here. Like he's going to be here tomorrow."

I knew I was about to lose her again. "Ayva, what happened? You obviously made it home. What happened with Tay?"

She looked back up at me, shaking her head. "I don't know. We got home. He seemed fine. He even talked with

Mom for a minute when he walked me to the door. I never would have let him leave if I had known anything was wrong. He just jumped back in his car and waved goodbye, smiling at us. As he backed out, Mom and I went inside the house. She'd just closed the door when we heard the crash. It was a horrible sound. Mom and I both ran back outside to see what happened. Everybody in the neighborhood was outside. People were running up the road, yelling for help. Mom and I ran up that way, too.

"Mom realized before I did that it was Tay's car. She tried to grab me and turn me away from it. To start walking us back toward the house. And then I knew. From the look in her eyes. I ripped away from her and ran toward the accident.

"I was crying, I think. Someone grabbed me and held me back. Then I was being pulled back toward the house. That's all a blur. I don't remember getting back here or coming inside. Then my dad was here, asking questions, and all I could do was scream and cry.

"The next thing I can remember is the doctor giving me something. I felt a little calmer until Dad started questioning me again. Who is Taydon Longshire? Where did I meet him? How did I know him? I got hysterical again and couldn't answer him. All I could think about was that Taydon was gone. Mom just held me as I cried.

"When Dad came back in next, he had the doctor with him again. Mom didn't want them to give me anything else, but Dad was insistent. When I stopped crying, he asked me if Taydon had been on anything, if I knew anything, if I was on anything. I started screaming at him to get out, to leave me alone, that my boyfriend had just died, and that I wouldn't talk to him right now. Deep down, I was scared, and as soon as they left me alone for a minute, I called Maddax and the twins. I didn't know what to say, what to do. Then I called you."

She looked into my eyes. "He's gone, and he's never coming back. I could have stopped him. I should have stopped him. It's my fault. All I had to do was tell him not to. Just a few simple words and he'd be here right now. Why didn't I tell him to stop?" She was crying again. Sobbing. I could feel her pain. The room was filled with it. Heavy. Tense. Suffocating.

I wanted to run out. To leave. To forget about Nock. To forget about Tay's death. But I couldn't. Ayva needed me to be here. To be strong for her. To help her deal with losing someone she loved and then to live on after. Because I'd done it.

But I didn't know if I could be strong for her. It was hard enough just being strong for me. Ana's face filled my mind.

We both jumped as Ayva's bedroom door flew open.

Audrick stood there, scowling. "There's someone here to see you. Come to my study." Then he turned and walked out of the room.

Chapter 25

I immediately started for the door, but Ayva just stood there. Audrick stopped, looked back, and his scowl deepened, and I quickly held out my hand to Ayva.

"Come on," I said softly, taking a step toward her. She slowly reached out and took my hand. Following Audrick down the hall, I could feel Ayva trembling, her walk unsteady. I looked at her eyes, wide with fear, and her face, an unusually light shade of green. I gave her hand a little squeeze and tried for a brave smile.

But I didn't really think it was successful. I felt like those damn butterflies from yesterday were back and gnawing holes through my stomach. *Who was here?* I sincerely hoped it wasn't Jaxx or Father. Not that security enforcers were a better option.

Rounding the corner into Audrick's study, I heard, "Oh my poor, sweet dear. It's so, so terrible. I can only imagine how incredibly awful you must feel right now."

Before I even I saw her, I knew who it was.

Dee.

She rushed up and threw her arms around Ayva, squeezing her into her chest. Ayva seemed to melt there, weeping, clinging to Dee. And Dee cooed and patted and stroked her hair, telling Ayva that she was there and that everything would be all right now.

Really? I closed my eyes for a couple of seconds and swallowed hard. It was obvious to me that Dee was phony. *How could Ayva be buying this?* Being syrupy wouldn't make this all better.

"Are you okay?" A soft voice from behind me whispered gently in my ear.

I forgot about Dee.

As I turned around, Maddax stepped forward and enveloped me in his arms. Closing my eyes again, I took a deep breath, laying my face against his chest. I drank in his scent, let it wash over me. He radiated strength and confidence, and I soaked it in. And suddenly, I felt okay.

And then I was aware again of where I was and what had happened. Shassa had her arm around Dee and Ayva, ushering them toward the couch. Audrick followed them. Maddax stepped back, took my hand, and walked me to the other side of the room.

He turned his back partially to them and hugged me again, leaning intimately toward my ear. "We don't have much time. Did she tell them about Nock?"

I looked up at him startled? What? Nock?

"Calyssa, focus. Yes or no. Has she told them about Nock?"

"No."

"Good. Don't worry. I'll handle this."

"Wha–" His stern look cut me off.

"Just stay quiet. Listen. And agree with whatever I say. Do you understand?"

I nodded.

He immediately turned back around, still holding my hand, and began to walk back toward the couch. I stumbled when he took off, and that earned me another sharp look. Then he dropped my hand.

As we approached the couch, Audrick turned to face us.

"Thank you for coming by, Dr. Steele. Especially at this late hour. I'm so sorry if we've inconvenienced you and your sister."

What? Dr. Steele?

My mouth dropped open. I looked from Maddax to Dee. She pursed her lips and gave me an almost imperceptible shake of her head. I got the message and clamped my mouth shut.

"... was no problem or inconvenience at all Mr. Banebriar. When my sister messaged me, explaining what had happened to one of her dearest friends, I immediately offered to come with her. She was so distraught for your daughter. I didn't want her to come alone."

"Please, call me Audrick. And, I understand completely. This has been quite stressful for all of us."

"Of course, Audrick, and call me Maddax. My sister, Dee, and I are here to help in any way we can. For both girls." He glanced at me. "Dee and I have known Lyssa for years. We're good family friends. And after she introduced Dee to Ayva, the three of them have been almost inseparable." He put his arm around me and gave a little squeeze. I smiled weakly.

"Lyssa, why don't you and Dee go tuck Ayva in for the night. I'm sure her doctor left something for her to help her sleep. If not, I can certainly prescribe her something." He reached out his hand to Ayva. She stood up, nodding, no longer crying, but not saying a word.

"That's probably a good idea. The doctor left an infuser for her tonight. We'll go grab it," Audrick said, stepping out of the way, then leaning over to help his wife up. The two of them left the room.

Dee hooked her arm through Ayva's. "Don't worry, Dear. We'll get you in bed and asleep. This will all just seem like a bad dream tomorrow."

As we started to leave the room, Maddax caught my arm. "Make sure to remind Dee that she needs enough to go to sleep immediately, and to sleep well into tomorrow morning." He let go as Audrick and Shassa reentered the room.

"Here's the infuser." Shassa had the small vial in her hand.

"I can take that, Mrs. Banebriar," Dee said sweetly. "I've volunteered at the local hospital for the last three years. I can administer infusers like a pro."

Shassa looked concerned, but right then Maddax added, "Audrick, Shassa, if you don't mind I'd like to talk with both of you for a few minutes while the girls are taking Ayva to her room. About what we were discussing before." Then he took a few steps toward a chair near the couch. The Banebriars looked at each other and followed.

Dee and I walked Ayva out of the room. "I'd like a drink of water," Ayva said, turning toward the kitchen.

"I'll grab it and meet you in the bedroom," I said. Dee didn't even acknowledge me. She just kept cooing at Ayva, walking her down the hall.

I turned and started toward the kitchen but paused again just outside the study door.

"... I know. But really, he's been under constant medical supervision. The seizures have been sporadic, and we really thought they were under control with the new medication. Maybe he forgot a dose. Being young, he would forget sometimes. I'm sure you remember, Audrick, what it was like to feel young and invincible. That nothing would ever happen to you, that you'd always be fine. Taydon never really accepted the fact that there was something wrong. He just wanted it fixed. Wanted to move on. We can only be thankful that Ayva wasn't in the car with him when he had the seizure."

Seizure?

Shassa's voice was strained as she asked, "Do you think he knew? Did he feel it?"

"Oh, no. I'm sure he wasn't aware of what was happening during the seizure, and from the report I read, I'd say death was immediate on impact."

"Well, at least he didn't suffer. The poor boy."

"I was worried when the enforcers first came to talk to me." Audrick's voice was strained as well. "The Longshire family is rather scandalous. Always in the news, caught up in something that borders on being illegal. I was worried that maybe he had gotten Ayva involved in something."

"He was a good kid, Audrick. I can vouch for him. I've known him for a while. He was trying to separate himself from his family. Make a better life for himself. Working hard in college. I think you would have really liked him."

When Dee's hand touched my shoulder, I almost let out a yelp.

"Don't worry about the water. She'll be asleep for at least the next 18 to 20 hours with the dose I gave her." Her smile wasn't sweet. She grabbed my arm and jerked me into the study with her.

"Maddax, we should be heading out and letting these poor people get some rest. They have to be exhausted, too."

"Ayva, she's asleep?" Shassa's face was still etched with worry.

"Yes. She looks so peaceful now."

"She'll probably need to sleep most of tomorrow as well. Mental trauma can be just as exhausting as physical trauma," Maddax added. "We'll take Calyssa home. I'll drive her. Dee can drive Calyssa's car and follow us. I don't think she should drive anywhere else tonight."

Okay.

This was too weird.

I wasn't sure how much of what Maddax had said was true. He sounded convincing. But the butterflies were back.

"Thanks, Maddax, but I can drive myself tonight. I don't want to put you and Dee out." Something felt off about this situation.

"Oh, absolutely not." Dee slipped her arm around my waist, looking very concerned. "We'd never forgive ourselves if something happened, would we, Maddax?" She leaned over, putting her head on my shoulder, and gave me a squeeze.

"No, we wouldn't. Goodnight, Audrick, Shassa." As he reached out to shake their hands, Dee already had me headed toward the door.

I tried to stop and turn around, but Dee whispered gruffly in my ear, "Don't even think about it, Sweetie. We need to talk. You *are* coming with us."

Chapter 26

Maddax stepped to the other side of me, and before I knew it, we were out the door heading for his car.

"I–"

"Don't say anything until we're in the car," Maddax said as he glanced over his shoulder back toward the house.

"But–"

He cut me off again. "Lyssa, I'm serious. Get in." The passenger side door opened automatically at his approach.

I felt helpless. I wasn't sure of what I should do.

"Now." Dee's hard voice startled me. I turned to glare at her. Amazing how all that syrupy sweetness had dried up, leaving cold anger in its place.

"Ladies, please. Not here." Maddax stepped in between us.

Leaning forward, he said softly, "Please, Lyssa. I'll explain everything in the car."

Really? What was going on here? I wasn't getting in that car until I had more information.

Then he leaned forward and kissed me gently. My resolve melted with the heat of the kiss, and I slid into the passenger seat.

"What's your audio car code?" Dee's glare was still just as intense, and it threw me for a second.

"What?"

"Your. Car. Code. Seriously. Pull it together."

Her words felt like a slap across the face.

My glare was back. "SRV2781G," then, "Door close." Dee jumped back as the car door silently shut.

In seconds, Maddax was in the driver seat beside me, and we were off.

We drove in silence for about a minute. This was not what I'd had in mind when I'd imagined my next visit with Maddax.

Maddax broke the silence first. "Lyssa, I know all of this is probably feeling a little overwhelming right now, but you were great back there." He reached over and took my hand.

His body heat radiated up my arm. I wanted to pull away, to ask him where he'd learned all those things about Tay, to question why he and Dee had come to Ayva's house, to–

But all that came out was, "Thanks."

Thanks? For what? It was like my mouth had control of itself and my brain was no longer connected to it.

Refocusing, I tried again. "Was that all true? What you said about Tay back there?"

Maddax looked over at me, studying me. His eyes narrowed and his jaw tightened. He pulled his hand out of mine. His eyes focused forward again.

"I take it you were eavesdropping on my conversation with the Banebriars?" A question, but not a question.

I swallowed hard. "I didn't mean ... I was going to ... I ... I ..."

The car slowed and pulled over. We were next to a dark building. I didn't see anyone around. Not even Dee.

When he looked back, there was anger in his eyes. "Don't question my decisions, Lyssa. I'll do whatever has to be done to keep everyone safe. To protect us all. Do you understand me?"

I swallowed again and nodded.

He reached toward me, and I instinctively pulled back. There was something weird about his eyes, like he was looking at me, but he wasn't seeing me. His hand dropped.

"Maddax?"

No response.

"Maddax?

Still no response.

A little louder this time. "Maddax, are you okay?" I reached out and touched his shoulder.

In a jerking motion, he reached out and roughly grabbed my wrist.

"Ow! Let go!"

And then he was there again.

"Lyssa, I'm sorry. You startled me."

I had moved as far away from him as I could get in the front seat, rubbing my wrist.

"I think you should take me home, Maddax."

He just sat there for a couple of seconds looking at me, then he started the car and pulled back out onto the street.

When he spoke again, his voice was much quieter, gentler. "I am sorry if I scared you, Lyssa. Sometimes I just get so focused on fixing a problem that I forget that I'm dealing with people. At our house, in the lab, it's all about efficiency and effectiveness. Emotions don't come into play, and I think that so much work has caused me to forget my manners. Are you all right?"

He looked at me again, and now his eyes were full of concern. He slowly reached out and took the hand I was rubbing. His thumb stroked it softly. "Forgive me, Calyssa. I can't stand to have you looking at me like that."

I knew I should have said, "No." Well, not just "No," but "Hell no!" and "Take me home right now!" but he looked and sounded now like the guy I'd met last night. And the words from *Instantaneous* suddenly started going through my mind.

"Can we go downtown and grab a nutrient drink before I take you home? Give me a chance to answer all your questions? I'm not ready for you to leave yet. I've been thinking about you all day. Well, actually, ever since you left last night."

We stopped at a little all-night drink shop. It had soft express lights, which all the signs claimed were "perfect for enhanced photosynthesis" when paired with their "top-of-the-line" drinks to "boost superior chloroplast processing."

Sitting in a booth across from Maddax, sipping my drink, I tried to make sense of his story.

He told me that he had multiple doctorates, so technically, he was a doctor. That his last name was Steele. And, that he felt like he'd known me for years.

"It's shocking really. I don't know how I can feel so close to you with only having met you 24 hours ago, Lyssa. It's a little scary to admit. I don't think I've ever 'needed' anyone, but I feel like I need you." He reached across the table and took my hand. "Do you feel it, too?" His stare was incredibly intense, and he didn't look away. Five seconds ticked by. Then ten. Twenty. Thirty. A full minute.

I couldn't handle it anymore. I looked away.

"I ... I ... this is just so ... fast ... I ..." My voice trailed off.

"Lyssa, look at me." Seconds again. "Lyssa."

Looking up, I saw tears in his eyes. That surprised me.

"Lyssa, I have to tell you something. I don't want you to say anything. I just need you to know."

He paused and cleared his throat. "Calyssa Brentwood, I believe I'm falling in love with you."

I was speechless. I wasn't sure that I believed that he could love me after only knowing me for such a short time. I mean, the only other guy who'd said that to me hated me now, and it took him a while to say it. But Maddax wasn't Gabe. I didn't think two guys could be more different.

Maddax stood up. "Let's get you home." He smiled and held out his hand.

Back in the car, he turned on music that filled the car with soft, crooning words. But I couldn't focus on it. Maddax held my hand, kissing it every few minutes for the remainder of the drive back to my house. But neither of us said anything.

We pulled into the driveway. Maddax jumped out and ran around to help me out of the car. Still silent, we walked up to the house. As we reached the door, Maddax stepped quickly in front of me, and the next thing I knew I was in his arms. Kissing him. A long, slow, passionate kiss.

When we finished, he stepped away and walked back to the car. Not another word.

And then my front door flew open.

Chapter 27

"Was that Maddax Steele?"

I couldn't tell if Livvy looked shocked or angry.

She stepped around me and watched the car leave our driveway.

Then her focus snapped back to me. "Where have you been? Some lady shows up with your car. I question her about where you are, and she tells me to 'relax,' that you're 'with the Doctor.' Then she laughs, and another car pulls up, she jumps in and takes off." Her arms were crossed. Foot tapping. Huge frown. Brows all bunched up. Angry. She was definitely angry.

"Sorry, Livvy. That was Dee. She brought my car home from Ayva's house. Maddax didn't think I should drive." At Maddax's name, Livvy froze.

"Maddax Steele?" she asked again.

"Yeah. You know him?"

"What in the world are you doing with Maddax, Lyssa? Why would you be involved with him? How do you even know him? He's like, almost ten years older than you." She stepped closer to me. "He's trouble, Lys. Stay away from him."

"What? How do you know him? I just met him recently, and he's been really nice. And, he's only like six or seven years older than me, not ten." Not that it mattered. What was Livvy's deal here?

"Trust me, Lyssa. I know from experience. Maddax is not a nice guy. Stay away from him."

"Are you being serious? How do you know him? Why would you say that?"

Livvy got quiet and a funny look crossed her face.

"Oh, now I get it. You dated him, didn't you? You dated him and it didn't work out and now you're trying to make sure that I don't make the same mistake you made. I get it." My voice dripped with sarcasm. "Just looking out for me, right?"

"I ... I ... I did date him. For a while. A couple of years ago. Right after I started college. Before ... before the virus." She started fidgeting. "But it's not what you think, Lys. I don't care that you're dating someone that I dated. Okay, actually, that is a little weird. But it's not about that. Maddax is not a good guy. Take my word for it."

"Why? What did he do, Livvy?" I felt my impatience growing.

She shook her head. "He starts out all 'Mr. Nice Guy.' I bet he told you how beautiful you are. How amazing you

175

are. That he loves being with you. That he needs you. Maybe even that he loves you. Has he got to that line yet?" She'd been studying me the whole time she spoke.

"What? No. You don't know what you're talking about!" I practically spat out the words.

Livvy laughed, a dry, humorless laugh. "Don't try to deny it, Baby Sister. He did the same thing to me. He's got you fooled."

"You're wrong, Livvy! You don't know what you're talking about!" My voice was getting a little louder with each word.

She laughed again. "Oh, yeah. That's why you're getting so worked up, right? Because I'm so wrong." She shook her head and smirked.

Something in me snapped.

"You're just jealous! You're jealous because I have a cute, smart guy that likes me and wants to spend time with me, and you don't have anyone! The only person who will even give you the time of day is a whacked-out rebel who's just using you to get Father's secrets! And he's gay, so he doesn't even have to pretend to be interested in you to get what he wants!" I was breathing hard, my hands balled into tights fists, waiting, hoping, challenging Livvy to yell back at me.

The cynical look on Livvy's face disappeared, and her lips began to quiver. She stepped back from me and turned around.

I felt my anger drain out.

Why had I said all those things to her?

I reached out and put a hand on her shoulder.

She immediately shrugged it off.

"Livvy, I–"

"Don't," she interrupted.

"But, Livvy, I ..."

She whipped around to face me. Her eyes were hard and fierce. She stepped so close to me that I could feel her breath on my face.

"You're wrong. Learn the hard way. I don't care. Maybe he's just what you deserve."

"Livvy–"

"And, you're wrong about me, too. You think you're so smart now, but there's so much you don't know." She stepped back and glared, looking me up and down. "You've definitely changed, Li'l Sis." Then she whipped back around and went inside.

I just stood there with my mouth open. Speechless. What did she mean?

Suddenly, I was tired. Tired of Livvy and her drama. And of secrets. Rebel secrets and security enforcer secrets. Father's secrets and Livvy's secrets and Jaxx's secrets. Even Dee and Maddax's secrets. Livvy still hadn't told me about the oh-so-important meeting that she had disappeared to. Probably ended up being nothing.

I was over it. All of it. I didn't want to think about any of it anymore.

In my room, I crawled under the covers once again. But this time, I tossed and turned. Covers on, covers off. Front, back, side. I couldn't get comfortable. I looked over and saw the Nock on my nightstand. Just one dose, and all of this would go away. One quick breath and I'd forget. One second to leave all these crappy feelings behind. I reached for the inhaler.

Chapter 28

But in the end, I just rolled back over, squeezed my eyes shut, and waited to fall asleep.

The next day, I stayed in my room working on homework. Lena popped her head in to see if I wanted her to make a nutrient drink. I told her I was fine.

Father stopped by for a minute to let me know that he would be going out of town on Tuesday for several days. I simply nodded and went back to work.

Livvy stood at the door and watched me for a minute. I could see her out of the corner of my eye in my mirror, but I didn't turn around. Eventually she left without saying anything.

Even Lulu chose to hang out somewhere else in the house, which was fine with me. I just wanted to be left alone. To focus on my schoolwork. I didn't want to think about anything else — not Ana, Gabe, Maddax, Livvy, Gunner, the rebels, the plan. It all made me exhausted again. This emotional roller coaster was draining.

Around noon, I noticed I had a headache. I rubbed my temples and turned up my express lights. Maybe I just needed a little more from my chloroplasts. But the persistent ache didn't go away.

I had to get the paper I was working on finished. It was due tomorrow, but I couldn't focus. Feeling irritated, I got up and kicked at one of my shoes. I caught it just right and it flew across the room, smacking into the nightstand by my bed, which caused a glass of water to tip over.

"Seriously?" My voice came out in almost a growl. I was ticked off, and I knew it, but I felt like I couldn't stop. Or didn't want to stop. Whatever. I felt my mood growing darker by the minute, and it felt horrible and good at the same time.

Screw all of them, I thought as faces crowded my mind. Everybody just wanted something from me. Wanted me to be someone. Wanted me to do something. It was never just about me.

I grabbed a towel off the floor and began to mop up the water on my nightstand, my bed, and the floor below.

And I saw my Nock inhaler. It must have fallen off when the cup tipped. I sat down on the floor, picked up the inhaler, and took a deep breath, letting the Nock fill my lungs.

Instantly, I began to feel more relaxed. I closed my eyes and felt the tension drain away. Why hadn't I done this earlier? I sat that way for about twenty minutes, just letting go of all the craziness in my life. When I opened my eyes, I felt refreshed. Stronger. Ready.

I got up and went back to my desk. I worked all afternoon, completing several projects.

Sometime that evening Father stopped by my room again. I wasn't sure how long he had been staring at me before I noticed he was there.

"I didn't mean to interrupt you. Been at it all day?"

"What? Oh, yeah. Lots to do for school. The term ends in just a couple of weeks."

"That's good, Calyssa. You seem to be ... doing well."

I turned to face him. This was an odd conversation. Father wasn't one for idle chit chat.

"I am. I've been working hard."

"That's ... good."

Seconds of silence ticked by.

He just continued to stare at me.

"Is everything okay, Father? You seem ..." *Weird? Different? Like you care? Like something's up?* I wasn't sure how to finish the sentence. But he did seem – off.

He straightened up and took a step back. "Oh. No. I mean yes. I mean everything is fine. Just checking on you." He took a second step back and then turned to leave, but hesitated. Turning back to me, he said, "You know, the older you get, the more you look like she used to look. Your mother. And sitting there, at your desk, so focused on your work ..." His voice trailed off.

Okay. This was definitely weird. He never talked about Mom. At least not to me.

I sat very still, hoping that maybe, just maybe, he'd say more.

Again, seconds of silence.

Finally, I prompted, "Like when she was in college?"

"What?" He looked startled. "No, no. I was just thinking about her sitting at her old research desk at AHGA. How much you look like she did then."

What? Mom worked at AHGA?

"When did Mom work at AHGA?"

Father's eyes narrowed. The moment was gone, but I wanted to know what he was talking about. Mom had never worked when I was growing up. At least, not that I remembered.

"Of course your mother worked at AHGA. That's where we met. You know that." His voice was dismissive.

"I thought you met in college."

"Well, we did. Meet in college. But we didn't start dating until she was working at AHGA." He was backing further out of the room.

I stood and followed him into the hall. He looked uncomfortable. I could tell he was done. But I wasn't.

"Wait, Father, don't go. Please, just tell me a little about it. About her."

His eyes softened. At first, I didn't think he was going to say anything. But then in a quiet voice, he said, "It was before you girls were born. She was brilliant. A research virologist. She set much of her work aside when Naleeva was born so she could stay home, at least part time, with her. And then you were born, and the two of you filled her time, so she stopped going in for a while. When you started school, she began going back in for a few hours each day, just while you girls were at school. But then ... she ... she ... died." I watched as his eyes transformed, hardening. I knew there would be no more talk.

"Anyway. Keep working hard. You'll be finished soon with your first year at the University. You need to find how you'll contribute to our society, Calyssa. Music is nice, but it won't change the world." And he turned and walked away.

I stood there. In the hall, by myself. Conflicted.

"You okay?" Livvy's voice from behind me.

I turned around and opened my mouth, but nothing came out.

"That was harsh. Even for him. Sorry." Livvy shook her head. "Our dad kinda sucks at being a father, in case you haven't noticed." She smiled weakly.

"Yeah. I've caught that once or twice." I smiled back. I guessed we weren't fighting anymore.

She threw her arm around my shoulder. "Don't worry, Little Sis. Whatever you do, it'll be far more than me. Face it, I'm gonna be the loser *yellow* sister who lives off the generosity of the family for the rest of her life. So, you better figure out how to keep me in the style I'm accustomed to." But her words were light-hearted.

I laughed. "Whatever, Rebel Girl."

"Whoa. That's top-secret information, remember? Or can't I trust you anymore?"

I turned and hugged her.

"You can trust me, Livvy." All the playfulness from my voice was gone. "I mean it. You can."

She hugged me back. "I know, Lys."

Stepping apart, we walked into my room together.

"Did you know Mom used to work at AHGA? That she was some sort of scientist before she gave it up to have kids?"

Livvy sat down on my bed, then leaned back on the pillows. "Yeah. Don't you remember going to AHGA as a kid? She'd run in to grab something, or sometimes one of our drivers would pick us up from school and drop us there, then she'd drive us home."

"I remember being there, and I think I remember the drivers dropping us off occasionally, but I don't remember going to her office, or wherever she worked. I only remember Father's office."

"Huh, now that you mention it, I don't think I ever went to her office either. Maybe she didn't have one. I do remember that the level where she worked was one where we weren't allowed to go. Besides, whenever we went there, all you wanted to do was look at the gallery pictures, over and over. I didn't get it. You were five. Why did you want to read the history of AHGA every time you came in? It's not like it changed or anything."

I picked up a pillow off a chair and tossed it at her. "Hey, don't hate me because I was a smart little kid."

"Don't confuse smart with easily entertained." She threw it back at me.

Livvy's hand came up as the smile disappeared from her face. Her eyes darted around the room.

I started to say something, but she shook her head, touching her ear to indicate an iBud call.

A few seconds later, she got up off the bed. "That was Gunner. We're meeting tomorrow to go over the file extraction plan one more time. To make sure I haven't missed anything. That you'll be ready to go in on Tuesday and get it for us." Her voice was back to business.

"'File extraction plan'? That makes it sound all official."

She shot me a stern look. "I'm being serious, Lyssa. I don't want anything to happen to you. Because of me. Because of something I asked you to do."

I sighed. "I know." The light mood had vanished from the room. Back to secrets and plans.

"Get a good night's rest, Sis. We'll go over everything one more time tomorrow night after you're done with school and work." She stood in the door frame. "I love you, Lyssa."

"I love you, too, Livvy. Good night."

After she left, I got up and closed my door. Looking over the things on my desk, I packed up what I needed for tomorrow, then crawled back into bed.

What a weekend, I thought. Ana's death, the realization that Gabe and I would never get back together, Livvy working with the rebels, Maddax and the twins, Nock, Tay's accident, and planning to steal a file from my own father's company. No wonder I was exhausted. Again. Remembering each event slowly drained me – the sadness, the anger, the apprehension. Individually they were overwhelming, but together – it was too much to process.

Tomorrow would be a new day. A new week. There were so many things in my life that I had no control over.

Tomorrow I would focus on the things that I could control. Change. Things that mattered.

"Music. Level 1." Soft music filled the room. I rolled over and tucked my arms under my pillow. As I drifted off, I realized that it was Hunter Green, singing "Instantaneous" once again to send me off to my dreams. I smiled. As I relaxed, Maddax's gentle kiss was the last thing I thought about.

Waking up, I felt well rested. A good night's sleep had been just what I needed to start today off right. I hustled around and grabbed a nutrient shake from Lena on the way out the door.

On Mondays, I had classes in the morning, so I headed straight to the University. My first two classes were lecture style, each an hour and half long: Global Inequities in Healthcare followed by Environmental History and Sustainability. Not really riveting presentations. I tried to stay focused.

When the second class finished, I decided to head outside and go for a walk. It was cold, but I'd bundled up today, and I really needed some fresh air.

Lots of students and staff were out walking through the courtyard, some individually and some in groups. Bright sunshine bounced off little piles of snow that bravely fought to keep their hold at the corners of buildings and edges of the walking paths. The air, crisp and invigorating, filled my lungs, and erased any last shadows of fogginess from my mind.

Watching a group of students laughing ahead to the left of me, I turned the corner at the Environmental Sciences building and ran right into a student who was standing there.

"I'm so sorry," I said, reaching down to grab the bag I'd dropped. "Totally my fault. Wasn't looking where I was going." I stood up, smiling.

The other girl was just standing up, too, after picking up something she must have dropped as well. As her long, lanky body unfolded, her piercing eyes stared down at me, so sharply that I couldn't say anything for a moment.

"Hello, Calyssa." No smile. Just spiky hair and hard, seafoam green eyes.

"Hello, El."

Chapter 29

We both stared at each other for a few awkward seconds.

El spoke first. "How are you feeling?"

"Umm, good. You?"

"Have you been using the Nock supplement inhaler daily since your last session?" She stepped closer to me examining my face. I stepped back and looked around.

"Should we be talking about that here?" I asked. I glanced over my shoulder at a group of people behind us.

"No one's close enough to hear. Nor would they understand what we're talking about even if they did overhear us."

I felt like she was analyzing every inch of me. It was disturbing. I pulled my jacket more tightly around me. She kept staring. "El," I finally said, "I'm fine. The way you're looking at me is creepy. People are going to wonder why you're staring."

"They'll probably just think I'm infatuated with you. People do that, you know. Make up stories to justify what they think they see. I don't care. It really doesn't matter to me what they think." She reached up to touch my face.

I pulled back. "Well, it matters to me. Stop it, El."

She dropped her hand and stepped back. Another awkward silence.

Okay. I had to do something. This was just uncomfortable. "Didn't Maddax tell me you're working on another degree?"

"Probably. He thinks it's a waste of time. But I find structural engineering fascinating. I'm headed right now to Experimental Fracture Mechanics. The complexity of comprehending static and dynamic loads requires a great deal of creativity and ... never mind. I can see you're not interested."

"What? I ... well, I ... you just lost me there after 'mechanics.' Sorry." I smiled.

No smile back. "It's fine. It's not for everyone. You're sure you've been feeling okay? I've told Maddax and Dee that a week is too long to wait for an observation, at least after the first dose."

"What? Really, I'm fine. And, I saw Dee and Maddax on Saturday night."

"Where?" she asked suspiciously.

"At Ayva's house. After Tay's ... accident." Surely El had to know about Tay. About his double dosing on Nock and his death.

El looked away from me. Without turning back, she asked, "You were there? Did you see Taydon?"

"No. By the time I got there his body had been taken away."

El started to walk away, but I quickly fell into step with her. "El, what really happened? Maddax told Ayva's parents that Tay had been having seizures. That he had been missing medication doses, and that it was probably a seizure that caused the accident. Do you think that's what happened?"

Surprisingly, when El looked back at me, her eyes looked softer somehow, not the usual piecing hardness I was so used to.

El slowly shook her head. "It doesn't matter what I think."

"It matters to me. Was Maddax lying?"

El kept walking.

"El. El. El, will you please stop? I just want to know if your brother was lying to me."

Abruptly she turned toward me and stood completely still. When she finally spoke, her voice was low. "I don't know anything for sure. I'm not a medical doctor. But from my research, I would say that Taydon probably did have a seizure."

"That's a relief. I mean it's sad, but at least it wasn't Nock."

"I never said that."

"What do you mean?"

"I never said that Nock wasn't involved."

"What do you mean, El? You just said his seizures probably caused the accident."

She shook her head. "No, I only said that he probably did have a seizure."

I took in what she was saying. "He didn't have seizures before?"

"Not that I know of. None in his medical history that I could find."

I let that sink in for a couple of seconds. "El, did you know that Tay double dosed that day?"

She didn't say anything.

"Do you think that Nock made him have a seizure?"

She still didn't say anything.

"Does Maddax know about this?"

Silence. She just continued to stare at me.

"El, how can you know about this and not say anything? What if this happens again? People have to know about the danger." My mind was reeling. Was it just the night before last that I had considered a second dose in one day? What if I had done it? The thought made me nauseous.

"Calyssa, listen to me. My brother and sister are very powerful people. Don't let their age fool you. No one will connect Nock with Taydon's death. No one has ever connected Nock with any deaths."

Deaths? My mouth dropped open. Was she implying that others had died from Nock? My mind raced back to my first discussion with Maddax about the drug. He had said there'd been "minimal issues," "some problems." And then – he'd kissed me, and I hadn't really given it another thought.

"El, you have to tell someone about this. You have to—"

She cut me off. "No, Calyssa. I don't. People take Nock because it makes them feel better. Better about themselves, or their jobs, or their lives, or whatever. But it's a choice. No one shoves that inhaler in their mouth every day. There are rules. Ignorant people break the rules. Breaking rules has consequences. But it's still a choice." Her eyes were hard again, no trace of softness now. Just cold and hard.

As she turned to walk away, I reached out and grabbed her arm. "But, El, you have to—"

Her head whipped back and she stepped right up next to me. Leaning over, she whispered in my ear, "I don't *have* to do anything. Taydon was a sweet boy, but he obviously wasn't that bright. Maddax was right. Nature finds a way to cleanse the gene pool." Then she roughly pulled her arm out of my grasp and headed into the next building.

I stood there. Unable to move. *Nature finds a way to cleanse the gene pool?* Was that truly what Maddax thought? Or just El talking? She seemed like the cold machine, like she didn't care about anyone. Not like Maddax. He was sweet and kind and – well, except when he lost it. Like when that guy grabbed Dee's arm. Or in the car when he accused me of eavesdropping. Which was the real Maddax?

Without really thinking about what I was doing, I went into the building where El had disappeared. I could hear a loud voice coming from one of the lecture halls. Maybe, if El was sitting near the back, I could try to get her to come out and talk to me some more.

As I entered the darkened room, I noticed various images flashing across the screen at the front where an older man stood talking. A bridge. A skyscraper. A dam. A cathedral. My eyes adjusted and I noticed that there must have been over 200 students seated throughout the room. I tried to scan the crowd as casually as possible. They all had their backs to me which made the task more difficult.

But all the way over to the left, in an aisle seat, I spotted her. That spiky hair helped in the identification. I started to walk along the back of the room until I came to the aisle where El sat. I could see she was taking notes on a digital tablet with a dimmed screen, drawing something freehand. Then she leaned over and whispered to the guy next to her. He leaned back and whispered something back to her. And our eyes connected. It was at that point that I realized the guy was a non-Green.

Gabe.

I froze as our eyes locked, then he said something else to El. She turned, looked at me and glared, and then whispered again in Gabe's ear. He snickered and shook his head. Then, keeping eye contact with me, he leaned back a little more and stretched an arm around El. She leaned in tight and whispered one more time to him, then they both looked at me.

And I took off.

Out of the room and out of the building. Out into the open air where I felt like I could breathe again.

Gabe knew El? The answer was clearly yes. And obviously well enough to be sitting with her in class – with his arm around her. Did El know that I knew Gabe? That I'd spent a week on his farm over spring break? That he'd sat with his arm around me? That he'd kissed me? That he'd told me he loved me?

Had he told her he loved her? Suddenly, I felt out-of-control angry. I wanted to scream. Or hit something. Or someone.

Even though I had one more class before heading to work, I found myself marching toward my car. I jammed my bag inside and threw the car into reverse. Two people had to jump out of the way as I flew out of the parking lot. *Screw them*, I thought. *I'm so tired of caring about everyone else, of helping everyone else, of being nice to everyone else. Nobody gives two shits about me.*

A car laid on its horn as I cut it off, taking a corner too quickly and way too sharply. Another slammed on its brakes to avoid hitting me in an intersection. I didn't care. It felt good to go too fast, to drive too crazy. I was out of control for the first time in my life. Out of control by my own choice, and I liked it.

I whipped around another building and sped up even more. I screamed at the top of my lungs. Then closed my eyes and screamed once more as loud as I could.

And when I opened my eyes, the scream that escaped my lips was one of absolute panic.

Chapter 30

I slammed on my brakes and twisted the wheel as hard as I could. And came inches from hitting a little girl standing wide-eyed in the middle of the road, holding a tiny, squirming animal.

Everything seemed to be in slow motion. I saw the top of the girl's head slide past my window as my car began to spin. I tensed, expecting to feel the impact of her small body against the side of my car, to see her go flying through the air, to hear her screams of terror and pain. I was going to be responsible for her death. But it didn't happen. I just kept spinning. Truly out of control. I'd been wrong before. I didn't like this feeling.

I'm not sure how many times I spun around before I felt the back of my car smack into something solid, and everything jerked to an immediate stop. I sat there, unable to move, unable to think. Until I heard someone crying. Jolted back to reality, I yelled, "Door open!" but nothing happened. I yelled twice more before it finally dawned on me that it wasn't going to work. I grabbed the emergency release handle and pulled. Nothing. I pulled again, as hard as I could, and the door flew open. Then I was out, running down the street.

There was a non-Green woman there now, jerking on the arm of the little girl, walking angrily toward me. The girl, who looked like she was probably five or six, was wailing. The woman was yelling. And the small animal, which I now realized was some sort of strange, hairless feline, was mewling and scratching, but the girl wouldn't let it go.

"I'm so–" I began but the woman cut me off before I could get anymore out.

"Look what you did to that nice Green lady and her car! Just look at it, Izzabellah! Your father is going to have a fit when he hears about this! I've told you and told you to stay out of the road! But you don't mind! No, you don't, and now look at what you've gone and done! Do you have a brain in there?"

Her yelling began to register in my mind. She blamed this little girl for what happened. The woman must not have seen me, my reckless driving. She didn't know. All I had to do was walk away, and no one would ever know. An unexpected calm came over me. I glanced back at my car. It wasn't good. I could just walk away and tell Father that I had swerved to miss a kid in the middle of the street, that even her mom said it was her fault. I could get their names and give them to him, and no one would ever know. Except me.

"... told you a thousand times that you can't chase that stupid creature! If it gets run over, so be it! It's obviously too stupid to live!"

And then the calm turned to anger and something in me snapped. "That's enough!" I yelled. And the lady stopped with her mouth open, staring at me. Even the little girl stopped crying. Only the animal continued its persistent mewling.

I kneeled so I was eye-to-eye with the girl. "Are you all right?"

She nodded.

"Is your ... kitty okay?" I looked at the hairless animal twisting to escape.

The little girl sniffled, then said, "It's not just a kitty. It's a Bobtail Sphynx. She's special, and she's super smart." The girl shot a glare at the woman still holding one of her arms.

The woman huffed. "Smart. Right. And I'm—"

I cut her off again. "She looks amazing. Can I hold her?" One of the little girl's arms was covered in scratches where the kitten had been trying to claw its way free.

"Well ..." The girl glanced from me to the kitten and back.

"I don't think so. I think we need to be going, since no one is hurt," said the woman, glancing around, as she pulled again on the girl's arm.

"Sure," said the girl, shoving the cat toward me and glaring again at the woman.

"Izzabellah! I said we're going!"

The kitten's claws grasped at the front of my shirt, catching the skin underneath. I tried not to jump as I gently repositioned the kitten in my arms. It nuzzled its hairless head in the crook of my elbow and stopped squirming.

"Ziffa likes you." The girl smiled, pulling her arm free from the woman's grasp.

"I like her, too." I smiled back.

"Give the girl her cat back. Or don't. I don't care. We need to go." The woman glanced around again.

The girl's eyes opened wide.

"Don't worry. I'll give your kitty back to you and your mom."

"She's not my mom. She's my nanny. And she hates Ziffa, but Daddy won't let her get rid of my kitty." Another glare.

"Well, wait until your father hears about the accident that Ziffa caused today. We'll see where that cat ends up."

The girl's lips quivered, and her chin dropped. Very softly she said, "I'm sorry Ziffa ran out in the road and made you wreck your car. Please don't blame her. It was my fault. I should have been more careful. I should have held on to her better. Please don't blame her. I'm sorry. If you're going to be mad, be mad at me." When she looked up into my eyes, I saw tears spilling down her cheeks. Then she dropped her head again.

I swallowed hard as I placed a hand under her chin and gently lifted it. "Izzabellah, I'm not mad at you. It's not your fault or Ziffa's fault. It's my fault. I was driving too fast. I'm just happy that you're okay. And, Ziffa, too."

The kitten was purring, resting quietly in my other arm. I gently picked up the kitten and placed it back in the girl's arms. "Hold her like I was. She likes that. She feels safe like that."

Izzabellah nodded her head, holding the kitten in the crook of her arm, stroking it softly with her other hand.

"Fine then. If that's the way you see it. I'd like your name and contact information to give to Izzabellah's father. In case, of any ... problems." She smirked at me, waiting for me to say something. Probably hoping I'd back out. Say it wasn't my fault, so she could blame the kid. I glanced down again at Izzabellah and Ziffa. But I wasn't going to back out and shift the blame. This was on me. Whatever happened when Father found out about the accident, I'd deal with that. It was nothing in comparison to if I had hit her. If I had killed her. And down deep, I knew I couldn't let this little girl take the blame for something I did. I just couldn't.

"That's fine. It's Calyssa Brentwood, and you can reach me at AHGA." I looked at the little girl. "That's where my father works, Izzabellah." Then I looked back at the woman. She let out a small gasp as the name recognition clicked in. Everyone in SciCity knew the Brentwood name. "Do you need me to give you the number to reach me there, in case Izzabellah's father needs to confirm it?" A hint of sarcasm in my voice.

"No. No. I'm sure we have it." The woman took a step back from me.

"My dad works at AHGA, too!" Izzabellah said with delight in her voice. "Maybe our dads know each other.

Maybe we could see each other sometime. And you could play with me and Ziffa!"

"Miss Brentwood is far too busy for that," said the woman, taking another step away. "We'll be on our way now." She grabbed the girl's sleeve and began to pull her toward the other side of the street.

"You can come see me anytime at AHGA, Izzabellah. And you can bring Ziffa, too. I'll even let you sit at my desk if you want to." Izzabellah nodded and smiled. The woman glared and continued to walk across the street.

"Bye, Calyssa!" A small hand twisted past the tugging arm to wave.

"Bye, Izzabellah! And, keep a good hold on Ziffa, okay?"

"Okay!"

I watched until they walked around the corner and disappeared. Then I turned, walking back toward my car. The back sat scrunched up against the base of a large statue. Something abstract, and, as far as I could tell, unharmed. Breathing out a heavy sigh, I walked back to the driver's side and got in. Pulling the door shut, I looked around. My stuff was scattered everywhere.

And that's when it hit me. I could have killed that little girl. Because I was having a pity party. Being selfish. Did I really, honestly think that I had it that bad? Getting ticked off at El and Gabe because I wanted Gabe to care about me, not her? Gabe had told me he was done with me. He'd said it to my face. But it felt easier to blame El. To blame Gabe. To blame anybody. Anybody but me. My mind wandered to my Nock inhaler. I hadn't dosed today. I'd probably feel much better if I did.

But deep down, I knew that was a cop out. Funny how easy it was already to choose dosing to deal with my life. But Nock didn't change anything. It wouldn't bring Ana or Tay back. And, it wouldn't make Gabe love me again.

Tears welled up in my eyes. My life would be so much easier if Ana was still alive, if Gabe still loved me, if I had never met Maddax or the twins, if Taydon hadn't used Nock, if Livvy had never gotten sick, if Father cared more about me, if—

Tears streamed down my face.

But my life was what it was. I had a home, a sister, a father, and friends. I was Green, so I never went hungry. I was attending the University. I worked because I chose to, not because I had to. I had my own car and all the tech I wanted. Truthfully, looking at my life, I realized just how easy I had it, compared to many other people. And I had thrown a tantrum that almost cost a little girl her life.

I wiped my tears away with the back of my hand and pressed the ignition button. Thankfully, the car started. I inched forward. Everything seemed to be working. At least I could drive it home.

At some point during the drive, I iBud-messaged work and let them know I wouldn't be in today. That I wasn't feeling well, and that I'd be in tomorrow. Luckily, I was only scheduled for a couple of hours, and I assured the secretary on our floor that I could make them up tomorrow.

Pulling into the driveway, I saw Livvy looking out the window. Before I could get out, she came flying out the front door, bombarding me with questions — what happened to the car, was I okay, did I need a doctor, where had it happened, who else was involved? When she finally realized that I wasn't answering, she stopped, took my hand, and led me into the house.

We sat down in the kitchen, and she made me a nutrient drink. That was a first. Then I told her about my day – about class, running into El, our conversation, seeing Gabe, leaving like a maniac, and the accident. She listened silently. When I finished, she simply said, "I'm happy you're okay ... and that you're here with me." Then she grabbed my hand, led me into the family room, and turned on an old classic movie, something we had loved as kids about a wizard kid going to magic school. It seemed kind of hokey when compared to all the digital enhancements in movies today. But it felt warm and familiar. And after about an hour of it, I drifted off to sleep.

And then I woke to Father's voice. "She's okay? There's some pretty extensive damage to the car." I could hear Livvy's voice. It was softer, and I couldn't make out what she was saying.

Father again. "Really? From AHGA? I hope this doesn't become a mess. And she didn't get a name? What was she thinking?" More from Livvy. Quite a bit more.

"Fine. Have one of the drivers take it in tomorrow. She can use your car since you're not going anywhere." Silence. "That's fine with you, isn't it?" Livvy said something, and then I heard Father's footsteps go down the hall to his study, followed by the door closing.

Livvy came back into the family room and noticed that I was awake.

"How'd he take it?" I asked.

"Better than you'd expect, I guess. I talked him down for you. Hopefully the girl's dad won't make a big deal out of it. If the nanny even tells him." Livvy frowned. "You're taking my car to work tomorrow. Be careful, please. I like it the way it is."

"Fine. I'll wait to take up professional racing until I get my own car back." I smiled. "And thanks, Livvy. For talking to him. He always listens better when it's you."

"You just have to know how to talk to him, Lys. Keep trying. He does love you."

"I know." I sighed. "I actually think I'm going to do a little reading for school and then call it a night." I got up and stretched.

"Oh, no you don't. Sit back down. Tomorrow's the day. And we need to review."

I didn't want to think about Livvy's plan right now, but she had just intervened with Father for me. So, I guessed I owed her.

"No argument? Now that's a shocker. Are you sure you didn't hit your head in that crash?"

"Just want to make sure that I get it right." Which was true. I didn't want to think about what messing up would mean. Livvy laughed.

We went through the entire plan again, twice. I recited directions. Repeated codes. Described procedures. Until Livvy was satisfied that I was ready. Then she handed me two black micro drives, noting that one had a silver stripe – it was the one I had to download the file on. The other one would automatically make a copy of the contents of the first when the two were laid next to each other. I stuck both in my pocket. Livvy hugged me, and I headed off to my room.

I tried to read, but I kept dozing off. Finally, I gave up, crawled under my covers, and immediately fell asleep.

Obviously, I'd forgotten to set an alarm because I woke up late. Then I found out that Lulu had chewed up my favorite lipstick and had somehow spread it across the carpet in my room. When I finally got out of the house, I realized the skirt I was wearing had a stain on it. Of course, I dropped my nutrient drink on my way into AHGA. And, to top it all off, it was sleeting. Not that my hair looked amazing today anyway. Crappy start to a crappy morning.

Sitting down at my desk, I took a deep breath and slowly exhaled. Reaching into my pocket, I felt the two micro drives nestled safely together. I took them out and placed them on my desktop. At least I hadn't forgotten those. I closed my eyes and took a few more breaths.

Then my iBud went off. It was Livvy. `Connect,` I thought.

`Lys, don't freak out, but there's been a change of plans.`

Chapter 31

Seriously? Don't freak out? What do you mean a change, Livvy? It took me forever to memorize the plans, and now you want to change them? My heart was already beating faster, and I was getting warmer by the second.

Don't stress, Lys. You're just going to have to go sooner than I thought. But everything else is the same.

Sooner? How soon? When? I felt like I was screaming in my thoughts.

Lys, relax, Livvy thought back at me. It's still the same plan. It's all good. No changes on your end. We're all good.

Okay. Fine. When do I have to go? I just want this to be over. I'd thought I'd like the spy stuff but snooping through files online was a lot different than actually breaking into a room and stealing one.

In five minutes.

What! Five minutes?! I'm not ready ... this won't work, Livvy. I can't do this. I—

Stop, Lys. Slow down. Relax. You can. In fifteen minutes, this will all be over. Look at the clock on your tablet. What time does it say?

9:16am.

Excellent. We're synced. At exactly 9:20am, walk over to the elevator, get on, and punch in the code 77511. Did you get that? 77511. That's the new code we needed to get you off at the twenty-fourth floor. I'll be watching you through the security system. I tapped in, and I'm watching right now. I can see you sitting at your desk, twisting your hair.

I immediately dropped the strand of hair I was tugging on and glanced around the room. There were cameras all over. She could have been watching me from any one of them.

Livvy, are you sure?

I'm right here, Lys. I'll be with you every step of the way. Now in just a minute, you'll need to take your iBud out and leave it in your desk drawer. We can't have any chance of anyone tracking you. Are you ready?

Yeah, I think so. I took another deep breath. Then I reached up to take out my iBud.

One more thing, Lys. I'm proud of you. I know this is asking a lot.

Thank me when we've pulled this off, Livvy. Then I thought, Disconnect.

I discreetly took the iBud out of my ear and placed it in my desk drawer. 9:19am. Slowly, I stood up and stretched, trying to look like I was getting up to go use the restroom or grab a nutrient drink from the staff lounge.

9:20am. I pushed my chair in and ambled slowly over to the elevator, pushing the down button. Putting my hands in my pockets, I casually leaned up against the wall as I waited. And then I realized the micro drives weren't in my pocket! I'd left them on my desk!

As I turned to go back, I heard the elevator door ping and slide open. Looking back, I saw it was empty. At least I wouldn't be drawing attention from someone there who might have offered to hold it for me. I grabbed the two drives and slid them in my skirt pocket, then headed back toward the elevators.

Once again, I hit the button and waited. I swore I could feel sweat pooling on the small of my back and at the base of my neck. When had it gotten so hot in here? When the door finally slid open again, I let out a breath that I'd been holding. I stepped on to the elevator, but as the doors started to close, I saw a thick, green hand slide in to stop them.

The doors opened again immediately, and Karsten stepped on.

"Hey, Lyssa." He smiled as he stepped in next to me, placing himself close to the code panel. "You headed down, too?"

I swallowed and nodded.

"Card or code?" he asked.

"Code." I croaked, then went into a coughing fit.

"You okay?" Karsten asked as he swiped his card and I tried to get the coughing under control.

I nodded as my eyes watered. "Sorry," I said. "I think I swallowed wrong." A couple more coughs.

Two floors down the doors opened again and Karsten stepped out. "This is my floor. You need help putting in that code?"

I quickly shook my head. "Nope. Okay now," I said in a raspy voice.

"See you back upstairs." Then Karsten was gone as the elevator doors slid shut.

I reached up and typed in 71155.

"Nonfunctional code. Please try again," a voice boomed through the elevator. I knew I'd visibly jumped, but I tried hard not to look up at the camera.

I tried again. 77115.

"Nonfunctional code. Please try again."

Crap! I knew that if I didn't get it right this time, the elevator would automatically take me back up to the lobby, and I would be met there by someone from the AHGA security team. Someone with lots of questions.

I rubbed my hands on my skirt.

One more time. 77511. The elevator began to move smoothly downward.

When the number twenty-four lit up above the door, it silently slid open. I stepped out into the hall, turning left to head three doors down. Just like Livvy and I had practiced a million times. Walking down the hall, I rehearsed my story, just in case anyone stopped me – I was looking for a patent for a research project that related to a school request that came in recently. It sounded okay on the surface, but anyone who did even a little investigating would know that I wouldn't need to come down here to get it.

The doors weren't numbered like Livvy thought they would be, so I glanced back quickly to make sure I really was at the third door on the left from the elevator. This code was supposed to be 98471. I held my breath as I punched it in. It slid open.

I walked into a huge room with three rows of digital stations that ran from the front wall to the back wall. At the far-left aisle, I found the fifth station and sat down, pulling up the air screen in front of me. Hearing voices, I paused, but they came from somewhere in the back of the room, and I didn't see anyone.

The prompting screen came up for the next code I'd memorized. "11190–" And I coughed.

A loud beep went off, and I just about flew out of my chair. I sat completely silent for the next five seconds, waiting to see if anyone was coming to see what I was doing. But nobody came.

Trying again, I completed the code this time, and a listing of the drive files came up. I flipped through until I found the file I needed, XRS-671-A88. I inserted the micro drive with the silver stripe that Livvy gave me, and a countdown began as the file loaded. It felt like the longest forty-five seconds of my life. When the screen flashed green that the process was complete, I grabbed the drive and dropped it back into my pocket with the duplicator drive. Thankfully, they'd do their thing without any help from me.

Closing the screen and pushing in my chair, I made my way back to the front of the room. I pressed the button on the panel to release the door. *Next stop, elevator,* I thought, *then my floor.* Almost home free. Holding my breath, I softly tapped on the wall panel to close the door behind me. Then, turning around, I ran smack into Jaxx.

Chapter 32

Without saying a word, he roughly grabbed my arm, quickly walked me over to the next door, and punched a code into the panel. Barely waiting for it to slide open, he shoved me into the room. As the door slid shut behind him, he pulled a small black square object out of his pocket.

The horror of being caught by Jaxx was just catching up with me. I started to say something, but he shot me a vicious look, shaking his head. Going to the center of the room, he placed the black box on a table. It let off an earsplitting, high pitched squeal for a couple of seconds, then went silent. I stared at him with my hands over my ears, my mouth open, my head aching. *What in the ...?*

Jaxx walked directly up to me and jerked my hands down.

"We don't have much time. The jammer will only work for a few minutes. It will look like a tech malfunction on the floor, but they'll get it back up and running quickly." He pulled out a small digital tablet from his pocket and punched in a series of numbers.

"Jaxx ... I ... I ..." *I what?* I couldn't think of a single thing to say.

"Stop, Calyssa. You don't know how lucky you are that I was the one monitoring the security system when you logged in at the elevator. I've been erasing your steps as you've been taking them, from the elevator to the room and back out. I knew you were up to something ... but this? Do you know how much trouble you could be in?" He looked furious. I felt like I was going to puke.

Then my mind latched on to what he had just said, replaying it – *how much trouble you could be in* – not how much trouble I was in. What? What did that mean? And why had he brought me in here? Why wasn't he marching me straight to Father? Or calling security? Or – or – ?

"Jaxx–" I tried again but he cut me off.

"Just listen." He glanced at his watch. "I know about what you've been doing. And Livvy. She's gotten really good lately. It's kept me busy. I thought I had everything under control, but then you two apparently started working together." He shook his head, looking down.

When he looked back up, he still looked angry, but he looked tired, too. Sighing heavily, he said, "The things I do to protect your father. Your family. I swear, you and your sister will get me killed, or at least locked up with the codes thrown away."

What? What was he talking about? As my brain played catch up, the questions started tumbling out.

"What are you talking about? What do you mean? What are you going to do with me? Why aren't you turning me in right now? Why—"

He cut me off again. "Be quiet, Calyssa." Glancing at his watch again, he continued, "We have about one more minute that the jammer will work, so we're getting back on that elevator, going back to your floor, and you're going to go sit back down at your station and keep working like nothing ever happened. Do you understand me?"

I nodded silently.

"There are things going on here at AHGA that your father doesn't necessarily know about. He's not the only one in charge here. My job is to make sure that things are taken care of. That he has plausible deniability. You must stay out of things here. Do you understand? Your little 'investigations' have to stop. Now. You're in over your head. This is serious."

The things he was saying weren't making sense. Father not in charge? Someone else? Things taken care of? Plausible deniability? Little investigations?

"Jaxx—"

He put up a hand. "I know this is your sister's doing, Calyssa. That she's got you working for her. I've kept the reins on her research, just giving her enough access to think she's discovering things. But she's getting out of control. And, now, recruiting you ...." He paused, like he was going to say something else, but then changed his mind. "Give me whatever you took from that room."

I swallowed hard. "Jaxx, I–"

"Don't say anything. Just give it to me. Whatever it is, I don't think it's worth dying over, do you?"

Dying over? I suddenly felt hot.

"Now, Calyssa."

I reached into my pocket and felt the two small drives Livvy had given me. I didn't know which one was which. Had the information been copied onto the second drive already? I didn't know. Livvy had never said how long it would take, just to put them together, and the information would transfer so we would have two copies. Just in case – just in case had become right now.

"Calyssa. We're out of time."

I handed him one of the drives. He looked at it, shook his head, grabbed the black box from the table and headed back toward the door. Instinctively, I followed.

Without speaking, we walked briskly back to the elevator where Jaxx punched in a code. Seconds later, we were on my floor. As I stepped off the elevator, Jaxx said in a low voice, "My office. Tomorrow morning. First thing when you get here." Then the door slid shut, and he was gone.

Chapter 33

I don't really remember the rest of the day. I went back to work at my desk until it was time to go to school. I don't even know what I did. I was just on automatic. I drove to school and went to my two afternoon classes. No recollection of what my professors had talked about. When the classes finished, I drove home.

As I came in the door, Lena was gathering her things to leave. "Calyssa, are you okay? You're so pale. Come over here and sit down."

I obeyed.

"Livvy, come here. Something's wrong with Calyssa." Lena poured me a tall glass of water and handed it to me. As I took it, everything from the day seemed to click into place. It was like all of a sudden, I watched my whole day flash before my eyes in fast forward: the crappy morning, the iBud message from Livvy, stealing the file, getting caught by Jaxx, finishing the rest of the work day, going to school, coming home. And then I started to laugh. Like hysterical laughing, not the ha-ha-that-was-a-funny-day laughing.

"I'm calling the doctor," said Lena, as Livvy entered the room. Livvy took one look at me, shook her head at Lena, then swooped in and threw her arms around me. As she hugged me, the laughter turned to sobbing, and I didn't even know why.

The next thing I knew, Lena was there hugging me, too. Just like when Livvy and I were little girls. After Mom died. Sometimes, I would just start crying, and Livvy would hug me, and Lena would pull both of us up onto her lap, holding us tightly, until my tears subsided.

When I grew quiet, Lena leaned back, brushed my hair from my forehead and gave me a gentle kiss. Then she leaned over and kissed Livvy's forehead, too. "It seems today was a little harder than most. It's good that we're all together." The same words she's said to me countless times growing up.

I nodded slowly and gave her a weak smile.

"Do you want me to stay for a while? Your father just left about an hour ago, headed out of town on a short business trip. He should be back sometime Friday. He told me I could take the next couple of days off if I wanted to, but I don't mind coming in and staying with you girls." She tilted her head to the side and wiped some of the dampness from my cheek.

Livvy looked at me, and I realized she was waiting to hear what I wanted. "No, Lena. I'll be okay. Thank you, though. There's just been so much happening lately. I think that maybe ... maybe it's all just catching up with me." I knew it sounded lame, but how could I sum up everything that had happened in the last week? Just thinking about all of it again threatened to bring more tears. "It's really okay. Livvy is here with me. We'll be okay on our own."

I watched a look of sadness pass across Lena's face. She was seeing it, too. Her girls were grown. We were as close as Lena ever came to having kids. She'd never married. Never had children of her own. When Mom died and Father dove even deeper into his work, it was Lena who stayed late, read us bedtime stories, and tucked us in for the night. She was the one who was here in the morning, who woke us up and made us breakfast, getting us ready for school. And it was Lena who was always here to make us a snack, help us with our homework, and make sure dinner was on the table. Over and over and over. For years.

Looking at her face now was like seeing her for the first time in a long time. When had she gotten so old? Her hair was gray, and wrinkles creased the skin around her eyes. Those beautiful soft brown eyes were the same, though. "I mean, of course, you can stay if you want to. I don't want you to feel like you have to go. I mean, you know you're always welcome here..."

Lena laughed, soft and gentle. "My girls. How time flies. Nope. I need to head back home. I have lots to do. And you girls could use a little sister time tonight, I think." She smiled again, then picked up her purse and jacket from the counter where she had placed them when I'd come in.

I smiled back at her. "Thank you, Lena. For everything." She just nodded.

As she reached the door, I added, "I love you, Lena."

"Love you, too, Lena." Livvy put her arm around me and rested her head on my shoulder.

Lena paused at the door, then turned back to us. "I love you both. Always have, always will." Then she turned and left.

Livvy immediately popped back up. "Lys, what happened? I lost camera access to you when you got off the elevator and didn't pick you back up until you were on your floor again. You never put your iBud in when you got back to your desk. You just slid it in your pocket." Her eyes were filled with concern.

I swallowed hard preparing myself. She wasn't going to like this.

"Jaxx caught me."

Livvy's mouth dropped open, but nothing came out. She closed it, then opened it again. Still nothing.

"He knows, Livvy. About you, about me, about what we've been up to. Maybe not all the specifics, but he's been watching you for a while. He said he's been feeding you information."

"What? Are you sure, Lys? I mean, did he actually say that?" She got up and started pacing.

"Yeah. He actually said that. This is serious, Livvy. I don't think he knew what I was taking from that room, but he knew I was in there and that I took something."

"How could he know? There are no cameras in that room. All you had to do was deny. Stick to the plan. You did, right? Stayed with the plan?" Livvy stopped and stared at me. "Lyssa, you didn't tell him anything, right?"

I paused, and Livvy slammed her fist down on the counter. "Are you kidding? Did you give us all up? How could you, Lyssa? *How could you?*" She was screaming at me now. In my face. I felt myself pulling back from her.

Livvy pressed both hands on the counter, staring at them. "Lyssa, what exactly did you tell him?" Her voice was calmer now, but it was cold.

"I ... I didn't say much. He did all the talking. He said something about knowing about your research, and that he had to protect our family, and that Father wasn't the only one in charge. That he had to provide Father with 'plausible deniability.' What do you think he meant by that, Livvy?" I studied her face as I spoke, watching a range of emotions pass over it.

"I'm not sure. Does he know about the rebels? About Gunner? That I've been meeting with him?"

"He didn't say anything about the rebels. I don't think he knows."

"Then maybe we're okay. Maybe he just thinks we're being stupid kids. Maybe–"

I cut her off. "He told me to report to his office first thing tomorrow morning. As soon as I get to AHGA."

"Probably no big–"

I cut her off again. "He made me give him a drive, Livvy. I'm sure he knows by now what we stole. That he's looking through those records, memos, whatever, and he's probably creating a cover story as we speak." I couldn't look at Livvy anymore. Disappointment had filled her eyes. "I'm sorry. He knew I'd taken something. He made me give it to him."

Seconds of silence ticked by.

Finally, she asked, "Did you give him both drives?"

"No, only one." I reached in my pocket, took out the duplicate drive, and set it on the counter. "I didn't have it for very long. I don't know if it had a chance to copy or not."

"Okay. At least this is something. I'm going to contact Gunner and see if I can get it to him and Jonathan tonight. Maybe it won't be a total loss." She picked up the drive and started to walk out of the room.

"Wait, Livvy, who's Jonathan?"

She hesitated. Slowly she turned around, and from the expression on her face, I could tell she had slipped. Said something that she hadn't meant to. "Uhhh ..." As her voice trailed off, her eyes darted around the kitchen, like she was trying to find the answer in there.

"Livvy, what aren't you telling me? Livvy? Who's Jonathan?"

"Don't worry about it, Lys. Let it go. It's not a big deal." She turned again to go.

"Obviously it is." That stopped her again.

"Let it go, Lys," she said, her back still to me.

"Tell me. I deserve to know. I'm the one who got that file for you. Or Jonathan. I think that should earn me some answers."

Facing me once more, she said, "You're right. You've earned some answers. But you have to be open-minded, Lys. You have to trust me."

I felt my eyebrows shoot up, but I didn't say anything. I just waited.

"He's Jonathan Fitting. But don't–"

"As in one of the Fitting brothers? Are you serious? Like Joshua Fitting's brother?" My mind raced as I remembered the night at the rebel camp when Gabe and I had heard Joshua speak. Panic gripped me all over again. "He's nuts, Livvy. Certifiable. I heard him. With my own ears. I heard him tell non-Greens it was okay to kill Greens because we're genetically modified. That it was their 'responsibility' to kill Greens. He compared us to diseased dogs!" It was my turn to shout now.

"Stop! Lyssa, just listen for a minute! Listen! I–"

But I didn't. I couldn't. My heart was racing. My breathing was ragged. I felt trapped in my own house. The Fitting brothers knew where we lived. They knew my sister. Those nasty, gnawing butterflies were back again. "How could you, Livvy? Do you hate Greens that much now? Are you willing to–"

"Stop it, Lys," she interrupted again. "Just shut up for once and listen. Jonathan is not Joshua. Since Jesse's death, he's been working toward legal ways to bring the corporations down. He's tired of people dying, and he doesn't want to lose anyone else. If you just talked to him, Lyssa, you'd see, you'd understand. He's not a bad person. Really. He's got some good ideas. Things that I believe in. Things that I think can work."

I felt my mouth drop open. And things started falling into place. Livvy wasn't just meeting with Gunner. She was meeting with Jonathan Fitting, too. She wasn't all googly over Gunner. She was falling for Jonathan Fitting! I tasted vomit in the back of my mouth. This guy had Livvy completely fooled. How could she not see it? See him for who he really was?

I shook my head. "You're not going to convince me, Livvy. I watched as Jonathan supported Joshua and what he was saying. As he cheered at his brother's hate-filled speech. As he urged others to take up their cause."

Livvy laughed. Which seemed totally inappropriate. "I wish you'd just meet him, Lys. You'd see what I see in him. He's not a fanatic. He's his own man. A good man. And, he's leading the rebellion in a new direction. One that we can all stand behind together. Regardless of skin color."

"Livvy, I don't know if he has you fooled or if you're just still not well. But there's no way that the man I saw has totally turned around his views. If you can't see that, something is really wrong with you."

Livvy's smile dropped. "So that's it, huh? I must be sick. I must not be in my right mind. Because I'm not Green, right? And you are, so you must be right. Done and done. Greens know best." She stared at me. When I started to say something, she immediately broke in. "You're not always right. Just because you don't believe me doesn't mean that I'm wrong. This time, you have no idea what you're talking about, Little Sis. I think it's you who's not thinking clearly." Walking right up to my face, we stood nose-to-nose. "You on something, Lys? Your eyes look weird."

"What? I haven't even Nocked today." And as soon as it slipped out, I wished that I could have taken it back.

Chapter 34

Livvy's eyes narrowed. "Nocked?"

"Never mind. It's nothing." Now I was the one who turned to walk away. But Livvy caught me by the wrist and jerked me back.

"What's Nock, Lyssa?"

"Nothing. I said never mind." I started to turn again, but Livvy had a firm hold on me.

"Oh, no. That's not the way it works. You don't get to make me answer you and then blow me off when I'm the one asking the questions."

"It has nothing to do with this situation, Livvy. Let it go." I jerked my arm away from her.

"This has something to do with Maddax, doesn't it?" That made me freeze.

"Oh my god, Lyssa. It's him, isn't it? What's he gotten you into? Are you on something? Please tell me you're smarter than that. That you wouldn't let him get you hooked on something."

"I'm not 'hooked' on anything. It's just an enhancer. That's all."

"That's all? That's all! Do you hear yourself? Let me guess. It's new. Developed by Maddax and his insane sisters. I'm sure they told you it's totally safe – that they've tested it and everything. Am I right, so far?" Her snideness was maddening.

"Stop it, Livvy. I'm fine. It's an enhancer. That's all. It's like an energy booster. With added chlorophyll. It makes you look greener. That's probably what you're seeing with my eyes. No big deal."

Livvy slowly started nodding her head. "Greener. Oh, I get it. That's what this is all about. Maddax always did have an obsession with that. Being 'Greener.' Because we all know that 'Greener' means better."

"It's not like that, Livvy. It's just a beneficial side effect. It's–"

"Beneficial side effect? Did we grow up in the same house? Do you hear yourself? In all your years living here, with a dad who works at AHGA, have you *ever* heard *anyone* talk about *beneficial* side effects? I can't remember even one, Lys. Not one. And you think I've been snowed." Her laugh was short and hollow.

"Livvy, I–"

"Save it. I think we're on two different paths. You go get Greener. I'm heading out to see Jonathan and Gunner. And

I'm taking my car, by the way. Don't bother waiting up. I don't know when I'll be home." Her lips curled in a smirk.

That was it. I was tired of all of this. "Fine."

"Fine." She stood there a few more seconds, then turned and left the room.

As I walked back to my bedroom, I heard a door close. Why'd I let Livvy turn everything around on me? Nock was stupid in comparison with the Fitting Brothers. And Livvy was headed out to meet one of them right now. She had no idea of what she was getting into – I'd seen Joshua Fitting and his brothers in action. I'd watched as they whipped up a fury in others, something that had turned malicious and ugly. I'd been caught up in the moment until I'd realized what they were really saying – that it was okay to kill genetically modified people because they were no longer "natural." And, Jonathan had never stepped in once to stop his brother, to rein in what was being said.

Why hadn't I stopped her?

Searching my pocket, I found my iBud and placed it in my ear. `Call Livvy,` I thought.

`Subscriber is currently unavailable,` a voice replied.

What? She just left. She must have turned it off. `Leave message.`

`Message function is unavailable. Please try again at a later time.`

Crap. Trying again, I got the same message. She must have taken her iBud out.

I tried to go to sleep, but I couldn't get comfortable. Eventually, my tossing and turning even got to Lulu, and she headed to her bed in the corner of my room. After catching up on a couple of digital episodes I'd missed, I tried messaging Livvy again. No luck.

Rolling over on my bed, I looked over at the inhaler on my nightstand. Then I stopped. What Livvy said was true. I didn't really know anything about Nock. About its side effects. About what it could be doing to me. I did know better. I just hadn't wanted to think about it.

"Play Zimmer. Level 2," I said.

Music filled my room, and closing my eyes, I felt myself begin to relax. Tomorrow would be better. I loved Wednesdays. No classes for me at the U.

When I opened my eyes, light cascaded into my room through the blinds I'd left open. I got out of bed and stretched. I needed to talk to Livvy. We had to talk.

I walked down the hall to the family room. No Livvy. I cruised through the kitchen thinking that maybe I'd find her eating. Not there either. Next, I checked her room. Opening the door, I got a sinking feeling. Something felt off. Then I realized what is was. I raced to the garage, then out the front door. Standing in the front yard in my pjs, I clasped my hands behind my head, trying not to panic.

Livvy hadn't come home.

Chapter 35

I tried her iBud and got the "unavailable" message again. My mind started racing through the possible scenarios. None of them were good. What if something had happened to her?

I walked back to my bedroom and sat down on my bed. Rubbing my temples, I thought about our last conversation. How we had left things. That sucked, but it also probably explained why Livvy hadn't come home. She was right. We didn't see things the same way. But that didn't mean we both weren't right. Honestly, I knew she was right about Nock. But I wasn't ready to accept Jonathan Fitting as a "good person," as her – her boyfriend? Was it to that point? Was that why she gotten so mad at me? Thinking about it just made my head hurt more.

As I considered slipping back under the covers, an iBud reminder went off. **Meeting at AHGA with Chayston Jaxx in one hour.**

I flew off the bed, panic flooding back. How could I have forgotten that I had to talk to Jaxx this morning? Just a little chat about him catching me stealing a file yesterday from my father's company. I really wished Livvy was here. Jaxx had the file. He knew what we took. Now I'd have to come up with some reasonable explanation that didn't involve rebels. Like – like – like what?

By the time I was ready to go, I still hadn't come up with anything solid. Just some lame excuse that Livvy and I were worried about Father. That he'd been acting "funny" at home. Not like himself. It was the best I could do. Anything else I came up with just led to rebel activity. For a second, I thought I was stuck, realizing that my car still wasn't back. But I remembered that Father was out of town, which meant his would be in the garage. Under normal circumstances, I'd never take out his Aston Martin Titanium 007XS, but these weren't normal circumstances, and I didn't know what else to do.

I tried contacting Livvy several more times on the way to work. Still nothing. Arriving at AHGA, I felt edgy. I saw my hand shaking as I reached for the door. Stepping inside, I tried to look casual as I walked over to the large windows. In the bright sunshine, I paused and took several deep breaths. I could do this. Jaxx didn't seem to know much. All I had to do was sit and listen. Talk as little as possible. Apologize. Focus on my concern for Father. Then, maybe, just maybe, I'd get out of this mess.

A hand clamped down on my shoulder, and I let out an audible yelp.

"Sorry to startle you, Miss Brentwood," a male voice said, "but I was asked to accompany you to Mr. Jaxx's office as soon as you arrived this morning." Glancing around, the man fidgeted with his jacket lapel and then his security belt. I swallowed hard, noticing the gun nestled at his side. Had AHGA's security team always carried guns? I hadn't noticed them before.

The man stayed with me as far as Jaxx's office. When the door opened, he and Jaxx simply nodded at each other, and then the man left.

"Since when have AHGA employees started carrying guns at work?" I asked as I walked toward his desk, not waiting to be invited.

"What?" Jaxx looked down, pressed a button at his desk, and the door slid shut behind me. "Oh, you noticed that. Good. It means that others probably are, too." He stood up behind his desk. "We've always carried guns. Now we're carrying them so they're visible. Your father's recommendation after the last bombing in the city."

"Oh." I couldn't think of anything else to say. Jaxx just stared at me, like he could see right into me. His eyes were penetrating, his frown unflinching, his jaw tense. I felt a little woozy. Reaching out, I took hold of a chair. Glancing back up, I saw a brief change in the look on Jaxx's face. Concern? Worry? Uneasiness? I wasn't sure, but I knew had seen it. *What's going on here?*

"Calyssa, sit down. I think you know we have a lot to talk about." Jaxx sat back down behind his desk as well.

I sat and tried to focus on my plan: listen, apologize, focus on concern for Father. I just had to stay on track.

Jaxx leaned forward, elbows on his desk, fingers steepled in front of him. Slowly he set his chin on his hands. Then he just stared at me, in silence.

I tried to sit completely still, to just stare back at him. *Stick to the plan, Lyssa.*

Finally, Jaxx let out a little laugh and leaned back in his chair. But he wasn't smiling.

"You have no idea how much trouble you could be in, do you? Sitting there all smug, thinking that because I didn't turn you in yesterday that you're safe today. What I can't decide is if you're dumb enough to blindly follow your crazy sister, or if you actually know what she's doing, and you're trying to protect her. Either way, it doesn't matter. You should have stayed out of this."

"What are you talking about, Jaxx?" I snapped.

Another little laugh. "Maybe you do know. The little sister finally looking beyond her beloved music into the real world. Regardless, I like the fire." And, this time, a smirk.

I crossed my arms in front of me and glared at him. *Screw the plan.* This guy was just another arrogant jerk. "Maybe you're just afraid that if I get caught, it'll actually be you who gets into trouble with Father. You're in charge of security at AHGA, and all of this has been happening behind your back."

That wiped the smile off his smug face. And for a second, I relished in that moment. But the look that replaced it was terrifying. His whole face seemed to darken. His eyes narrowed, cold and hard. I saw his jaw clenching, grinding his teeth. A large blood vessel that ran along his temple stood out. Deliberately, slowly, he stood back up. A thunderstorm ready to erupt in violence, looming over me.

"Your father is the least of my concerns. Do you really think he'll care that you and your sister stole some old building plans? They don't contain any relevant research information. The rooms are just numbered, and areas are indicated by letters, and some of the floors have had changes over the years. Offices have moved, staff on levels have changed, and security measures aren't even identified. The only thing it's good for is a history lesson of AHGA. It's–"

I interrupted, standing up, too, unable to stop the words that came tumbling out. "That's a lie and you know it! That file contained memos that prove that AHGA's been involved in illegal land sales! Don't try to cover it up with some–"

"I am *not* lying!" His voice boomed over mine. And I dropped back into my chair. Then silence.

Jaxx left his desk and walked over to a window, his steps rigid, his hands in fists at his side.

"Maybe that's what your sister told you, Calyssa, but I've looked at the files. Have you?" He didn't turn around.

I didn't answer.

"I didn't think so." In the next second, he was right next to me, grabbing my chair, whipping it around so I faced him. As his hands firmly gripping the chair on both sides of me, he lowered his face until we were eye level. It was like time slowed down. I noticed a small trickle of perspiration running down the side of his cheek. A movement in his jaw.

His eyes searched mine like he could see into my soul. I felt like I was in a trance, holding my breath, waiting between heartbeats.

When he stood up, the trance broke. I took a deep breath and clasped my shaking hands together on my lap in front of me. Sitting back behind his desk, he closed his eyes and shook his head.

When he opened them, he looked weary. "Tell me what you think you know, Calyssa."

"I ... I ... I don't know anything, I guess."

He shook his head again. "That's not what I asked."

I just sat there.

"How about I start us off, then? I'll tell you what I know that you know." He waited for me to respond.

I said nothing.

"Fine. I'll take your silence as agreement. You and your sister have been secretly searching files at AHGA. I believe you were doing this separately, at first. That you each weren't aware of what the other was doing." He paused.

I remained silent.

"I'll take that as a yes. You, I believe, were looking for a connection between AHGA and the killing of Jesse Fitting. Oh, don't look so shocked, Calyssa. Did you really believe that I wouldn't put two and two together when that picture of Jesse Fitting with the Star in his hand surfaced? With you and all your babbling about the security enforcers murdering someone in a field? Your father came to me with the whole story. I told him it had already been taken care of."

I felt pieces snapping together in my mind. My memory bracelet on Father's desk. The missing pictures. I opened my mouth, but Jaxx started up again before I could say anything.

"Catching up now? Yes, *I* erased those images. Do you realize the predicament they would have placed your father in? His daughter turning in evidence against the SciCity Security Enforcers? That she had been 'with' the rebels? You would have immediately been made out as an accomplice. And Gabe Stayton, too. Had you thought about him?

"We might have been able to get you off, but only by throwing the boy to the wolves, giving them a story about him kidnapping you, trying to trade you to the rebels, to Jesse Fitting, that it went bad, and then, fortunately for you, the enforcers showed up just in time. It was a plausible scenario, one that we considered, but I also knew that Andrew Stayton's well connected and wouldn't give up his son easily. That he could have caused just enough trouble to push for a larger investigation, and then it would be out that you'd been to that rebel camp.

"Again, surprised? I told you I already knew. Remember those pictures you took of the cute kids playing in the river? And the woman, the one who claimed security enforcers had killed her husband and taken her land? Oh yeah, I know about her. She'd been listed as a rebel sympathizer before she disappeared off the grid. And you had pictures of her. On your memory bracelet. Which meant you knew where to find her. Do you think the enforcers would just let something like that go?"

I sucked in a breath, feeling like he'd just punched me in the stomach. My heart was racing. He knew. Jaxx knew about the rebel camp. He knew about Leah and her kids. But did he know about Gunner? I tried to remember what other pictures I had taken. Just the ones at the river, and then the ones of the shooting, I thought.

What did it mean? If he knew all of it, why was I still here, going to University, working at AHGA, living at home with my family, like nothing had happened? "But, Jaxx, if—"

"No, Calyssa. Don't say it. Don't say you could have explained it. Or fixed it. Or whatever story you're concocting right now. I fixed it. For your father. For your family. That's what I do. What I've been doing for years now."

"But why would Livvy lie to me? About the file I copied for her?"

Jaxx sneered. "Copied. You say it like it was yours to copy. You mean stole?"

I felt myself blush as my face heated up. "Yeah. The one I stole."

Jaxx laughed, but it wasn't quite as curt this time. "At least you admit it. I don't know why Livvy would have you take it. I've looked at it from every angle I can think of. Maybe she thought it would show more than was actually there. And, I don't know why she thought it would contain land purchase information. Livvy has been very thorough up to this point. I haven't seen her make many mistakes. Her research patterns have been well thought out. Why do you think Livvy wanted you to get it for her?"

Because Jonathan Fitting had told her the rebels needed it. But I wasn't going to say that to Jaxx. Despite everything he knew, it didn't seem like it included her connection to the Fitting Brothers.

"I know that she thought it would provide proof that AHGA had been involved in some illegal land sales, and we'd hoped it would show us whether or not Father was involved. You're positive there wasn't anything like that in the file?"

Jaxx just looked at me like I was being ridiculous and crossed his arms, leaning back in his chair.

I had to know if he knew anything about Father. Not that he would tell me, but I had to ask. "Jaxx, you told me that there are things going on at AHGA that Father doesn't know about. That he's not the only one in charge here. That you make sure he has plausible deniability. What'd you mean by that? I know enough to recognize that AHGA is involved in some shady dealings with several security enforcers. Does Father know?"

Jaxx steepled his fingers in front of him once again, this time tapping them against his lips. I couldn't tell if he was going to answer me or not. I wanted to reiterate the questions, to reword them, to just keep asking until he finally answered. But I didn't think that would work with Jaxx. So, I waited.

"What you really want to know, Calyssa, is if your father is a 'bad' man. Has he done, or condoned, horrible things? Isn't that really what you want to ask me?" His eyes narrowed.

I bit my tongue to keep from yelling at him. Recrossed my arms and crossed my legs. And glared some more.

"You're learning. There's value in patiently waiting for an answer. In letting your opponent wonder what you're thinking instead of just blurting everything out. But you've made a mistake. I'm not your opponent. In fact, without you ever knowing it, I've been your greatest ally. I've been the one watching over you, covering your tracks, hiding your clumsy attempts at rectifying the wrongs of the world."

Jaxx was my ally? Right.

Pain in my butt? Yep.

Spy? Definitely.

Creepy old guy? Absolutely for sure.

But an ally? That was it. I couldn't keep quiet any more. "You've been my ally, huh? Looking out for my best interests all along, huh? Just trying to make my life full of sunshine and rainbows? Hmmmm. Well, all I see is some weird guy who spies on me and erased my pictures because he thought it would be better than handling the fallout. Wasn't it you, Jaxx, who told me life was all about making choices and being adult enough to deal with the consequences?" I gave him my best sneer. His face went blank. I'd expected him to get mad again or something, but this time he just sat silently.

Sometimes, when Jaxx looked at me, he seemed to be seeing something else, like now. I actually looked behind me to see if someone or something was there. It felt eerie, like we were just sitting there waiting for something to happen.

When Jaxx spoke, his eyes focused back on my face and his voice was low, so low that I had to lean forward to hear him. "You want to know what I've done for you, Calyssa? Fine, let's just talk about the last few months, okay? Let's see, besides taking care of the pictures that would have crucified you and your family, I paid off some low-life scum reporter who tried to make some money off you after you *gave* him the Jesse Fitting photo, which you weren't supposed to have. He had an intricate plan of blackmail that would have made some real problems for you and the family. And you were clueless.

"Oh, and I've hidden your little drug escapades from your father – oh, yes, I know all about your adventures with your new 'boyfriend.' I had to run Maddax off once before when he got a little rough with Livvy. She never told you about that, did she? Well, he's been more persistent with you, and he did help smooth over the whole car accident thing at the Banebriar's.

"Which reminds me that I had to call in a few favors from some enforcers I know to keep you from being questioned after that kid OD'd on your new party drug. Fortunately for you, your father called when you left the house. I tracked you to the Banebriar's neighborhood and cut into a surveillance camera in the area. And guess what I intercepted? A call that was going into the Enforcers HQ with your license plate and car information. I got them to let you through the blockade to go 'comfort you friend' with assurances that you'd never been in contact with the boy in the accident.

238

"And, let's not forget the promotion I just had to arrange for the tech analyst on level sixteen. You know, the one whose kid you almost killed. Remember that? The day when you wrecked your car. And then you thought that throwing your Brentwood name around would keep you out of trouble. Just the opposite in fact. He immediately tried to see your father. Demanded a meeting. Good thing I was there to intercept. It cost your father some money, but the guy won't bring it up again.

"I'm the one that's always there for you, Calyssa. I always have been. That's what I do for your family. It's what I've done for the last fourteen years. Since your mother's incident. I protect all of you. I do the hard things that your father doesn't want to dirty his hands with. I've cleaned up after all of you for years. Your father, you mother, your sister, and now you. I don't need you being the one causing the problems, instigating the issues. I shouldn't have to protect AHGA from all of you ..."

His rant continued. I sat in shock. Jaxx had a hand in almost every aspect of my life. As my mind grappled with everything he'd just told me, something was nagging at me. Something small he'd said. Something that wasn't that important. Or was it? What had he said?

I interrupted, "You're still protecting all of us?" He stopped mid-sentence, silent for a couple of beats.

"Every day." He looked perturbed.

"On top of everything else you do, you have to watch out for the four of us? Cleaning up our messes, fixing our mistakes? Protecting the family name?"

His voice was harsher this time. "Yes, Calyssa. It's a full-time job that you're not making any easier."

And then I knew. He'd answered without really thinking about it. Honestly. Because he was tired of all this.

I stood up and stared down at him. Intently, just like he'd done to me. My pulse quickened. I placed my hands palms down on Jaxx's desk to keep them from shaking. A deep breath. My turn. "Jaxx, how long have you known that my mother is alive?"

Chapter 36

Seconds ticked by. Five. Ten. Twenty. Thirty. We just stared at other. The longer he waited, the more I knew I was right. He'd slipped up. *My mom's alive! Where? How?* Question after question flooded my mind, but I stayed silent. I'd wait him out. No matter how long it took.

Finally, after what seemed like forever, Jaxx sat back and closed his eyes. Without opening them, he said, "I've always known, Calyssa. She never died. People just assumed that she did, and we let them. For five years, scientists and doctors kept her alive with machines. Your father couldn't let her go. He kept believing that somehow, he'd come up with a way to bring her back. We talked at first about telling you girls, but he decided it would be too hard. You have to understand, at that point, the doctors told him there was very little hope. She was in a deep coma with minimal brain activity. He was worried that you and Livvy would have to go through losing her all over again. So, he waited, silently. Only a few key people at AHGA knew that Layney was alive." Jaxx opened his eyes.

I slowly sat back down, afraid my legs would collapse out from under me. I hadn't heard anyone say her name in a long time. "I want to see her," I said quietly. This was unbelievable. Maybe that was it. Maybe Jaxx was lying. Mom couldn't be alive. If she was, she would have come back to us.

Jaxx just sat there staring at me.

"I want to see her." Louder this time, my heart racing.

"No, you don't," Jaxx said softly, his eyes changing again. He looked – sad?

Even louder, almost yelling, I said, "Yes, I do, Jaxx. If she's really alive, prove it. Show me."

"She's not the woman you remember."

"You're lying! You're just trying to work me! You're just trying to ... to..." My voice trailed off. I couldn't think. *My mom's alive.* That one sentence just kept repeating itself over and over in my head.

"Calyssa, let me finish the story. Do you want to hear what happened? Do you want to know the truth?"

What could the explanation be? I wasn't sure I really wanted to know, but I found myself nodding my head.

Jaxx sighed. "About eight years ago, for some reason, your mother started having seizures. Her doctors tried neurosurgery and electroconvulsive therapy to get it under control, but nothing seemed to be working. Our neuropsychopharmacology department talked your father into experimenting with transcranial magnetic stimulation in the hope that by sending electrical currents to the vagus nerve in her brain, they could terminate the seizures."

I must have looked lost, because Jaxx stopped.

"Do you understand any of this?"

"Not really." I felt confused. My mom was alive, and Jaxx was talking about parts of the brain that I didn't understand. "How do you know all of this? Why are you telling me?"

"I haven't always been in this position, Calyssa. I have multiple degrees, including a medical doctorate. Don't look so amazed. It's one of the reasons your father hired me. I understand the significance of what's happening here as well as the importance of protecting it."

What? Jaxx was smart, like super smart? I'd never thought of him as anything but old and creepy.

"And I'm telling you all of this because it affects your mother. Scientists and doctors inserted tiny electrodes in your mother's brain in the hopes that deep brain stimulation would stop the seizures."

"Did it?" I was just wrapping my mind around the idea that my mom might still be *alive*, and the thought of her suffering from seizures made me feel sick.

Jaxx nodded. "The seizures stopped. And a few days later, your mother opened her eyes. She didn't move, she didn't speak. But your father was adamant that somehow, these electrodes held the key for bringing your mother completely back to him. Doctors warned him not to get his hopes up, that this deep brain stimulation process had never been used in this way, and that it was known to cause depression and mood alterations in other situations, but he said it didn't matter. He personally oversaw the creation of a new neurocybernetic prosthesis system that was networked through Layney's brain. Many were skeptical, but that didn't stop him. You know how he is."

I nodded again. How did Jaxx know all of this? It was way too elaborate to be fake, wasn't it?

Jaxx continued, "For the next two years, it was all your father worked on. Once your mother started to speak again, it was obvious that there was very little that she could remember. She knew her name was Evalayne but didn't remember being called 'Layney.' That was your father's nickname for her after they got married. Some of the doctors started referring to her as 'Eve,' the first woman brought out of a coma through this process. She liked Eve, so everyone started calling her that.

"She seemed to remember her childhood, and her training as a virologist seemed to come back to her as well. But she never said anything about you or your sister, or about her marriage to your father.

"Your father didn't push it. He thought it would all come back over time. He kept redesigning her neuronet, implanting more electrodes, pushing the tech further and further. As your mom got better, she became more involved in the research. In terms of science, she seemed to understand things at an incredible rate, like whatever they'd done to her somehow increased her thinking and processing ability. But it also changed her, Calyssa." Jaxx paused. He looked uncomfortable.

"What? What is it? What do you mean it changed her?" My stomach tightened. I knew I wasn't going to like the answer.

"I knew Layney before. She was sweet. Kind. She obviously loved you girls. She loved your father. He was different then, too. More – caring – I guess."

I'd never heard anyone refer to my father as caring. Smart? Yes. Efficient? Yes. Effective? Yes. But caring? No. Not that he didn't care. He just didn't really show it much.

"Eve was clinical. Calculating. Focused. She never seemed to laugh or cry. Never really happy or sad or mad or ... or anything emotional at all. About a year after she was 'better,' your father thought that seeing you girls might trigger some sort of emotional response in her. But he didn't want you to see her, just in case it didn't work, if she didn't remember you.

"He brought you and Livvy to AHGA and had you both wait for him in an observation room. Neither of you had any idea of what was going on. I was with him. He asked Eve to join him and to tell him what she observed."

Now my stomach was in knots. Our mom had seen us? Why hadn't she asked to talk to us? To be with us?

"When Eve didn't have much to say, he finally broke down and told her everything – that she was his wife, that you were their children, about your life together. He told stories about you two growing up. About how much she loved you girls. About how much he loved her. Eve watched you and Livvy for the better part of an hour while he talked. And I watched her.

"I knew what was coming, Calyssa, but I could see that your father had no idea. When he finally finished, he took her hands in his and told her he was still in love with her. And she told him that she had no feelings for him at all. That everything he said may have been true, but that she had no recollection of it, so it wasn't true for her ... that his 'stories' meant nothing to her. He begged her to try to remember. He pleaded for her to look closer at you and Livvy. He yelled and cried and banged his fists on the table. But Eve just stood there and watched him. He finally walked over and kissed her.

"I'll never forget what happened next. When he stepped back with a smile on his face, Eve simply said, 'There's nothing there, Kassius. I feel nothing for you or those girls. You are not my family any more than anyone else here at AHGA. Please don't ever touch me again.' Then she turned and walked out of the room. Your father just stared after her. He started toward the door, and I grabbed him. Told him to give her some time ... that maybe something would come to her ... that maybe ... well ..." Another big sigh.

"Your father was different after that. Like he just turned everything off that didn't have to do with running the business. He didn't go visit Eve. He didn't work on her project anymore. But it didn't matter. Eve was working on her own research by then. She was fascinated with continuing brain research. Eventually, Kassius was running the business dealings at AHGA, and Eve was running the research projects. At that point, she was officially hired as Director of Special Research, choosing to go by Eve Huxley, her maiden name. She's always stayed behind the scenes, and rarely chooses to leave the facility, not seeing any reason to.

"About two years ago, she started becoming more secretive with her research. She's become obsessed with some old files that she found, ones that dated back to the founding of the company. She has her own team that now spends all its time on her research. Even I don't know much about it."

My mind was reeling. I looked down at my lap and realized that I'd been squeezing my hands together so tightly that my fingers were white. Rubbing them, I wasn't sure what ached more, my fingers or my heart.

My mom was alive but didn't remember me.

She was here but didn't want me.

She had seen me but didn't love me. Not anymore. Maybe Father was right. Maybe it would have been better to never know.

I felt tears begin to slide down my cheeks. I didn't try to stop them. I didn't care that Jaxx was there, or that I was probably still in trouble for stealing the file. Memories of Mom flooded my mind. Her reading to me at home. Walking through the park with her. Playing our instruments together. How could she not remember those things?

Jaxx brought me a bottle of water. I sat with it in my lap, unable to wrap my mind around everything he'd said. But the more he had talked, the less I doubted his story. I still didn't understand why he was telling me now. Was it a punishment? Because I had been messing around in the files at AHGA?

As if he could read my mind, Jaxx said, "Take a drink, Calyssa. There's more to the story. More that you need to hear. I need you to listen. You need to know."

Okay. That sounded ominous. What more was there? What, finding out that my mom was alive after thinking she was dead for the last thirteen years wasn't enough? Or being told that she not only didn't remember me, but that she didn't want anything to do with me now? Or that she worked right here for the last four years in the very facility that I had probably visited at least weekly, but I'd never seen her?

How could that be? How could she have been so close, and I didn't know it, didn't sense it, didn't feel her here? Then a memory, fuzzy at first, slowly came into focus. When Livvy was so incredibly sick and I came here to see her. To one of the deepest security levels. I'd bumped into a woman who was getting on the elevator as I was getting off. She was writing notes on her digital tablet and hadn't even bothered to look up. I'd paused as I stepped out. Something had caused me to look back at her, a familiar feeling, a trigger of a memory just out of reach, but the elevator door slid shut before I got a second look. Then I'd turned my focus back to Livvy, and forgotten the entire incident, the feeling. But now I knew, without a doubt, it had been her.

"Calyssa." The voice startled me, pulling me back to the present.

I opened the water bottle and took a long drink. My heart was telling me to run out of the room, to go find my mother, to help her remember me. But in my gut, I knew I needed to hear what Jaxx had to say next. So, I stayed.

"Go ahead."

Jaxx leaned back in his chair once more. "I didn't want to tell you this part, Calyssa, but looking at the situation now, I think it's important you know before you make any decisions about what you're going to do next.

"When Livvy and her friends were infected with the PKPH virus, your father wanted them to be brought here immediately. As soon as Eve heard, she demanded to be on the team. Several of her recent projects had involved viral studies, and she was the top virologist at AHGA. I think your father secretly hoped that maybe it had something to do with it being Livvy." He frowned and shook his head.

"Eve and her team went to work running tests on Livvy and the other boy they'd brought in with her. Your father had made it clear that treatment of Livvy, if possible, had to wait for his return. So, Eve started with the boy. Some new experimental drug her team had developed. When your father and I arrived, he met immediately with Eve. She reported that the boy had died, but she thought she knew what had gone wrong, and she was just getting ready to try again. This time with Livvy.

"That was the closest I think I've seen Kassius to losing it. He told Eve she couldn't touch Livvy, that under no circumstances could this drug be used on her. That he would be handling her case personally. Eve laughed at him. Told him he was a washed up 'has-been' who abandoned the research lab years ago, and that he should leave treating the subjects to people who knew what they were doing. That he should stick to what he was good at — making money to keep her research funded.

"Kassius slapped her across the face before I could get in between them, and Eve turned terrifyingly quiet. While I was trying to calm him down, Eve just stood there. Didn't say anything. Didn't leave the room. Nothing.

"Once your father had himself under control again, he apologized to Eve, saying that Livvy was their daughter, not their test subject. Eve disagreed, saying that Kassius was missing the real opportunity here, that PKPH was going to be the next pandemic, and that AHGA had a chance before anyone else to get in front of it, to develop new genetically engineered superior chloroplasts, and that it tied into some of her current work. She actually seemed excited.

"Kassius looked at me. I knew it was then that he truly understood that there was no part of Layney left in Eve. That Livvy was no more to her than the boy that had come in — just another possible test subject. He told Eve that it was non-negotiable, that she couldn't test anything on Livvy until they knew it was safe. She reminded him that she was Director of Special Research, and that she had final say over all experimental research and treatment in the facility. That he'd appointed her to that position, and that Livvy's treatment was ultimately her decision.

"Kassius was desperate. I tried to calm him down again, but at that point, someone came in and told us that Livvy had taken another turn for the worse. Eve told your father she could stabilize Livvy, and then she would leave the treatment decisions up to him, but he'd have to agree to something in return. As soon as she said that, I knew we were in trouble. I don't know if Kassius didn't catch on, or just didn't care."

I found myself leaning forward, holding my breath again. "What did she want?" I whispered. The gnawing butterflies in my stomach told me I wasn't going to like the answer.

"Access to you."

Chapter 37

"Me?" I said, jumping up out of my seat. "You said she didn't want anything to do with me." Suddenly I felt really hot, aware of more than just a trickle of perspiration making its way down my back. I started to pace around the room. This didn't make sense. Mom, or Eve, or whoever she was now, wanted to trade a sick Livvy for me? Nothing good was going to come out of this – she hadn't said she wanted to get to know me, or hang out with me, or – or anything that sounded even relatively good. Just access. Cold, clinical, scientific, experimental – not good.

"Eve told your father that she wanted to run tests on you. On your DNA. Somehow, she had found out that you had been engineered using genes that she had specially chosen for you from her own DNA. It has to do with her research on identifying superior genetics. Her premise is that customers will pay a premium for a guarantee of superior human chloroplasts, and that, with enough time and research, her program could create a modified organelle that could be introduced into the hereditary DNA of an individual that could be passed to offspring."

"Passed to offspring? Like children being born Green?" I was shocked. I'd never heard of any successful research in this area.

"Eve believes she's on that track, and that she may be able to use a hollowed-out form of the PKPH virus as the carrier for this new genetic modification. She wanted to be able to compare her own DNA with her offspring's, so she wanted access to you and your DNA. And, she needed more infected test subjects."

My mouth felt dry. My heart was racing. My palms sweaty. "What did Father tell her?"

"They came to an agreement. Your father would have sole discretion over Livvy's treatment and Eve would do everything she could to help stabilize her. In return, your father agreed to give Eve access to all medical and genetic files on you as well as blood and tissue samples, but he refused to allow her physical access to you at any time. Because of that, she also demanded that he do whatever he could to bring other people infected with PKPH to AHGA for her research project, something she was calling the Viridis Eugenics Project, and that he would stay completely out of it."

"Viridis Eugenics?" I stopped pacing and stared at him.

"Viridis is Latin for green, and Eugenics comes from Greek meaning good genes. It's based out of level 30, so it has the highest security requirements. I told your father not to agree, but he shrugged me off. He just wanted Livvy protected from Eve's testing, and you kept away from her. He was worried about both of you."

I sat back down heavily in the chair in front of Jaxx's desk.

Viridis Eugenics Project.

I remembered the tablet in the staffroom that I'd found. It belonged to Dr. Morlan. No wonder she'd been upset when she forgotten it. "Does she ... Eve ... go by V now?"

It was Jaxx's turn to look shocked. "How do you know that? Has she contacted you?"

"No, I saw a memo that I'm sure I wasn't supposed to see. It didn't mean anything at the time, but now, things are starting to fall into place."

"Her team has started calling her V now. I'm not sure why. She doesn't fill me in on much, and I just try to make sure she doesn't do anything to put your father or the company in jeopardy. She's incredibly secretive."

I rubbed my forehead, closing my eyes. I needed to talk to Livvy. How would I explain all of this to her?

"Calyssa, there's one more thing."

I opened my eyes. *Not more*, I thought. *What else could there be?*

"From what I've put together, we think that your mother had one of the very earliest cases of the PKPH virus, before anyone knew what it was. When we saw your sister, she looked identical to how your mother looked when your father brought her here so many years ago. Some of your sister's treatments were the same things that had been successful in stabilizing your mother." Jaxx grabbed another bottle of water. This time he opened and drank the whole thing. Wiping his mouth with the back of his hand, he sat the bottle back on desk.

I sat silently, biting my lower lip, a feeling of dread passing over me. *What is he* not *saying?* I started to ask, but he put a hand up.

"I'm worried about Livvy. She's been up to something lately. The things she's tracking on the server, the files she's accessing, even some of our recent conversations."

"What are you saying, Jaxx?"

"I think Livvy is starting to exhibit some of the same characteristics as Eve. I'm worried that whatever they did to stabilize her may have affected her brain the same way it affected Eve's. I think she's changing, Calyssa. And not in a good way."

"What? Livvy's ... fine." Even as I said it, I was thinking about her unpredictable behavior lately. How much she'd changed. But mostly it was for the better, right? We'd ween getting along better. We'd finally been talking, really talking. But what about her involvement with the rebels, with Jonathan Fitting? What if Jaxx was right? What if something was wrong? Or if they'd done something to her brain? What if–

"I just thought you should know, Calyssa. I know you love your sister, but she may not be the person you thought she was. Be careful. Don't blindly follow her. She may not be fully competent right now. Think about what you've seen from her lately. Is this making any sense to you? Do you–"

Jaxx's door opened behind me, startling both of us.

"Sorry to interrupt, Sir, but your iBud was off." A man wearing a security uniform stepped in. "We've just received a report that there have been sightings of unauthorized civilians around the dam. I've sent two teams out through the front, but I thought you'd want to know immediately, given the trouble in SciCity lately."

"Absolutely, Mace. I want two more teams to enter from here through the tunnels and come at it from the other side of the dam. You go with them. I'll join the ones from this side."

"Yes, Sir."

Jaxx was already halfway to the door by the time the other man was gone. He stopped and checked his gun as well as his scanner pack.

"I have to go, Calyssa. Think about what I said. We should talk more. Come in and see me tomorrow." Not a request.

I nodded as I got up out of my chair. And then Jaxx was gone, too.

I went back to my desk and tried twice more to reach Livvy by iBud. Still no answer. But this time the message function was back on. That was a good sign.

Livvy, you need to message me as soon as you get this. We have to talk ASAP. It's important. Like super important. I had my meeting with Jaxx today and there's way more going on than we knew. Livvy, I have to tell you something, but I don't want to do it in a message. Please, please get ahold of me. I'm working at AHGA today, but if you message me, I can come meet you somewhere. And, Livvy, I love you. Then I disconnected.

Back at my desk, I pulled up a file I'd been working on, but I couldn't focus. So, I gave in and decided to see what I could learn about Eve Huxley. I did a mainline search first, which pulled up documents that everyone in the company had access to. Eve was mentioned in 129 documents. Seriously? How did I not know of her? But then again, AHGA did employ over 1,200 people. Most of the documents that mentioned Eve had something to do with new research updates. Every once in a while, she was quoted, but nothing stood out.

Next, I looked at the Class 1 and 2 files. More of the same, just research projects currently in development, which meant this information hadn't been released to the public yet. Still nothing new to learn.

After doing a quick double check to make sure no one else was around, I used a code I'd found on Father's desk at home that allowed me to view Class 3 and 4 files. Here I did find some images of projects that included the scientists working on them. Two included Eve, but even after I enlarged them up, they weren't great. One was a partial profile, and in the other she was looking down.

I was about ready to give up when I found an image of her from four years ago, just after she'd been hired in Director of Special Research position. It was of all the directors, including Jaxx as the Director of Security and Father as the CEO of the company. There were a dozen people in the picture. All beautiful and handsome, all Green, and all smiling. Except one. I blew up the picture and looked more closely at it. Short, dark green hair, sharp but striking features, solemn expression. But when I focused on just her eyes, without everything else, I could see some similarities to Mom. Well, the Mom I remembered anyway. From when I was five years old. Sort of. How could someone look so different?

I searched further back in the archives and found a picture of "Kassius and Evalayne Brentwood," one from just before she got sick. Cropping everyone except Mom/Eve out of both images, I manipulated the two pictures on the screen, so they appeared next to each other. Even like this, they looked like two different people. It was only after I enlarged both pictures until all I could see was their eyes that I knew for sure. An identical shade of emerald green. The same eyes. But one set looked happy, full of love. The other pair looked analytical, almost cynical. Funny how much feeling was expressed through the eyes.

Then a shrill siren filled the air, and red lights began to flash near the elevators.

Chapter 38

I jumped up, looking around, and heard people coming down the hall. I hurriedly closed the images on my screen.

"Calyssa, to the elevator. Immediate evacuation." I heard Karsten's voice before I saw him, but we both arrived at the elevator at the same time.

"What's happening?" I'd never been in any kind of a drill like this before at AHGA, and I'd never heard of a building evacuation here.

"I don't know. I just know that red lights mean get out ASAP." Karsten looked worried. He pushed the elevator button like ten more times, as if pushing it more would bring it faster. When the door did open, it was already crowded with people, but they moved over to squeeze us in.

When we reached the lobby, security officers were everywhere, directing people out of the building. What was going on? For the most part, people were quiet, streaming toward the main doors. I jumped in line and followed the surge out to the parking area.

Once there, I noticed people gathered in small groups based on who they worked with. I scanned the crowd for Eve but didn't see her anywhere.

A hand on my shoulder from behind made me jump, and I let out an involuntary yelp as I spun around to see who it was.

Jaxx.

"Miss Brentwood, are you okay?" Back to Miss Brentwood. No hint on his face of the heart-to-heart we'd had earlier today.

"Uhh, I'm fine. What's going on?" I waited as Jaxx scanned the area around me.

Ignoring my question, he spoke into some sort of old hand-held tech, saying, "Red Team has Mermaid. Clear from building. Griffin and Siren aren't in today. Who is still unaccounted for?"

A voice came through device. "Blue Team has Minotaur and Pegasus. Clear from building."

A different voice, "Black Team has Sphinx, Nymph, and Centaur. Clear from building."

Another voice. "Orange Team is bringing up Dragon, Elf, and Manticore right now. ETA to front door is two minutes."

One more voice. This one sounded frustrated. "This is Yellow Team. Phoenix is refusing to evacuate until we have confirmed this is not a false alarm. I also have Basilisk ready to go. We're at Level 30. What do you want us to do?"

Jaxx breathed out hard through clenched teeth. "Bring Basilisk up. I'll come in after Phoenix."

"Good luck with that, Boss. Yellow Team on their way up."

Jaxx turned to a younger officer standing behind him. "Escort Mermaid to her car. Drive her to the Brentwood estate. Stay with her until I contact you." Then he took off back toward the front door.

My eyebrows shot up. "Mermaid?" I asked.

"Yes, Miss Brentwood. Every Director as well as each member of the Brentwood family has a mythological codename to be used in emergency situations. That way, if anyone taps into our tech, they can't target someone specifically. It's for your safety." He took my arm. "Let's head to your car, Miss." His face stayed completely neutral. No hint of smile. His eyes constantly scanned the crowd around us as we walked briskly to the parking lot.

"Obviously Griffin and Siren are my father and sister, since they both aren't at the facility."

The officer looked uncomfortable. "If you say so, Miss Brentwood."

That made me laugh. I mean, I knew whatever was going on here was some sort of an emergency, but the thought of all those mythical creatures coming out the front door at AHGA just formed a ridiculous picture in my mind.

"Which director is Phoenix?"

"I'm not allowed to say, Miss."

"But I'm a Brentwood."

No comment from the officer.

"Well, the Yellow Team seemed happy enough to get out of that escort."

"Phoenix can be ... prickly."

"Ahhh. Huxley." I gave him an I-know-how-she-can-be look.

He slipped a quick, studying look in my direction. "Can't say, Miss." But his lips twitched a smile.

Spot on. Eve seemed to be unpopular with more than just Jaxx. That was already how I was thinking of her, as Eve. Not as Mom. Not as Layney. Eve.

"Can I at least ask your name?"

He glanced at me and then continued his scan of the area. "It's Trygg Matson, Miss Brentwood. Please feel free to call me Trygg." We arrived at Father's Aston Martin parked in my space. Trygg let out a low whistle as he came around to help me into the car.

"Then you have to call me Calyssa. Or Lyssa. That's fine, too."

"Lyssa it is then." Still scanning the crowd, he closed the door behind and climbed into the driver's side. "Ignition code?" He looked like a kid in a candy store as he sat ready to drive the car.

"TXJ3346R." The car started and Trygg pulled out. "Why aren't you using iBuds? Seems it would be easier than the old tech Jaxx was using."

"Most people don't have access to the old tech anymore – Jaxx calls them 'walkies.' Less chance of interception."

"Oh." That didn't really make sense to me, but Trygg seemed to agree with Jaxx. "Can you tell me what happened back there? Why we had to evacuate?"

"I'm sorry. I can't. When it's clear, they should send out an iBud message to everyone. You'll have to wait until then."

We rode in silence. I was lost in my thoughts again, replaying my conversation with Jaxx, so I was surprised when we pulled up to my house. "I didn't realize you knew where I lived."

"The whole security team does, Miss Brentwood. I mean, Lyssa." He jumped out and ran around the car to offer a hand to help me get out. As we entered the house, Trygg pulled a walkie out of his inside jacket pocket. "Red 3 with Mermaid at Olympus."

Jaxx's voice squawked back, "Confirm Siren's presence, Red 3."

Crap. I didn't think Livvy was here. Her car wasn't out front or in the garage.

"Can you grab your sister for me? I need to speak to her briefly so I can report in."

I rattled off the first thing that came to mind. "She went to stay with Lena today, our domicile attendant. Father gave Lena the week off, but she always invites Livvy and me over. Livvy hates to stay alone." And, remembering that Livvy usually left her car tracker in the garage, I added, "Lena was picking her up this morning when I left for work." Trygg wouldn't know that Livvy's car wasn't here. At least I hoped he wouldn't. I tried for a relaxed smile, but it came out as a nervous giggle.

Trygg looked skeptical, but he picked up the walkie and said, "Siren is spending the day with the help. Got picked up this morning since Griffin is out of town and Mermaid had to work."

Silence.

Finally, Jaxx came back on. "Fine. Stay as directed. Red 1 out."

Trygg walked over to the panel by the front door. Pressing a button, he spoke into the panel, "Security and perimeter check. Code clearance 7-9-2-alpha-tango-red-3." The panel spewed back numbers, times, and codes, all which seemed acceptable to Trygg, as he finally seemed to relax a little.

"So, what's next?" I asked, staring at him, which seemed to make him uncomfortable all over again.

"I'll just stay here, posted at the door, Miss Brentwood. I mean, Lyssa."

"Well, that seems ridiculous. We have the best security in SciCity. At least that's what Father says. Seems like you could sit down and relax for bit. Since you apparently have to hang out here for a while." That made him look perplexed. And that made me laugh. "Really? Come on into the kitchen. I'll make us both a nutrient drink."

Another look around and then a smile. A real smile. "Okay. Lead the way."

We sat in the kitchen for the next couple of hours, talking about our lives. I learned that Trygg was six years older than I, the last of four boys, all of whom had followed in their father's footsteps to become SciCity Security Enforcers. Trygg had been recruited by Jaxx straight out of

Enforcer Academy to work in the private sector. That hadn't made his family happy, but he said any time they got on his case about it, he reminded them that he was the youngest and making more money than any of them.

Trygg was easy to talk to. He told stories about growing up with three brothers and a mom that could whip all of them into shape with a single look. He spoke proudly of his brothers and their service, as well as his Father, who was a lieutenant in the West Metro precinct. He worried about them with the rebel attacks lately. He talked about his brothers' wives and kids and said that they all talked every night to check in with each other. And that on the last Sunday of the month, they all still met at his parents' house and had a barbeque for the grandkids, since none of them were old enough to go Green yet.

He went on to explain that each of the four brothers had worked hard in school and had earned Green scholarships during their time at the Academy. They seemed like a fair, honest, kind family who loved each other and were good members of the community.

"Sounds like you've got a great family."

Trygg smiled. "The best. My dad always says, 'Live the life you love, and you'll love the life you live.' That's what we Matsons try to do. Serve, protect, and whoop up on each other in the annual precinct softball tournament. They have to draw straws each year to see who will get me." He winked at me.

Just as I was starting to tell Trygg about Livvy, my iBud chimed to let me know I had a message. Trygg said to take it, and that he needed to check the security system again.

As he got up and headed back to the front door, I accessed the message, hoping it was from Livvy. But it wasn't. It was the explanation message Trygg had referred to before. It stated that there had been a bomb threat at AHGA earlier today, and that rather than risk employee lives, they'd chosen to evacuate the entire facility. Multiple checks had been performed and no bombs or other terrorist paraphernalia had been found. The message ended by stating that AHGA would be open tomorrow, operating at regular business hours. That meant that I had work in the morning again.

Trygg walked back in about the time I finished listening to the message. I could tell right away that something was wrong. Tension lines ran along his forehead, mouth in a frown, eyes darting around the room.

"What is it?" I asked.

"My father messaged me. There's been another bombing downtown around 132nd and Powell at an express lighting shop. He can't reach my oldest brother, Teigen. His precinct is in that area. He's on duty tonight."

I could see the worry and fear etched in Trygg's face, and I remembered when Jaxx had come to the Stayton farm and told me that my sister was dying. "Go," I said. "You need to be there. Help look for him."

"I ... I can't leave you here alone. And Jaxx isn't answering." He looked frantic, clasping his hands behind his head, his face all scrunched up.

"Are you kidding? I'm in the most secure house in SciCity. Leave Jaxx a message. Tell him what's going on ... that I told you to go. He can send someone else if he wants to. I'm here alone all the time." I swallowed hard at the lie. I didn't really like being here alone, but I seemed to be finding myself in that situation a lot more often lately.

"I ... I ... I'm not—"

"Well, I am sure. Go. Think about your brother. Your family. They need you right now. I don't. I'm home safe. I'm fine. Go, Trygg."

"You'll get a hold of Jaxx, or me, or somebody, if you need anything?" His eyes were on the front door.

"Yes!" I put my hands on his shoulders, and softly said, "Go, Trygg."

He stared into my eyes for a couple of seconds, then leaned in and hugged me, whispering in my ear, "Thank you, Lyssa. I'll come see you tomorrow. If that's okay with you."

I nodded, squeezing him tight one more time, then gently pushed him toward the door. "Go help your brother."

At the door, he turned one more time to look at me. Handsome, kind, and brave. *That's a good man,* I thought. *One that's worth getting to know better.*

And then Maddax's face filled my mind. Followed by Gabe's. Three men. So completely different. I sighed as I reset the security at the door panel. *How do you know when you've found the perfect man?* I wondered. Was it more important that he's calm? Or exciting? Stable? Or a risk taker? Kind? Or adventurous? A family-oriented guy? Or one who wants to see the world? What did I want? It made my head hurt to think about it.

I headed to my bedroom. All I wanted to do was crawl under the covers, curl up with Lulu, and go to sleep. Not think. Not dream. Just sleep.

And then I woke to another shrieking security alarm. Someone was in the house.

Chapter 39

I leapt out of bed before I even really knew what I was doing. It was pitch black, and as I scrambled toward my bedroom door, I tripped over something, and found myself sprawled across the floor. Then an iBud alarm went off in my ear, too. And a voice, telling me that Chayston Jaxx was trying to connect.

Calyssa, what's happening? Jaxx's voice filled my mind.

I … I … On my hands and knees, I reached for the door, grabbing the handle to stand up, when it flew open, whacking me in the head and knocking me off my feet again.

"Moooooooooo." From somewhere in the dark, Lulu added her voice to the confusion.

Calyssa!

Suddenly, a blinding light filled the room. I threw my hands up over my eyes, trying to focus on the shape that filled my doorway.

Jaxx! Someone's-

Then Livvy's voice. "Oh my god, Lys! Are you okay? I messed up on the code, but only once. Why was it set at such a high security level? I—"

Calyssa! Are you alright? I have security enforcers en route! I'm only minutes away!

No, Jaxx! It's-

Then a male voice. "Her head's bleeding! What happened?"

Finally, my eyes focused. Gunner.

Gunner? Gunner! In my house with security enforcers and Jaxx on the way!

Livvy and Gunner were both trying to help me, and Lulu was there nuzzling me, too. But it was all just making it harder to get up. "Stop! Both of you! Just stop for a minute! You, too, Lulu. Get back!"

Calyssa! Calyssa! Can you answer me? Calyssa!

Jaxx. Stop. It's okay. It's just Livvy. She set off the alarm by accident. Call off the security enforcers. I'll go reset the alarm right now. I'm fine. Really, I'm fine.

Are you sure? There's no danger?

I looked at Gunner. He'd grabbed a wet towel from somewhere and was dabbing it at my forehead. I swatted his hand away. I'm sure.

I'll call off the enforcers, but I'm still coming over. ETA two minutes. Be ready to let me in the door. Then he disconnected.

"Shit." I tenderly touched my forehead and my fingers came away sticky with warm, red blood.

"Oh, Lys! I'm so sorry! What were you doing on the floor? I—"

"Livvy, stop. Jaxx is going to be here in like one minute. Hide Gunner. And do it good because you know he's going to search the house." Looking at her for the first time, I took in her dirty clothes, disheveled hair, scrapes on her hands. "Oh my god, Livvy. Are you okay? Actually, don't explain now. Hide Gunner. Get changed. And at least wipe the dirt off your face." I threw the wet towel at her that Gunner had tried to use on me. "I've got to get that freaking alarm turned off."

I got up and staggered toward the door. Gunner grabbed my arm to steady me. "I said go! Both of you! Now! I'm fine!"

Gunner and Livvy looked at each other and took off down the hall.

Walking toward the front door with Lulu on my heels, I realized that my head was starting to hurt. I touched it again. That was a mistake. Punching in the code on the panel, the alarm paused, and a voice asked for a verbal clearance code. "Calyssa Grace Brentwood. Clearance code 65001." Then I waited for the eye scan, but it seemed to take forever. Finally, the voice stated that it was all clear, and the house was silent again.

Picking up Lulu, I leaned against the door and closed my eyes.

Until the door slid open and Lulu and I toppled outside. Right into Jaxx.

"What? How in the—" Once again, I was struggling to get up. Lulu jumped off me and ran back inside the house.

Jaxx just scooped me up with one arm like I was rag doll while his other arm held a gun out in front of him.

"Jaxx! What are you—"

"Stop thrashing around and be quiet," he snarled, eyes darting around the house.

Then a scream. Livvy dropped a cup she was holding, and it shattered against the floor. "Jaxx! What are you doing to Lyssa!" Not really a question since she screamed it at the top of her lungs.

"Set me down!" I yelled, too. Which made my head hurt even more, and I must have moaned or something, because Jaxx and Livvy both got quiet.

"Bring her in here," Livvy said as she moved toward the kitchen. Jaxx followed and carefully set me down on a stool. Livvy ran a towel under water at the sink and brought it over, gently wiping at the blood.

"Stop it. I can do that. You're just making it hurt worse." It came out more harshly than I intended. Jaxx and Livvy exchanged a look. "Sorry. It just hurts." I winced as I touched my forehead again.

Livvy handed me the towel. She looked better. Her face was clean, and her hair was tucked up in a messy bun. She had on a baggy t-shirt and sweats. Only the scratches on her hands remained. She saw me looking at them, and pulled them away, but not before Jaxx noticed, too.

"Does somebody want to tell me what happened here? You two look like you've been in a war zone, and I'm not used to rushing over here at 2am with an intruder alert waking me from a dead sleep. And with your father out of town." He shook his head, sitting down on a stool next to me. He looked tired.

"We're fine. You can leave." Livvy's voice was curt.

"Give him a minute, Livvy," I snapped. Her eyebrows shot up and her mouth dropped open. She probably thought I'd gone crazy, or had brain damage, or something. I just closed my eyes and shook my head. Mistake. I needed to hold my head very still.

Jaxx looked at Livvy. "Can you get your sister a bag of ice? That bump over her eye is starting to swell."

Seconds later, a bag of ice was being pressed against my head. It hurt but felt good at the same time. I held it in place.

"Now, does someone want to tell me what in the hell is going on here?" Jaxx looked back and forth between Livvy and me. "Well?"

Livvy just looked at me.

Really? Fine. I started to spin what I hoped would be a reasonable story. "Sorry, Jaxx. Livvy got up to make herself something to eat. She realized she left something in the car and when she punched in her code to go out and get it, she hit a wrong button or something. Trygg left it set at the highest level, so it immediately went off."

Livvy mouthed, "Trygg?" but I just gave her a small shake of my head. Which made me grimace again. Which made Jaxx turn and look at Livvy. "Sorry" she said, smiling apologetically, "I was tired, and I'm still forgetful sometimes." She used her weak voice, the one she'd played me with so many times before.

I went on, hoping Jaxx would just turn his attention back to me. "The alarm startled me, and I jumped up out of bed, tripped over something on the floor, and hit my head on the door as I came crashing down. I'm not so nimble, I guess."

"Why'd it take you so long to answer your iBud?" Jaxx eyes were stern.

I wasn't sure he was buying this. I knew I had to sell it. "Really? I was dead asleep. My absent-minded sister sets off the alarm of all alarms, like a wake-the-dead and run-from-the-zombies alarm. I trip and hit my head at the exact same moment you message me, demanding answers, then she comes running in screaming at me when she sees me bleeding, also demanding answers, and I'm still half asleep. Except now I have a splitting headache. It took a minute to get to both of you."

Jaxx sat there for a few seconds. "I was worried after what happened today at AHGA. With your father out of town, I'm responsible for you girls." Then looking at Livvy, he added, "And what happened to your hands?" Livvy looked down studying her fingers like she was just seeing them for the first time.

"She was picking berries with Lena today. Scratched them up. She really likes those berries." Livvy's head shot up, and she rapidly nodded in agreement.

Jaxx just shook his head. "You know you can just buy those, right?"

She smiled sweetly again. "Just trying to fill my time. Between naps."

Jaxx's eyes narrowed.

Too much, Livvy, I thought. "Whatever. Can we all just go back to bed? I'm exhausted."

"Maybe I should stay. You may have a concussion." Jaxx was staring at me again.

"Livvy and I will stay up for the next couple of hours and watch a movie or something. She can keep an eye on me and call you if anything seems weird. Right, Livvy?"

"Absolutely." She was nodding again.

Jaxx was looking back and forth between the two of us.

"Really, Jaxx. We're adults. We do stay home alone." I tried to make my voice sound smooth and relaxed.

"Fine. Just let me do a quick sweep of the rooms for my own peace of mind, then I'll head outside and do one there as well. If everything looks okay, I'll take off and check in with you in the morning."

"That sounds great." I tried to smile. I hoped Livvy had hid Gunner well. I knew there was no way Jaxx was leaving until he felt satisfied that all was normal at the Brentwood house.

Livvy started to get up, but I shook my head. Then gritted my teeth. No head movements. Why couldn't I remember that?

We sat silently in the kitchen until Jaxx returned. We all said our goodnights, and finally, he left.

"That was intense." Livvy undid her messy bun and ran her hands through her hair.

"Yeah." Gunner walked in.

"How'd you know Jaxx was gone? He could have caught you walking in here like that," I said, trying to hold still while I talked.

"Livvy hid me in her room under a pile of dirty clothes. Stink-eee. No way Jaxx was going to rummage through that. As soon as he cleared her room, I dug my way out. You're both lucky I didn't pass out and asphyxiate in there!" He looked serious, but he couldn't quite keep the laughter out of his voice.

"Whatever." Livvy bent over and picked up Lulu, stroking the pink hair that grew from the top of her head. "You've had an exciting night tonight, Girl. You need to head to bed." Turning back toward my room, Livvy carried Lulu off.

Gunner pulled up the stool next to me that Jaxx had vacated. "Let me take a look," he said, gently pulling the ice pack back from my forehead. "Ooooow. Yeah. That's gonna be a doozy of a bump. Keep the ice on it."

"Thanks for the advice. I'll try to keep it in mind."

Gunner sat silent for a minute. When he turned back toward me, his eyes were serious. "You didn't follow my advice last time. About Gabe."

I sighed and closed my eyes again. He'd told me not to tell Gabe I loved him unless I was sure. I had been sure, but then we witnessed two murders, I found out that my sister was dying from a mutated virus, we'd almost been blown up at his farm, and I was whisked back unconscious to the city. And, I'd found out that his dad and brother had almost been killed because of me. I hadn't stopped loving him. I just knew that by being around him and his family, I put them all in danger. I couldn't live with that.

"I asked him to come here to the city with me, you know."

"Gabe would never be happy in the city."

"I know," I said softly. "But it doesn't matter anymore. He hates me. He thinks I'm responsible for Ana's death."

This time it was Gunner's voice that was soft. "I know. He's wrong about that, Calyssa."

I tried to smile at him, but I couldn't quite make it happen.

Livvy walked back in. A look passed between them but neither one said a word.

I was too tired and sore to deal with this. And Livvy owed me some answers. "Where have you been? And why haven't you been answering your messages? I've been *really* needing to talk to you, and you've just been ... where? Off playing rebel?" It came out meaner than I meant it, and Livvy winced. But I was tired of saying sorry. I wasn't sorry. Livvy had taken off and left me to deal with Jaxx and the stolen file mess. Same old Livvy. Just bailed out when times got tough. I scowled.

Gunner nudged her. She looked at him, and he gave her a nod. "A lot has happened, Lys. Some really serious stuff. When I got your message, Gunner and I came straight here. I'm sorry we were gone so long." She hesitated.

"My 'stuff' is serious, too, Livvy. I had to face Jaxx alone. *Alone*. With no help from you. And guess what? That stupid file you had me steal for you isn't even what you thought it was. There are no land memos there. No proof of illegal dealings. It's just old building plans for AHGA. And besides that, I also found out that our–"

"I know, Lys. That's what Gunner and I need to talk to you about."

"About our mom?"

Livvy shook her head. "What? No. Focus, Lyssa." That ticked me off. It was Livvy not listening to me, not the other way around. I had to tell her about our mom. What could be more important than that?

"Lyssa!" she shouted.

"What!" I closed my eyes, my forehead throbbing.

"We know why those old building plans were important. Lyssa, Joshua Fitting is going to blow up AHGA!"

Chapter 40

"Right. We've heard that for years, that the rebels are going to bomb AHGA. No way. AHGA's security is top-of-the-line. All the newest tech. There's no way they're getting by all of that. They can't do it."

The whole time I was talking, Livvy was shaking her head. "Usually I'd be right with you, saying all the same things. But we overheard things in the last couple of days. It's going to happen."

"When?" I asked, unable to hide my sarcasm.

"We don't know yet. But we're trying to find out."

"How, then?"

She hesitated. "We don't know that either. But Lyssa, they wanted those plans for a reason. They—"

"Jaxx said there's nothing in them, Livvy. He's been through all of it. He says it's a waste of time."

Livvy's eyebrows shot up. "Oh, that's right. You and Jaxx are best friends now, huh? I noticed that earlier. What'd he say to win you over? I can just imagine you and Jaxx sitting in his office, sharing a nutrient drink, discussing AHGA business—"

"He told me Mom's alive, Livvy."

"What?" She let out a snarky laugh. "Right."

I just stared at her, keeping my lips pressed firmly together.

"Mom died. When we were little. Remember that, Lys? Maybe that bump to your head was a little worse than we thought."

I just continued to stare at her.

Finally, she threw up her hands. "What?"

"She didn't die. Father took her to AHGA, then he told us she was gone. But she wasn't dead. She was in a coma for like five years. They did some sort of experimental brain procedures on her, running electrical currents through her brain. She finally woke up, but she didn't remember much. And she's ... she's not the same now. Not like she was when we were little."

"Are you sure this isn't some story that Jaxx concocted to get you to talk to him? I mean, it just doesn't seem realistic that—"

I interrupted, "It's true, Livvy. And she still works at AHGA, but she goes by Eve, or V, now instead of Evalayne or Layney. And by her maiden name, Huxley. I've looked her up. Found files at AHGA. I've seen pictures. She looks different, but it's her."

Livvy sat there, silent, with her mouth hanging open.

"But why wouldn't she ... if she was there ... how come she didn't ...." Her voice kept trailing off mid-sentence.

So, I told her everything that Jaxx had told me. About the virus. The operations. Father's devotion to helping her get better. When he brought us in. That was when Livvy started crying. But I didn't stop. I needed her to know it all.

But by the time I finished, I was completely exhausted. I felt like I could barely keep my eyes open. Livvy came over, her cheeks still damp from her tears, and hugged me. "It doesn't matter what she thinks or who she is now. We have each other." She was trying to be brave, but I could see that all of this was a way bigger deal to her than she was letting on. "Go get some sleep. You've been up for Jaxx's mandatory two hours."

"What about you? And Gunner?" He'd been so quiet, I'd almost forgotten he was there.

"We're going to stay up for a while longer. We have some research we can do here before we go back."

"Go back?"

"To meet with Jonathan. He really is worried about the bombings that Joshua is encouraging. But don't worry about that right now. I'll keep you in the loop as I find things out."

Livvy walked me to my room and tucked me in like she used to do when we were little. She kissed the non-injured side of my forehead, and I was asleep before she even closed my bedroom door.

When I opened my eyes again, it was light outside. I touched my forehead. Still tender, but now just a dull ache rather than a stabbing pain. I could live with that. Checking the time, I realized I had about an hour before I needed to be in at work. It was Thursday, so I only had to work for a few hours this morning, and then then I had my two music classes in the afternoon. That made it a light day. Touching my forehead one more time, I was pretty sure I was going to be home early and back in bed.

Lulu ambled over, and I picked her up to snuggle for a few minutes. Life had been so crazy this last week that I hadn't spent much time with her. She nuzzled under my chin, and I felt her body go limp as she fell asleep. Slowly, I got up, trying not to disturb her. I figured I'd just let her sleep in my bed. She looked so peaceful.

Before getting out of the car at AHGA, I took one more look at my forehead in the mirror. It wasn't quite so swollen, and makeup had helped cover the bruise that was forming.

Walking in, I was headed straight toward the elevator when I heard one of the front area receptionists call out to me. "Oh, Miss Brentwood. Mr. Jaxx has asked that you come to his office upon your arrival. He said he wasn't sure when you'd be in because you'd had a minor accident last night."

She looked inquisitively at me. She probably couldn't see my forehead from across the room, and I didn't feel like walking over, showing her, and having to explain.

"Thank you," was all I said as I stepped into the elevator. Second day in a row with a morning meeting with Jaxx to start my day. Feeling on edge, I closed my eyes and gently rubbed around the sore spot. *Well, today's meeting can't be any worse than yesterday's*, I thought.

Jaxx's door slid open just as I raised my hand to knock.

"Calyssa, come in. Sit down." His voice sounded – strained. Now what? "How are you feeling this morning? Any problems last night?"

"No. I'm okay."

"Good. Why don't you drop in and see the staff physician today before you leave just to make sure everything is good? With your father coming home later tomorrow, I want to make sure everything is in order."

"I really think I'm fine, but I'll stop in if it makes you feel better."

He nodded. "I know I gave you a lot to think about yesterday, but I'd like to ask you not to contact your mother in any manner until I've told your father about our talk. I'm feeling I may have been remiss in making that call without consulting him." He adjusted how he was sitting. Twice.

"Okay. I hadn't really thought about how to deal with all of this yet anyway."

He looked relieved.

As I stepped out the door, another security officer passed me, stepping into Jaxx's office. "Is it true, what I just heard? Matson was killed last night?"

Overhearing his comment, I stopped and turned around.

Jaxx was frowning. "Unfortunately, it is."

The officer stood in front of Jaxx's desk, shaking his head. "He and I were planning a road trip in a couple of weeks with his brothers. We were going to take the nephews camping. Their first guys' trip. It's unbelievable."

Then the connection hit me. Matson.

I stepped back into the office, asking, "Are you talking about Trygg Matson?"

Surprised, both Jaxx and the other officer turned to look at me. The other officer looked back at Jaxx uncomfortably.

"It's okay, Nelson. Matson's the one who took Calyssa home yesterday, wasn't he?" he said turning back to me. "I'd forgotten about that."

"It was him?" I felt sick.

"Yeah. Trygg Matson. He was a good kid, great officer here."

"What happened? When he left my house, he said he was going to look for his brother, Teigen. Something about a bomb going off in his precinct."

Jaxx cocked his head to the side, giving me a funny look.

"I spent several hours with him yesterday. He seemed like a genuinely nice guy. Are you sure it's him?" *Trygg is dead?* I couldn't seem to get my mind wrapped around that.

Jaxx hesitated. "He ... he was killed when a building collapsed ... looking for his brother. I don't know all the details. Just that there was another rebel bombing downtown. Matson was told that his brother and another enforcer had gone into a building to look for survivors when they'd heard a call for help. It sounds like the structure was dangerous, badly damaged, whole sections were falling in. Other enforcers were there waiting for an operational support team.

"When Matson arrived, and his brother and the other officer hadn't come out yet, he went barreling in after them. Not long after he went in, the rest of the building collapsed. His body, along with his brother's and the other enforcer's, were identified earlier this morning, and I was notified."

The other officer pounded his fist against Jaxx's desk. "These rebel terrorists are totally out of control! Good people are dying! Teigen had a wife and three little kids! Who's going to be next? They don't seem to care who they kill!" His voice seethed with anger as he pounded the desk twice more.

"Nelson!" Jaxx's voice was sharp. The officer sharply pulled his hand back and dropped his eyes.

"Sorry, Sir." He turned brusquely and left the office.

Jaxx and I both stood in silence. I thought about the short amount of time I'd spent with Trygg, and what I'd learned about him and his family. They sounded like wonderful people. Even though they were SciCity Security Enforcers. Trygg's family reminded me of the Staytons – families that valued spending time together. They just wanted be with each other.

I thought about what Livvy had told me, that Joshua was encouraging the rebel bombings. He obviously didn't care who was killed along the way. And, I was sure he'd believe he was justified in taking down some extra Greens, especially security enforcers. Just a few more diseased dogs.

Trygg and his family were not diseased dogs. I felt so angry. I wanted to pound my fists against the walls, too. To yell. Scream. Maybe it was the rebels that should be put down.

And then I thought about Gunner. And Kye. And Leah with her six little kids.

Why couldn't this just be easy? Good guys. Bad guys. Clear lines.

Good people. Good families.

And that made me think about my family ... about Mom. Well, Eve, now. I reached up and rubbed my forehead. It was starting to ache again, but I didn't think that this time it was from hitting it against the door. *Why can't my life ever just be easy?*

I looked back at Jaxx again. "Do you—"

He threw up his hand to interrupt me, a serious look on his face. His eyes were moving around, and I could tell he must have been listening to someone on his iBud.

Focusing on me, he walked rapidly across the room grabbing my arm and pulling me with him along the way. "Another bomb threat. Evacuation procedures will begin in thirty seconds. I'm putting you on the elevator. An officer will meet you at the top. Wait for me outside."

Then he pulled out the walkie from inside his vest as he pushed me toward the elevator. "This is Red 1. Begin protocol for Priority Evacuation. Authorization code beta-delta-seven-one-niner. All teams, on my mark." As the door slid shut, he said, "Now."

Just like yesterday, the siren and red lights began. When the door slid open, a new officer was there. For a second, I hoped they were wrong — I hoped it was Trygg. But it wasn't.

Without a word, the officer escorted me out the door, toward the parking lot. About five minutes later, Jaxx was standing next to me. "Calyssa, you might as well head to the University. We're not sending everyone home today, but it may take an hour or so to get this all sorted out. These bomb threats are ridiculous. A waste of time and corporation money."

I thought about what Livvy had told me. "But what if—"

"It's a false alarm. I've had special units at the doors all morning. I just double checked all sensors. No way any explosives could have made it into the building without being detected. I talked with your father. He'll be home tomorrow, first thing in the morning now. He'll put a stop to these absurd bomb threats and the panic with the employees."

I wasn't sure. Jaxx seemed confident in what he was saying, but ... "What about the bombs going off all over the city, Jaxx? Isn't it better to be safe than sorry? I mean, how do you know, absolutely, positively know, that AHGA isn't a target?"

By now, Jaxx was looking annoyed. "Because it's my job, Calyssa. Let me do it. Head to the U." And, with that, he turned and left.

I arrived at the U about an hour earlier than usual, so I grabbed a nutrient drink and sat down at one of the outdoor tables. It was chilly, but the sun was shining brightly. I thought about pulling up current articles on the news tablet embedded in the tabletop, but that made me remember the last article I'd read here. When I'd found out about Ana. Had it only been a week ago?

Instead, I just sat there, watching the world go by.

Hearing raised voices behind me, I turned around to see a tall, thin, Green couple across the courtyard in an argument. I couldn't quite make out what they were saying but I could tell from their body language that they were upset. As the voices got louder, they started drawing more attention from people around them. Suddenly the man reached out and pushed the woman, and a non-Green guy came out of nowhere, stepping in between the two. I jumped up as well and headed in that direction.

As I got closer, I started picking up pieces of the conversation.

"... don't know what you're talking ..."

"... only an idiot ..."

"... you'll regret ..."

When I was just a few feet away, the Green man thrust out both hands, this time pushing the other guy. Not hard enough to knock him down, but hard enough to make a point.

The push caused the non-Green to step to the side, and the Green turned partially, too.

And I stopped dead in my tracks. It was Gabe and Maddax.

Chapter 41

Gabe saw me first. Frowning and shaking his head, he stepped away from Maddax. Maddax turned, saw me, and smiled. El stepped out from behind Maddax and ignored me.

Maddax was the first to speak. "Lyssa, good to see you, darling. I was just telling El that I'd hoped I'd run into you here today."

Gabe let out a sarcastic laugh. "Of course, you two know each other. That makes perfect sense." Maddax looked curiously at him.

El piped in, "Oh boy, the ex and the current boy meet. Isn't this fun?" But she didn't sound like she was having fun.

"Your ex? A non-Green? I am surprised, Lyssa." Maddax had a disapproving look on his face.

"Don't worry about it, Maddax. It was a long time ago. Before Calyssa was Green." Gabe looked like he had just eaten something that tasted horrible.

"Oh, that makes much more sense."

I'd been standing there with my mouth open, but that was too much.

"What? No. I mean yes. I mean no. I mean–"

"Poor girl, you two have perplexed her." El's sneer was followed by a sharp laugh.

I threw her a glare and tried again, choosing to ignore the conversation that had just taken place. "What was all the yelling about over here?"

El's turn to glare. "Maddax and I had a ... misunderstanding. Gabe interpreted it wrong. We're all fine. You can run along to class," she said as she flicked her fingers at me.

Furrowing my brows, I said, "I don't think so."

Maddax laughed. "Now, now, ladies. Seems a little tense here." And with a huge smile at Gabe, he continued, "Perhaps we can talk more later. I'm interested in learning more about the non-Green boy who's captured El's attention. And, although I'd love to whisk you away to lunch, my dear Lyssa, El and I are needed at a meeting. But we're still on for Friday night, right?" He added a wink in my direction, which earned me another sarcastic laugh from Gabe, and a scowl from EL.

"Maybe ... I have a lot going on right now ... we'll–"

"Of course we are." He walked over, kissed me on the cheek, then turned, taking El's arm, and headed down the path.

"Have fun with that," Gabe said as he started to turn to head in the other direction.

More than a little annoyed at all three of them, I snapped back, "What's that supposed to mean?"

Gabe stopped. "Just what I said. You two are perfect for each other. El's told me about Maddax's obsession with becoming 'Greener.' You two should get along great."

"I am so sick of you being such a jerk, Gabe Stayton. I'd forgotten just how arrogant and self-righteous you are."

"Oh, you're one to talk. To think that you had me fooled at one point, that a Brentwood could care about anyone but themselves. I warned Gunner about your screwed up, yellow sister, too. I'm sure that apple hasn't fallen far from the tree either."

What? Gabe knew about Gunner and Livvy?

"Surprised I know? Not everyone keeps secrets from their friends, Calyssa. I just hope your sister is more reliable than you were. Although it sounds like she's taken a shine to one of those Fitting brothers. Maybe it'd just be best if she dropped Gunner and spent all her time with the Fittings."

Talk of the Fittings brought back the seriousness of the conversation that Livvy and I had. "Knock it off, Gabe. It sounds to me like Gunner is just as tied up with Jonathan Fitting as Livvy is. Aren't you the least bit worried about them? Especially with all the rebel bombings lately? What if they get hurt? I thought Gunner was your best friend."

"Things change, Calyssa. You should know that best of all of us." He started to turn to go again.

"So, it's just whatever? If he dies, he dies? You're unbelievable. Have you really become that unfeeling?" My voice was rising. I couldn't help it. I wanted to walk over and slap him across the face. To tell him to get over his pity party, and to go save his friend. And my sister.

Gabe stopped and turned back around slowly. "I care about the people who care about me. Gunner has other priorities right now. He'll be back when he sees things more clearly. And my priorities are at the farm, which is where I'm headed. Since Nana Jane's accident—"

"Nana Jane had an accident? What happened?" I took several steps toward him until he held up his hand.

"Not for you to worry about, Calyssa. You're not a part of my family. I'll take care of things at my house. You take care of things at yours. I mean, if anyone wants you there."

His last words were like a punch in the stomach. I'd confided in Gabe about how I'd never really felt like I was a part of my family after Mom was gone. I couldn't believe that now he was turning those words against me.

He shook his head and walked away.

I wanted to cry. But I didn't. Instead, I turned my thoughts to Nana Jane. She'd been in an accident? I had to find out what had happened.

I headed to my car to use my cellular connection there to call a digital landline at the farm. Nana Jane didn't use an iBud, so Andrew still had an old hand-held phone for her to use. After four rings, she answered.

"Nana Jane? It's Calyssa. I heard you were in an accident. Is everything okay?"

"Oh, Calyssa, I'm fine, really. It's just a fractured wrist and dislocated collarbone. A short cast and an immobilizing splint for a week or two, and I'll be good as new."

"What happened?"

"It's silly, really. I took Ben out riding the other morning. Something startled the horse, and it reared up. I wasn't holding on the way I should have been, and I slipped right off its back. I think it scared poor Ben more than it hurt me." She laughed.

"Are you sure? Really? You're okay?"

"I'll tell you what. Why don't you swing on out by the farm for lunch tomorrow? I'll add a nutrient drink to our homemade pasta and a fresh garden salad, and you can see for yourself. Plus, I'd just love to visit with you again. What do you think?"

"I ... I ..." I wasn't sure what to say. I really wanted to see Nana. But I didn't want to run into Gabe.

"Don't worry. It will just be Ben and me. Gabe and Andrew have committed to helping out on a neighboring farm with some hive issues they've been having. Something about the robobees malfunctioning. Andrew told me that they're heading over late tomorrow morning and won't be back for several hours. They won't be here for lunch." Good old Nana Jane. She always knew the right thing to say to put me at ease.

"Okay. It'll be around noon. I have a couple of classes in the morning, but then I have about a two-hour break until I have to be back for my afternoon classes."

"Perfect. I'm looking forward to it. We'll see you then."

Hanging up, I smiled. Maybe some time with Nana Jane was just what I needed. A bit of consistency and wisdom in my crazy life.

Feeling better, I remembered that I should have been heading toward my Creative Orchestral Composition class. It was more difficult than the class that followed, Appreciation of Western Music of the 21st Century, but it was still my favorite class this term. It was the first time in a while that I'd been challenged in a music class, and that felt good. I grabbed my cello from the back of my car and began walking to the music building.

Call Ayva, I thought to my iBud as I walked. I realized that I hadn't talked to her in a few days. Not since I'd gone over after Tay's accident. That made me feel guilty. Friends needed to be there for each other, as Gabe so glibly reminded me.

Calyssa? I was just thinking about you. I'm so happy you called. I know I've been out of touch recently, but I'm pulling it back together.

I'm sorry I haven't been over again, Ayva. I should have-

Don't worry about it. I wasn't in much shape for visitors anyway. But I'm dealing with it better now. With Tay's death. At least I can say his name without crying. Dee has been over a couple of times. She's so sweet. She's been helping me through it.

Dee? She would have been one of the last people I would have wanted to spend time with. But Ayva did sound better.

Are you coming in for any classes today? I asked her. I knew she had one afternoon class on Thursdays.

No, but I'll be back on my regular schedule tomorrow. That means I'll see you in Dr. Penning's speech class tomorrow afternoon. Did I miss anything on Monday?

Umm, I missed class on Monday, too. So, I guess we'll find out when we get there.

Perfect. If we have to start something late, she'll probably let us work on it together. Oh and, Calyssa, do you mind driving us to Maddax and the twins' house for the Nock party? I'm not driving again yet. I just don't feel comfortable behind the wheel. Mom's dropping me off at the campus tomorrow. I told her I was going to spend some girl time with you, and we'd be home later tomorrow night.

You want to go Nock, Ayva? After what happened to Tay? Really?

It's okay, Lyssa. Dee and I have talked about it a lot. We both feel it's important for me to get back on a regular schedule. But I need you with me. To be there. Please. I always feel better when you're around.

I didn't tell her that I hadn't used Nock in several days. That I wasn't planning on using it anymore. In the end, I told her I'd take her to the party. I needed to talk to Maddax anyway. To let him know that I was done in terms of Nock. I hadn't decided yet if I was done in terms of Maddax. I needed to think seriously some more about that.

After my two music classes, I got back in the car to head home. On the way, I tried to get ahold of Livvy. No reply, but I left a message for her to get in touch with me. At home, I made myself a nutrient drink, fed Lulu, then curled up in my bed with soft music playing. It was Zimmer. And I finally felt relaxed. Tomorrow, I would have lunch with Nana Jane. I went to sleep happy.

I woke up the next morning to a recorded iBud message.

Message sender? I thought.

The reply jolted me upright in bed. **Eve Huxley.**

Chapter 42

Suddenly, my mouth felt dry and my heart was racing. Why was Eve messaging me? What did she want? I thought about what Jaxx had said, that she wanted "access" to me.

`Play message.` I held my breath and listened.

`Calyssa, it's Eve Huxley, Director of Special Research at AHGA. I'd like to schedule an appointment to see you at 8am on Monday morning. I'm looking forward to meeting you.`

That was it. Nothing else. Not a "let me know if you can make it." Or a "call me back if you want to reschedule."

I lay back down on my bed. Was this good or bad? Had she remembered something? Did she finally want to get reacquainted with her daughter? Or did she just need me for some sort of research?

I had to tell Livvy. I jumped out of bed and ran down the hall to her room, then the family room, then the garage. No

Livvy. This was getting old. Father would be home today, and then I wouldn't be able to cover for her. I left her another message, telling her Father was going to be home this morning, and that she'd better get home ASAP if she didn't want to have to explain to him how she "miraculously" got better while he was gone. I thought about telling her about Eve's message but decided to wait. Maybe I'd swing by AHGA after my visit with Nana Jane and see if Jaxx knew anything about it.

Both morning classes were lectures again. I tried to focus and take notes, but I had more on my mind than cost analyses of new limb prosthetics in Eurasia, or rates of ice caps melting in the early 2000's. When class was over, I was at my car before most students were even out of the building.

Driving back to the farm, I drank in the beauty of the land. I was just as mesmerized by it as I had been the first time I'd seen it out of the window of Gabe's truck. I paused, just before a small bridge, to let an oversized hauler pass first. I wasn't sure we'd both fit at the same time, and I wasn't in any hurry. The guy driving waved out his window as he drove by. That was one thing I truly loved about being out here in the farmland. Everyone seemed so friendly.

A few more miles, and my iBud chimed. It was Livvy. Finally.

Livvy, where have you been?

Lys, just be quiet and listen. It's happening. Today. Gunner and I worked our way into a group that we'd heard had connections with the bombings. We—

What? Livvy, where are you? What—

Stop interrupting, Lys. This is important. They won't tell us the exact details yet but we're with them right now. We're close. You should hear some of these people - it's scary. They just keep ranting about the world getting Greener and Greener, and how it's our job to stop it before becoming Green is no longer a choice, but a requirement. I've convinced them that I'm incredibly angry about being rejected by all the Greens since I contracted the virus. That I made a mistake and don't want to be Green. That I was pushed into it by Dad. And that now I want to help their cause. That I want to wipe out the Greens' ability to continue Enhancements.

Wipe out the Greens? What?

Lys. Listen. I just said all that to get Gunner and me in. Something's happening at AHGA today. Something big. This group is the one that's been calling in the bomb threats. They're estimating reaction time for maximum exposure. It's—

Connection lost, my iBud reported. I pulled over and jumped out of my car, trying to reconnect with Livvy. But I just kept getting the connection unavailable message. I checked my connection status. Last time I'd been at the farm, I didn't have service out here, but since then, I'd had Father add the extender satellite software with global connectivity. I still had full access – the dropped messaging wasn't on my part. It was Livvy that couldn't connect right now for some reason.

Call Father, I thought. I didn't know what I was going to say, but I had to warn him.

It went to message twice, but on the third time, he connected. **What is it, Calyssa? This is not a good time.**

It was never a good time. **Father, you have to listen to me. I think the rebels are planning on bombing AHGA today. You have to get everyone-**

They're only threats. Pranks. There's no way-

Father! Listen! They're not just pranks! They're trying to-

Lyssa! Stop! I don't have time for this! Jaxx and I are dealing with these "so-called" threats. We've had two more this morning already. I have the SciCity Security Enforcer Director sitting in my office right now. What I don't have is time for my teenage daughter to tell me what I need to be doing. We'll talk tonight.

But, Father! Livvy said-

Call disconnected. Would you like to leave an additional message?

What? He'd disconnected me? I tried to reconnect several more times, but Father didn't answer. I tried Jaxx. Same thing. I tried Livvy. Still unavailable. I felt completely helpless.

Pacing around the outside of the car, I tried to recall exactly what Livvy had said. It sounded like she and Gunner were with a group right now, one that had been doing at least some of the bombings. And that she knew AHGA was going to be next.

Why wouldn't Father listen to me? Why wouldn't anyone listen to me? I screamed as loud as I could. A few startled birds flew away in the field next to me.

I had to think. What was left to do? Should I turn around and drive back to AHGA? Make Father listen to me? But what if Livvy had it wrong? What if the rebels were just playing her? Using her to disrupt our work at AHGA? They'd certainly accomplished that in the last couple of days. I doubted that many Enhancements were going on with the evacuations happening.

But AHGA wasn't the only enhancement center in SciCity. There were two more large facilities downtown, as well as several boutique companies that had sprung up, offering deluxe accommodations with exceptional aftercare in pampering environments for recovery. Had any of those places been bombed? I tried to remember. Something about a medical building, maybe? Could it have been an enhancement facility? I wasn't sure.

I thought about calling the SciCity Security Enforcers. But what would I have said? Their director was already with Father at AHGA. And I didn't have any specifics, other than the fact that my sister was working with a rebel group responsible for some of the previous bombings that had taken place. That sounded fantastic. I was sure they'd love to hear that. So would Father.

"Come on, Livvy. Call me back." I stopped and leaned up against the car. I tried one more time to message Father. Still no answer, just the option to leave a recorded message. *Fine.* Leave message.

Father, I really need you to get ahold of me right away. This is important. Extremely important. It has to do with the recent bombings around SciCity. Please, please - I need to talk to you.

I disconnected. I didn't know what else to do.

I thought about going to the farm and explaining everything to Nana Jane. Maybe she'd know what to do. I was sure she'd try to help. But was I really going to bring "Green issues" into that house again? That hadn't turned out so well for the Staytons the last time I was there.

My iBud chimed. It was Livvy!

Lys. Oh, my god, Lys. I was wrong. It's not AHGA that they're targeting. They wanted the old plans because they show all of the original access points to AHGA, including those from before everything went down with the PK virus. Back when AHGA was just a visitor center. For the dam. That's what they wanted. Entry to the dam. That's the target, Lyssa. They're going to blow the dam!

Wait! What? What do you mean, the dam?

We're inside it right now. There are old access tunnels from the visitor center to the control room in the dam, several levels underground. No one uses them anymore, but they're there. And, there's an old emergency escape tunnel that comes out on the opposite side of the dam, across from AHGA. It looks like it had been partially blocked a long time ago, and it was gated and chained. But they got through all of that. That's what they've been doing the last couple of days. It's why they kept calling in the bomb threats. It kept everyone focused on the AHGA side of the dam.

Suddenly something Livvy had said registered. Wait, Livvy! You're inside the dam right now? What are you doing? You have to get out! Now!

I can't, Lys. Gunner and I have to try to stop them. If the dam blows, it's going to kill everyone in SciCity! Think of all those people. All those innocent children! Lys, I can't let that happen! I've got to try!

Livvy, no! Leave! Go over to AHGA! Father is there right now with the Director of the SciCity Security Enforcers and Jaxx! Go over there and tell them everything! They'll listen to you! They'll help you!

For a few seconds, there was no response.

Livvy! Livvy, are you there?

Lys. Stop and listen to me. I've tried to call Father. He's not answering. I called the Security Enforcers - no one believes me.

Livvy! Please! Just get out of there.

Jonathan just showed up. He and Gunner are talking to them right now. Jonathan's telling them that this isn't the way. He's reminding them about all the non-Greens in SciCity, that they'll be killing all of those people, too. And Gunner's saying that many of the rebels in their group still have family there. That they'll be killing ... Her voice was gone again.

Livvy? Livvy? Livvy!

I think they're listening to Jonathan, Lys. The leader of this section is a woman they call Dally. She's - oh my god! Lys! Dally just shot Jonathan! Oh my god! He's … he's … there's blood everywhere! I'm trying to stop it, but … No! She shot Gunner, too!

Livvy! Livvy! Get out of there! Livvy!

Silence.

Livvy!

Lys. Listen to me. I love you. I want you to know that. And tell Father-

No! Livvy! You have to get out of there! Livvy!

…I love both of you, and I wish I'd told you both that more often. I'm so proud of you, Lys. Of who you're becoming. You're an incredible woman.

Livvy! Stop! Run! Get out of there!

Silence.

Livvy! Livvy! LIVVY!

Call disconnected. Subscriber is currently unavailable, a voice stated.

"NOOOOO! LIVVY!" I jumped back in my car.

At that moment, an iBud alert went off as well as an emergency broadcast alert through the speakers in my car. "This is an emergency. This is not a drill. There has been an explosion at the SciCity Dam. Anyone in the area is directed to evacuate immediately. Again, anyone in SciCity, including all of New Tech Valley, needs to immediately get to higher ground." The message kept repeating.

Call Livvy.

Subscriber is currently unavailable.

Call Father.

Subscriber is currently unavailable.

Call Jaxx.

Subscriber is currently unavailable.

Emergency - call SciCity Security Enforcers.

Due to the extreme volume of user activity in your area, this transmission is currently unavailable. Please try your call again momentarily.

Chapter 43

Driving back toward the city, I had to slam on the brakes, not believing what I was seeing. The small river I had crossed earlier was at least three times wider than it had been before. And the bridge – the bridge was completely gone!

I just sat there for a minute staring at the turbulent, murky water that swirled angrily out of sight. How was I going to get back? I tried again to reach Father and Livvy. Nothing. The emergency broadcast kept repeating over and over. It was on every station.

Who else could I contact? Who would know what was happening in SciCity? I tried Lena. No answer. Then Ayva. Nothing. Then Maddax. It didn't seem to matter. No subscribers were available.

I had to get out to the farm. To Nana Jane. She'd know what to do, who to call. Where we could get some answers.

My car careened recklessly as I pushed it way beyond what it was made for, especially on the gravel roads in the area. As I reached the farmhouse, the front door flew open, and Nana Jane rushed out, followed by Ben. I ran to meet her.

"Calyssa! You're here! You made it! I'm so happy you made it! It's so terrible–"

"Nana Jane! I can't get a hold of anyone. Not Father or Livvy or any of my friends! And the bridge down the road is washed out! I can't get back to the city! I can't get back to help them!" I was hysterical. Tears rolling down my cheek. I felt trapped. How was I going to get back to the city?

Gabe's truck came racing down the driveway, sliding to a stop with a spray of gravel. He and Andrew jumped out, leaving both doors open, rushing toward us.

Gabe looked shocked as recognition registered on his face. "Calyssa, what are you doing here?"

I ignored him, running toward Andrew. "Andrew, I have to get back to the city! I can't get ahold of anyone! Father, Livvy, my friends! But the bridge isn't there anymore! How do I get back?"

Andrew held up his hand. "Slow down, Calyssa. Reports are coming in from farmers in the outlying areas. I won't lie to you. It's not good–"

"Oh my god! Oh my god!" I started to rock back and forth. I felt like I was losing it. "What if ... No. They can't be ... There'd be emergency procedures in place. But Livvy! No, Livvy! She was in the dam! She was–"

Andrew grabbed my shoulders and gently shook them. "Calyssa, slow down. I need you to focus. Talk to me. Livvy, your sister, she was inside the dam?"

I nodded, tears still flowing down my cheeks.

"With your Father?"

I shook my head this time. "No with a rebel group. The one that's been doing some of the bombings. She and Gunner and Jonathan were trying to talk them out of it. But they shot Jonathan! And Gunner! Oh my god—"

Gabe interrupted, "Gunner's been shot?"

"Gabe, not now!" Andrew's voice was gruff. Softer, he said to me, "Come over here with Jane. I'm going to go inside and make a few more calls to see what I can find out. Jane, Ben, let's get Calyssa inside. Grab her some water and a blanket. Gabe, make some calls to see if any of the farms have heard of a road that's still open to the city."

Nana Jane put her arm around me, pulling me in close. As I leaned against her, I realized I was shaking uncontrollably. I started to say something, but Nana Jane just hushed me and hurried us toward the front door.

Ben had a blanket ready to wrap around me once I sat down on the couch. Gabe came in with a glass of water for me.

"Calyssa, how do you know Gunner was shot? Where was he?" He knelt, and looked directly at me, his face searching mine for answers.

"He was with Livvy, and Jonathan Fitting, and the rebel group inside the dam. One of the rebels shot him. I was messaging with Livvy when it happened."

"Are you sure? Really sure? Maybe you got it wrong?"

I heard my voice beginning to rise. "I know what I heard, Gabe! I know what she told me!"

"Why would he have been there? What was he doing? He assured me that he had nothing to do with the bombings, that– "

Suddenly I felt an overpowering anger. "You knew that Gunner and Livvy were working with the rebels! With Jonathan Fitting! You knew when we talked about it yesterday! And you said you had different priorities! And now he's dead! They're probably both dead! Does that make all of this your priority now?" I stood up abruptly, knocking the glass of water from Gabe's hand. I watched the glass as it seemed to fall in slow motion, smashing into thousands of tiny pieces as it hit the ground, the water splashing across the floor.

"Gabe, Calyssa! Enough!" Nana looked back and forth between the two of us, her face matching the harsh tone of her voice.

Just then, Andrew walked in. "Everyone is scrambling for information, but no one knows much. I can't seem to find anyone who's found a way back into the city that hasn't been washed out somewhere between here and there." He was shaking his head. "I'm not sure how we can get back."

"Nana Jane, there's call for you in the kitchen." Ben's soft voice. We all looked toward him standing in the doorway. "The man said it's important. He said he's with the Department of Homeland Security."

Nana Jane and Andrew exchanged a brief look, and Nana immediately left the room. Ben walked over to me and put his hand on my shoulder. "Please don't cry, Calyssa. Dad and Gabe will help you. Won't you?" He turned to look at them.

Andrew stepped in beside his son and put his arm around him. "Of course, we will, Ben." Ben's hand dropped from my shoulder, and he sat down next to me.

Everyone was silent. Seconds ticked by.

"Charlie Simpson could fly Calyssa back to the city." Ben said matter-of-factly, breaking the silence.

Kneeling in front of his son, Andrew asked, "What are you talking about, Ben?"

"He has a hovercopter at his place right now. He's been working on it. I saw it earlier this week when Nana Jane and I rode over to their ranch. He let me look at it while Nana Jane was helping Missy with something in the kitchen."

Andrew stood up. "I'm going to make a few more calls. Good thinking, Ben." Ben nodded his head.

Looking over toward Gabe, I saw he was picking up pieces of broken glass from the floor. I knew I should help him, but I couldn't make myself get up. I kept replaying my last conversation with Livvy. Could she have made it out? I had to believe that she could still be alive.

After several minutes, Nana Jane and Andrew walked back in the room, both with somber looks on their faces.

Nana Jane spoke first. "I've been asked by the Federal Emergency Management Agency to be the Federal Coordinating Officer and head up the Emergency Response Team for this situation."

"But Nana, you haven't worked for them in a long time." Gabe dropped the glass pieces he'd collected in a small trash can next to the desk. "Why are they calling you?"

"It sounds like everyone else was in the city. I'm the only retired FCO that they could reach that is currently within several hours of SciCity. Right now, they're setting up an Emergency Operations Center at one of AHGA's research fields just to the north of the city. It has a warehouse located at the top of a hill there, and it sounds like the water didn't flood it. Once the EOC is in place, others will be joining me for a Joint Preliminary Damage Assessment." She was looking now at Andrew as she spoke. "I told them I'd get there as soon as I could. It's a long drive to take all the backroads to that warehouse."

"Charlie just messaged me back. He still has the hovercopter at his ranch. He said he'll be here in fifteen minutes to get us to SciCity. I'm sure we can drop you at the EOC on the way, Jane."

"I'm going to grab a bag. I'm not sure when I'll be back to the farm." She headed upstairs.

Andrew reached out and took Ben's hand. "You're going to need to stay here, Ben. I'm going to ask Stan and Jill if they'll come over and stay with you until we can get back. Are you okay with that?" Ben silently nodded his head. "Okay, then. Let's see if we can find one of them in the barn. They were working with the new horses today."

Jumping up off the couch, I reached out and grabbed Andrew's arm. "I'm coming with you, to the city, right?" The scratchiness of my voice startled me. I sounded so desperate.

"Absolutely, Calyssa. Wait right here for me."

Then it was just Gabe and me in the room.

"Calyssa, I–"

"Don't, Gabe. I don't have anything to say to you right now."

"But–"

"I'm serious. Just leave me alone." I got up and walked out of the room, heading back toward the front door.

I just kept thinking about everyone I knew in SciCity. What had they been doing today? Surely some of the areas had to be okay. I mean, some of those buildings were really big. I was sure they'd be able to make it through the flood of water. And, if Livvy had run – she could have made it out through the tunnel to the other side. She could have made it. Same thing for Father. AHGA was set up as high as the dam. He could have made it. I didn't want to think about anyone else right now. About my friends who were down in the valley, in the city.

I saw Andrew and Ben making their way back toward the house with a woman at about the same time that Nana Jane and Gabe joined me on the front porch. Hearing a soft whirring, I shaded my eyes, noting a hovercopter headed in our direction.

It landed on the driveway away from the house, and all of us took off toward it. Only Ben and the woman remained on the front porch.

The pilot nodded his head at Andrew and then at the seat next to him. The rest of us followed him in and sat in seats in the back. Nana Jane showed Gabe and me how to buckle in. She'd obviously done it before. After buckling her own belt, she slapped the back of the pilot's seat and I felt the hovercopter begin to lift.

I'd been in AHGA's hovercopters before, but they weren't like this one. It had open sides in the back, and the air whipped though, pulling on my clothing and tugging at my hair. I grabbed a hair tie from my jacket pocket and pulled back my hair into a tight bun, trying to keep it out of my face so I could see.

The pilot flew above the road I had driven on earlier. We passed over the bridge that was no longer there and saw whole sections of the road gone. I tried to prepare myself as we got closer to the city. I knew it was going to be bad.

Rounding a big corner, we got our first look. And I immediately knew I was wrong. This wasn't just bad. It was complete and utter destruction.

There was water everywhere. The pilot flew down closer to the surface of what now looked like a huge lake. A lake with thousands of parts and pieces of buildings, broken and floating, as far as the eye could see. And as I looked closer, I was horrified by a realization – many of the floating objects were actually bodies.

Chapter 44

It was like watching a movie. No way it was real. For miles, in every direction, nothing was like it used to be. Some buildings were completely gone. Others were still standing, but just barely. Death was everywhere.

When we arrived at the research fields where the EOC was being set up, we all got off the hovercopter. Nana Jane was immediately met by several federal officers, who introduced themselves as part of her Emergency Support Team. They asked Andrew and Charlie if they would talk to some of the other pilots that were gathering there, to help coordinate a search grid for a rescue operation. Gabe and I were asked to wait at the copter.

"Calyssa, I'm sorry about Livvy. I—"

"Don't say it, Gabe. She may still be alive. She could have made it out. I told her to run. She knew—"

"I didn't mean ... I mean ... I just ..."

I walked away. Gabe called out after me, but I didn't stop. When I reached the door of the building that Nana Jane had entered, I paused for a minute as I looked inside. The entire floor had been completely transformed from a warehouse into a high-tech command station. Nana Jane stood in the center, barking out orders, and people hustled to complete each command as fast as she could give them. No one seemed to question the gray-haired grandma now in charge. Just lots of "Yes, Ma'am's" and head-nodding.

She saw me and waved me over. Tentatively, I walked through the moving parts as the set-up was being completed around us. Nana Jane had a different air about her. Authoritative. Commanding. Imposing. Experienced.

Three people approached just before I got to her. "FCO Rutherforse, this is Lieutenant Colonel Epeli. He is familiar with the new comsat-imaging system that we can use to help identify areas that may have survivors. And this is Master Sergeant Chen. She will head up the search for the terrorists responsible for the attack. Both will be reporting directly to you, and you'll be my liaison."

Nana Jane nodded once sharply. "Excellent. Lieutenant Colonel, Master Sergeant, digital tables and prepped stations have already been set up at the north end of the building. Let's meet there in ten minutes to discuss what each of us knows at this time."

Everyone nodded in agreement, and all three walked away. Staring at her, I realized how different she looked. I felt like I didn't really know Jane Rutherforse at all.

Turning to me, she smiled and held out her arms. Stepping toward her, she pulled me in to a big hug. This was the Nana Jane I knew.

"We're all going to do everything we can to find your family and friends, Calyssa."

Hearing a loud whistle, we looked back toward the entrance. Charlie was there, motioning me back toward the door.

"Go, Honey. Charlie's been a hovercopter mechanic in the reserves for years. He can fly just about anything they can put in the air. I've asked him to lead the unit heading over to AHGA."

"Thank you," was all I managed to get out before I sprinted for the door.

Charlie was loading up the hovercopter by the time I got there. Andrew and Gabe were already on board, as well as five other men and women. I jumped into the empty seat and fastened myself in.

Once again, we were in the air. I'm not sure how long the flight was to AHGA. I simply sat and watched the devastation go by under us. And tried not to think about what might lay ahead.

Following the valley, we rounded a corner and I gasped. The once massive dam was almost unrecognizable. Not much of it was still there. I immediately looked to the left and sucked in a deep breath. AHGA was in shambles. All of the beautiful floor-to-ceiling windows were shattered. Chunks of concrete and metal were jutting precariously out of places where they shouldn't have been.

But there were people! Some of them running around, others motioning for us, a few lying in the entrance area in front of the building while others tended to them. I scanned everyone, looking for faces I knew. For Father. For Livvy.

As we landed, I spotted Jaxx. He'd made it! Father should have made it, too, then! He and Jaxx were together not long before the dam blew. Jumping out and running toward him, I heard yells coming from behind me, but I didn't stop. As I got closer, I could see Jaxx's bloody face and torn clothing. Another man was trying to attend to the jagged gash on his cheek, but Jaxx kept waving him off, like a pesky mosquito.

"Jaxx!" I yelled as I got closer. "Jaxx! Is Father with you?"

Looking in my direction, I saw the grimace that crossed his face before it went neutral again.

I stopped. I knew it before he spoke. I'd seen it in his face. He walked the rest of the way to meet me.

"Calyssa, you're okay." Grabbing his walkie, he said, "Mermaid has been located. She's fine." Then back to me, "How'd you escape the water? I thought you were at the U today for classes."

I just stood there. I couldn't say anything.

"Calyssa? Calyssa, are you okay?"

A medic was there again, trying to clean up the wound on his face.

"Knock it off. I'm fine," he snarled. The guy stepped back from him.

Jaxx stepped closer to me. "Calyssa. Answer me. Are you all right?"

"My father, where is he?" My voice was almost a whisper.

"He ... he ... to be honest, we're not sure. We haven't been able to find him yet."

"So, he's not ... dead?"

"We're still hopeful. I've got men sweeping the building now."

"But you were with him. I talked with him on his iBud not long before the dam blew. He was with you and a SciCity Security Enforcer. You were—"

"Not when the explosion happened. Right after your call, we were going to head over to the dam. Your call concerned him, more than I think he wanted to let on. I said I'd go check things out. Your father was going to go with me, but at the last minute he got a call from someone in research who needed to see him. He told me to go and report back if there was anything suspicious.

"I took six or seven officers with me. We thought we'd do a perimeter search first. We'd just gotten off the elevator and were walking through the lobby when the bomb went off. It knocked me unconscious. I'm not sure how long I was out for, but when I woke up, there was shattered glass and smoke everywhere. Sirens, lights, bodies sprawled out all over. It was chaos. We started moving everyone we could to the front entrance to assess damages." He paused and shook his head, which must have hurt because he winced and lightly touched the bloody laceration. "Damn it," he said through gritted teeth.

"Jaxx, my father. Do you know if he's in one of the lower levels? I can go in and help look for him." I started walking toward the door, but Jaxx grabbed my arm and swung me back around.

"You can't go in there, Calyssa. We have emergency workers clearing floors one through three right now. It's structurally unsound."

"What about the rest of the levels? From four to thirty? What about the people down on those levels?"

Jaxx closed his eyes, just for a second. When they reopened, he looked tired. "There's an old underground connecting tunnel on level four. From AHGA to the dam control room. When the dam blew, water filled the tunnel, and as far as we can tell, it's flooded all the levels below it."

I was stunned. At that time of day, hundreds of people would have been working on those levels. "Do you think Father went down there?" I felt panic rising again. "We have to get in there! To go look for him! What if he's alive, trapped down in one of those levels?" Suddenly I felt nauseous, and I tried to pull away from Jaxx. I had to get in that building. I had to find Father.

"Calyssa! I already have emergency divers in there. They have oxygen reserves with them. If they find anyone, they'll get them back up to safety. There's nothing you can do."

And then another thought. "What about Eve? Have you found her yet? Did she make it out?"

"Not that I know of."

Looking out across where the dam used to stand, I asked, "What about the other side? Do you know if anyone made it out over there?"

Jaxx's eyes narrowed. "You mean like the people responsible for this whole mess? Rebels?"

I cringed as he said it, realizing that probably wasn't something that I should know.

"Or your patrols. Don't you have men patrolling that side of the dam as well?"

He studied me for a few seconds. "We usually do, but with multiple bomb threats this morning, I had most of my men sweeping the complex area. Your father wanted to keep it business-as-usual. He was stressed about the amount of time lost in the past two days due to the earlier threats." He shook his head, started to say something else, but then stopped when two other officers approached him.

"Jaxx, we need you over by the hovercopters. They're going to fly some people out that need immediate medical attention, then come back for others. It sounds like they're using Warehouse 375 as an emergency evacuation center."

"Stay here, Calyssa. I'll be back in a few minutes."

Like I was going to go somewhere. I had nowhere to go. My father and sister were missing. The woman who I'd recently discovered was my mom was missing. Except for Jaxx and the Staytons, pretty much everyone I knew was missing. And, from the flight in, I thought that my house was probably gone.

And that made me remember Lulu.

Chapter 45

And that's when the enormity of it all hit me. Thinking about poor, sweet Lulu. It was silly really but – I didn't think she knew how to swim. I sank to my knees right there and began to softly cry. What was I going to do? Leaning over, my hand splashed in a pool of water that had been trapped in a concave section of the concrete.

I could see my reflection as I gazed into the water. It wasn't the face of a drowned woman, although it could have been. If I had stayed at the U. If I hadn't gone to see Nana Jane.

Can you drown in grief? I thought.

I turned away sharply, angry at my weakness. I didn't have time for self-pity. I was still here, still alive, still able to help others who needed it. I pulled myself back to my feet. There was nothing I could do for my family or for Lulu right now, but there were a lot of people here. And as the afternoon sun was sinking, it was getting colder and colder. People were wet and injured, a dangerous combination. We had to get them out of here. There had to be something I could do to help.

Looking over the area, I saw Andrew helping a woman toward a hovercopter. I ran after them. For the rest of that afternoon and well into the evening, I assisted medics with bandaging and splinting, I checked off missing people on the AGHA staff roster as they were found and identified, and I helped load people onto the shuttles that were taking them to the emergency evacuation center. Later in the evening, I even helped carry the body bags so they could be taken to an identification center.

When it was dark, they brought in lights. Still, the rescuers continued their searching, and the divers dove back down repeatedly. Finally, Andrew found me and said that we needed to go back to the farm. We would come back tomorrow, but there wasn't much more that we could do tonight.

"But we haven't found any of my family, Andrew. We have to keep looking." Rubbing my hands together, I realized I was incredibly cold and tired.

"We'll come back, Calyssa. Tomorrow. All of us." He and Gabe looked as tired as I felt.

The flight back to the farm was silent. When we landed, Andrew and Charlie made a quick plan for pick up again in the morning, and then Charlie was gone. I followed Andrew up the stairs to the porch and into the house. Jill and Stan told Andrew that Ben was already asleep. They also made plans for the morning. Then they, too, headed out.

I spent the night in the spare bedroom that I had used when I'd come to the farm with Ana last spring break. Lying down in the bed, everything caught up with me, and I cried myself to sleep.

For the next three days, we just kept repeating what we'd done on Friday. We'd go to an area with other evacuation workers, assist the medics, identify people, make lists of those in the area still missing, and load the shuttles. On the third day, we found a family trapped in an upper level of a tall office building, one that had toppled over into another close to it. Using harnesses and straps, we were able to get all five of them up into hovercopters. Their whole family had made it. They were alive and they were together. But most of the time it didn't end like that.

I kept busy during the days, helping others, keeping my mind busy. But the nights –well, once I was back at the farm in bed – each night was more difficult than the last. I knew that with each day, there was less of a chance that we'd find Livvy and Father alive. Or Eve. The divers were pulling fewer bodies out of the lower levels of AGHA as each day passed. There were areas that they couldn't get to, and many employees were still missing. I wasn't sure if it was better to not find a body and to keep hoping, or if it would have been easier to know that someone was dead. Every day, family members went back and waited for the divers to come up. Every day, some left knowing that they'd never see their loved one again while others knew they'd be returning the next day.

On Monday afternoon, Gabe showed up where I was working. I hadn't seen him much in the past few days.

"Calyssa, I need you to come with me."

"I'm busy, Gabe."

"Calyssa, Nana Jane sent me to get you," he said softly.

And for a few seconds, I thought my heart stopped beating.

"What did—"

"She didn't tell me anything. She just said to find you and bring you to her."

And I knew.

I silently followed Gabe to a hovercopter that took us to the EOC where Nana Jane met us as we landed.

No one said anything. Nana Jane just held out her hand, and I took it. We walked around the huge warehouse to the back. As far as the eye could see, there were large white tents set up.

"Part of my job is to make sure that bodies are being identified, and next-of-kin notified whenever possible. Fingerprints, dental records, skeletal remains, DNA matching, we're using every means possible to put an identification with a body."

I just nodded. My heart was racing now. Who had she found? Was it Father or Livvy? I hadn't told her about Eve, so I doubted it was her.

"Calyssa, you don't have to see the body."

"I need to."

Nana Jane led the way into one of the massive tents. "Everyone in here has been identified."

Rows and rows of body bags on the ground. Hundreds. And this was just one tent.

About half way down on the right side, Nana stopped, leaned over and scanned a tag on the bag. "Are you sure you want to do this? We clean each body up the best we can here, but death is never pretty."

I nodded and knelt next to her.

Nana Jane unzipped the bag.

Yellow, tangled hair spilled out. And part of me felt guilty, because I had wanted it to be Father, not Livvy. She loved me. She cared about me. She was proud of me. It wasn't fair to lose her. We were finally more than sisters. We were friends.

Uncontrollable tears streamed down my cheeks. I brushed some loose hair from her forehead. She was so cold, so still, so quiet.

Nana Jane leaned over and kissed me on the forehead. "Take your time. I'll be outside."

So, I sat there, on the cold, hard ground, grieving for my dead sister.

How much loss can one person take and still survive? I thought about Livvy and Ana. So different, yet each so beautiful in her own way. Both of my sisters were gone now. My heart ached in a way it never had before. Like it was being crushed, squeezed to a point that it would never return to the way it was before.

I cried until no more tears came. Then, I just sat there with her. Because I didn't want her to be alone. I remembered all our squabbles as kids. All the times she annoyed me, made fun of me, laughed at me. How she would make me so, so angry, and then tell me to "lighten up."

I remembered the times she held my hand in the dark when I was afraid. When she'd read me stories after Mom was gone. When she'd helped me pick out a dress for my Junior Formal. When she'd bought me my first iBud, my first memory bracelet, my first express lights.

I thought about our time together in that last week. How I'd seen a completely different side to her. How much she'd grown up. How much she'd hurt. How much she'd worked for what she'd believed in.

And then I thought about our last conversation. She'd said she was proud of me, of who I was becoming. And that she wished she'd told me more often that she loved me. Like a knife twisting in my already ravaged heart, I realized that I hadn't said it back. I hadn't told her I loved her, too. And now, I'd never be able to do that again.

At some point, it had gotten dark, and soft lights enveloped the tent. I knew I should be going, but I didn't want to leave her. Because this time, when I left, I knew I'd never see her again.

I jumped when I felt a hand on my shoulder. Turning, I saw Gabe.

And a cold hatred like I'd never known before filled the fresh, gaping hole in my heart.

Chapter 46

"Don't touch me." My voice was harsh as I brushed his hand off my shoulder.

I could see the shock and hurt in his eyes, but I didn't care.

"Calyssa, I–"

"Don't say it. That you're sorry. Or that any of this matters to you."

"But–" There were tears in his eyes, but I didn't care.

"No! No buts! This is on you, Gabe! You could have stopped them! You could have talked to Gunner! He would have listened to you! I told you he might die, but you said it wasn't your priority!" I was screaming at him now.

"That's not what I said. I–"

"Whatever, Gabe! Wasn't it you who told me that actions speak louder than words? What did you do?

Nothing! And you could have! You blame me for your sister's death? I'm not sure what I could have done to stop Ana, but we both know exactly what you could have done to stop Gunner and Livvy!"

"But–"

I yelled right over the top of him. "You told me you care about the people who care about you, but those people keep ending up dead! Thank god you don't care about me!" I knew what I was saying was wrong, that I was hurting Gabe – I could see it in his eyes. The realization, the pain, the regret was there. But I couldn't stop. I didn't want to stop.

"You were right, Gabe. Things change. I've changed. You made sure of that. You wanted me out of your life. Wish granted. Who has the fake tears now? Like you said to me, I don't want them or need them. I'm lucky you're out of my life. You're the most horrible, miserable, arrogant, selfish human I know, Green or non-Green. I can't believe that I ever thought I loved you!"

Standing there, breathing ragged, hands clenched at my sides, I waited for him to respond. Daring him to. Hoping he would. But he just stood there. In silence.

"Finally, the wonder boy has nothing to say for himself! I'm glad I'm not you, Gabe Stayton! I don't think I could live with myself!" Then I turned and stormed out of the tent, never looking back.

Heading toward the hovercopters, I realized I had nowhere to go. My sister was dead, my father was missing, and my house was still underwater, if it was still there at all.

Frustrated, I veered down a hill and took off walking. I didn't know where I was going, and I didn't care.

Screw everyone. And everything. I'm done caring. There's no one left to care about me.

I walked and walked and walked.

Until I noticed the sun peeking over the edge of mountains. Then I stopped right where I was, and I sat down, and I cried again. But this time, the anger was gone, drained out over the course of the walk. And all that was left was an empty sadness.

That's where they found me. Andrew and Nana Jane. I didn't even notice the hovercopter landing, but it must have, because they loaded me onto it, wrapping a blanket around me. They were talking to me, but I didn't hear anything they said. They took me back to the farm and tucked me into bed. Nana Jane stayed in the room with me, and Andrew brought me a drink that I refused to take. I curled up in a ball and closed my eyes. And hoped that I'd never wake up.

But I did.

When I woke, it was dark. Walking through the house, I ended up on the front porch. I sat on the stairs and looked up at the stars. It seemed to take all my energy just to sit there. I didn't want to think about anything or anyone. There were no more tears. I just wanted to be empty.

I heard the front door open, but I didn't turn around. I'd hoped that whoever it was would just leave me alone.

"Glad to see you're up, Calyssa." Andrew's voice. "Can I join you?"

In my mind, I told him to go away. But nothing came out.

So, he sat down next to me.

At some point, Andrew reached out and put his arm around me. And, a little later, I leaned over and rested my head on his shoulder.

As the sun began to rise, Andrew sat up a little straighter, and I lifted my head. Without turning towards me, he said, "Pain is a shapeshifter, Calyssa. I know this from experience. It may feel like this for a minute, or a day, or a year, but eventually it will change, until one day you realize that something else has taken its place. How you live with your pain will determine what it becomes. But it will always leave a scar that reminds you of what happened.

"See this scar, right here?" He held out his hand in front of me, palm up, rubbing the tip of his pinky. "This one reminds me of the time I was teaching Gabe how to build an engine for his truck. We were talking and laughing, and I cranked down on something, and my hand slipped. Tore the skin open and cut clear to the bone. But it healed. The scar will always be there, but it doesn't stop me from teaching my children how to work on things on the farm.

"And this one?" He turned his hand over, and I saw a scar that ran from between two of his fingers down his hand, curling around to his wrist. "This one was from a time that I had to cut a calf out of a jumble of barbed wire. My neighbor said we should just put it down. But when I knelt next to it, that calf stopped struggling and just watched me with its big, brown eyes. And I knew I had to try. I don't know who was bloodier by the time I was done, me or the calf, but I got her out, and she made it. And I'd do it again, in spite of the scar, because these animals are my responsibility."

Andrew dropped his hand.

"But it's the scars that we can't see that affect us the most. The unseen marks humans leave on each other. Sometimes, they do something or say something. Sometimes, they don't even know what they've done. And sometimes, they leave us. The truth is every person you meet might hurt you someday. But life is all about finding the ones that are worth hurting for."

Andrew turned, looking at me, waiting until I looked back at him. "My scars are mine, Calyssa, and I wouldn't trade them for anything. When my Lydia died, I thought my life was going to end. I couldn't imagine a world without her in it. I didn't want to be a part of a world where she wouldn't be with me. But then, I looked at my three, beautiful children, and I saw little pieces of Lydia there. In Ana's smile. In Gabe's laughter. In little Ben's eyes. And slowly, I felt her all around me. In the beauty of the lilacs, in the whispers of winds, in the way a mama horse nuzzled her foal. And I realized that she was still with me. In that beautiful scar that reminded me why I loved her so much. If it hadn't hurt so bad, maybe I would have let her go. Just moved on. But I realized I wanted to remember.

"It still hurts, when I rub that scar on my heart, but not like it used to, and each time I think about it, I remember all the incredible things about her, about what she brought into my life, about what I would have missed out on if she hadn't been a part of it. And I'm thankful for the time I spent with her, no matter how short, because without her in my life, I would have missed out on the best parts.

"Ana's scar ... it's still raw. But like Lydia's scar, I would never trade it, because that would mean she wouldn't have been mine. And I couldn't bear that. Right now, I just have to focus on her love, and her laughter, and the way she felt when I hugged her, because if I let the anger and the resentment take over, I might forget some of those things. And that's just not worth it to me."

Then he leaned forward and kissed me on the forehead before heading back into the house.

Gradually, I let the memories back in. Ana's laughter as we rode horses together. Livvy's determination as she sat on the couch working on her files. Father's confidence walking across the lobby of AHGA. Mom's grace when she played her violin.

Andrew was right. I didn't want to lose those. I didn't want to forget. I didn't want to be empty.

I headed back inside, showered, got dressed, and met up with Andrew as he headed back outside to wait for the hovercopter. I'd decided to go back out today. To make a difference where I could. Andrew just nodded as I fell in step beside him.

As Charlie landed, he waved us over. "We're going to make a stop at the Atkinson farm down off the south fork of the Colorado River. I got a call that several bodies had washed up there this morning. I said we'd take them to the EOC for identification." He looked at me. "A couple of them are Green citizens."

Chapter 47

I climbed in and belted up. Every time we picked up a body of a Green citizen, I'd wondered if it might be Father, or Eve. One of the Greens did end up being an AHGA employee, but it wasn't someone that I knew. More bodies were being discovered each day, and occasionally someone that had been missing showed up and was reunited with their family. But Father and Eve remained unaccounted for. I talked with Jaxx several times. He thought that Eve's body was probably trapped under the water in one of the lower levels at AHGA. Slowly, the water was receding, but I was told that it would probably be months before all the levels would be fully accessible again.

SciCity, or what was left of it, and the surrounding areas were in chaos. Everyone had massive losses, Greens and non-Greens alike. Each day revealed the name of someone else I'd known who had died because of the bombing at the dam. And every night I grieved the new loss. Ayva and Shassa. Dee and El. Mr. Hazelbrook. Karsten. Jessalyn's parents, Dom and Maria. Dr. Penning. Even Kelly Green from G-Cubed who'd been visiting his grandparents in SciCity the day of the explosion. Every family was touched by the tragedy – it didn't matter if they were Green or non-Green, farmers or security enforcers, shopkeepers or government officials, adults or children. The losses were staggering.

On the Friday following the bombing, Joshua Fitting put out a broadcast, announcing that his heart went out to all of those who had lost loved ones, and that he, too, had lost his last brother. He declared that this horrible "accident" was "God's way" of telling us we needed to get back to all things "natural." That this was the second time God had used a flood to "cleanse" the earth.

It was the spark that lit the fire of hatred, and all the pain fueled the ensuing violence. Attacks in the streets. Raids on farms that had opened their doors to Greens, or non-Greens, or both. It didn't seem to matter. A couple of assaults even took place at the EOC, one resulting in an identification tent being burned to the ground with over two hundred unidentified bodies still in it. Their families would never know what happened to them.

Everyone referred to "us" and "them," and the need to watch out for "those people." More deaths. More panic. More fear. More anger.

After two more weeks, just over 20,000 bodies had been identified, and over 35,000 were either among the unidentified dead or still missing. Most communication networks were still out, like iBuds and digital news, but radio waves filled the air. Just about everyone had something to say, and almost all of it was full of prejudice and bigotry.

"Watch out for the Greens – they're already rebuilding tech to kill off plants so all the non-Greens will die!" *Really? Even the Greens needed the plants to produce oxygen to breathe.*

"Kill any non-Green with a gun before they kill you! Only rebels would be flashing their guns around in days like these!" *Seriously? And what were the other guys going to kill the "rebels" with? Oh yeah, their guns.*

"Keep your eyes on the farmers. They're hoarding food, supplies, and tech for themselves. Maybe somebody should go teach them a lesson about sharing." *Sharing? Or taking? And isn't that the same stuff they've had at their farms all along?*

"The security enforcers are all out-of-control thieves now. They're all as bad as the rebel terrorists!" *Right. All of them? Not a good one out there, huh?*

It was terrifying.

Andrew and Nana Jane had invited me to live with them on the farm. It worried me – any place that had Greens and non-Greens living together seemed to be targeted by both groups. But I didn't have anywhere else to go. And I loved spending time with Ben and cooking in their kitchen again in the evenings. Nana Jane came home about once a week, and we always had a nice, big dinner waiting for her. Andrew still went out about every other day, helping with body recovery, tracking down leads on missing people, and starting to rebuild in areas where the flood waters had receded.

Gabe and I had silently agreed on unspoken civility. We didn't really talk, but we didn't fight anymore either. We lived under the same roof, but we both acknowledged the distance that had grown between us. I didn't think that I really hated him, but things had gone too far to get back any old feelings.

Six weeks after the explosion, although much of the water had receded or been diverted, lawlessness was still rampant in the city and the areas around it. A "town hall" meeting was called to discuss the future of SciCity. Everyone was encouraged to attend, Greens and non-Greens. I'd heard that Joshua Fitting would be in attendance as well as one of Trygg's brothers, Tobias, who was now an acting Director for the SciCity Security Enforcers. Nana Jane had been asked to provide security for the venue, and she chose a mix of Greens and non-Greens, people who were willing to work together for the betterment of the community.

The day of the meeting, tension was running high. Nana Jane had located a large fairgrounds building with stadium seating that the flood waters had missed. She arranged for weapons checks at the door. No weapons inside. No exceptions. We got there early to help with the set-up. Gabe and Andrew had used some of the equipment from the EOC compound to enhance an older sound system to make sure that everyone could hear. People had filled out forms for presentation time in front of the audience. Each had been allotted three to four minutes to make a specific point.

At noon, the building opened to the public, and I began to worry. We were expecting over 10,000 people to show up. Other than in high school, which was tiny in comparison, I'd never seen so many Greens and non-Greens together in one place. And, like high school, the seating was very segregated. The air felt tense, and my stomach hatched a new set of butterflies.

"Good afternoon, ladies and gentlemen. My name is Jane Rutherforse, and I will be facilitating today. Welcome to the first of many town hall meetings. Thank you for taking time to join us here." She went on to review the procedure for the speakers and the expectations for the audience.

The first man was a non-Green who spoke about the importance of getting the downtown area of the city up and running again as a hub for everyone to use. For the most part, the audience was quiet and attentive.

Next was a Green woman. She focused on the number of single parents trying to raise kids now, and about the number of parentless children. Someone in the audience stood up and yelled something about non-Greens taking in the kids since no one would be going Green anymore, and that started an argument that ended in a fist fight that security had to break up.

Speakers continued for the next two hours, covering all sorts of topics. Water filtration, repairing the dam, allotments of food, concerns about lighting and electricity, reopening of schools, continuing searches for those still missing, looting that had taken place in houses and buildings in the city – the list went on and on.

A man in a long jacket and hat stepped up to speak next. He removed the hat, and shocked murmurs rippled through the audience. Joshua Fitting. As he'd promised. There were hoots of support and threats laced with obscenities from throughout the building. Several fights broke out again, but it was back under control quickly.

"Brothers and sisters! By God's grace, each of you made it here today. Take a good look around. I'm here to talk to you about choices. More specifically about making good choices. Standing here today, I am a free man. I live the life I choose. No one tells me what I have to do, where I have to go, if I have to eat, who I have to love. Those are my choices, mine alone. You no longer need to have your worth based on what you can become rather than on who you are. No longer must you become more to mean something." Voices in the crowd were starting to pick up, either agreeing with him or telling him to shut up. Officers were looking nervously at each other. Nana Jane looked ready to approach the podium.

"Now, friends, we must recognize that overconfident advancements in technology threw us headfirst into a crisis that has basically wiped out our beloved city, and almost our entire population. Unrelenting scientists and corrupt corporations pushed and prodded and forced nature to do unnatural things. And our beautiful, incredible planet struggled and fought, frail, on the brink of devastation, extinction, total annihilation ... only through God's grace, it slowly found a way to return to us ..."

I'd heard this speech before – almost the exact same one at the rebel camp! This was not going to end well. Nana, Andrew, and several officers were now making their way across the stage.

"... hearts, search your souls. Look inside you for what you know is right. Today, I ask that those who hear the call deep inside themselves, those who no longer are willing to be shackled by science's stranglehold on nature and man, step forward to join me and the others who chose to–"

Nana Jane grabbed the microphone away, and fights once again erupted in the audience. Chants of "Let him talk!," "Lock him up!," and even, "Kill the drone!" rang out from different sections of the audience. Joshua had stepped back from Nana Jane with his hands in the air and an injured what-did-I-do look on his face. Then he was smiling and waving to the crowd.

It took several minutes to get the audience under control again. Next was a Green scientist. His proposal that the priority of the city should be bringing genetic modification facilities back online brought many of the same shouts from the audience, but now it was "Kill the gimp – genetically modified people don't deserve to live!"

Again, the microphone was taken away before the speaker could finish. If this was how it was going to continue, I didn't think anything more productive was going to come from this meeting.

This time, though, it was Andrew who hushed the crowd. For several seconds he stood silently, staring out over the sea of human faces. When he spoke, his voice was strong and sincere. "Ladies and gentlemen, we cannot and must not pretend that things in our city can continue the way they are. Violence will not hold the key to rebuilding our community. It is time to say, 'Enough is enough.' If we are to move forward, we must come together, we must pull together, and we must stand united."

I watched the faces in the crowd as Andrew spoke, some were nodding, some were scowling, but most were quietly listening. Then, to my right, about twenty rows back, someone caught my eye. I couldn't be absolutely sure from this distance, but I thought it was Eve! I had to get closer. Was it her? Had she somehow made it out of AHGA? And if she had, why didn't Jaxx know about it? I began trying to make my way toward her.

As I moved through the crowd, I heard Andrew continuing. "During my lifetime, I have dedicated myself to the people of SciCity, in the ways I know best, through science and through farming. Those of you who know me, know I feel that everyone has the right to make their own choices on the issues we're discussing here together. I have spoken against rebel radicalism and against corporate tyranny. I have supported free trade in the farming community and new research that improves the lives and health of our citizens. I value the ideal of a free society in which all persons, Green and non-Green, can live together in harmony and with equal opportunities."

This set off murmurs through the audience. Two women directly in front of me leaned in to hug one another and cut off my movement momentarily. As I stepped around them, I realized I couldn't see the woman I'd been trying to reach. I looked desperately around, and spotted her in the next aisle over, headed down the stairs. I pushed through the crowd to the aisle closest to me and started down as well.

"Violence against another whose skin is a different color than our own cannot be tolerated in any form, in any context, in any circumstance, by any political leader, by any corporation, or by any government. We must consider what kind of world we want our children to grow up in. Every child has the right to survive, grow, and be protected from all forms of violence. They have the right to learn and explore, and to ultimately make their own choices for themselves. And that includes the choice of going Green, or not going Green. Our children are our most precious gift. We have all been given an opportunity to make a difference, and we owe it to our children and our children's children to start today."

I was almost parallel to her when Andrew paused, and I glanced up, noticing him making a point to look all around the building. I refocused. If I went down two more flights and across one more section, I'd be right next to her. To see if it actually was Eve.

"We've all lost loved ones. But we are still here. We owe it to each other to move forward, to help one another, and to share our gifts to make life better for all of us. It cannot wait. The time to change is now. My name is Andrew Stayton. Regardless of the color of your skin, if you need my help, and if I can help you, I will. And I'm challenging each of you here to make that same commitment." And at that point, people stood up, many applauding, but some were stepping out to leave. And I lost sight of the woman.

Frantic, I tried to push my way through. People were yelling again, some in support of what Andrew, and others simply spouting the same mindless rhetoric they had been before.

Feeling a sharp tug on my wrist, I turned to shout at whomever had grabbed on to me. I shook my arm vigorously to try to shake off the hand that was grasping mine. But it wouldn't let go. One more look toward where the woman had disappeared, and then I grabbed the person's wrist with my other hand and jerked it toward me.

"Let me go! I have to–" My voice caught in my throat as I looked into the person's eyes.

His voice was soft, but somehow, I heard it over the shouts of the crowd. "Do I know you? I think I know you."

Father.

Chapter 48

He looked different – so – not like him. His head had been shaved, and his hair was just starting to grow back. I could see a jagged cut that went from his forehead up into his hair, closed with what seemed to be twenty or thirty stitches. He had a scraggly beard and heavy bruising around one eye and the bridge of his nose. His lip had been split but was now in the process of healing. He was thinner and a paler green than I'd ever seen him, and his other arm was in a cast, hanging from a sling around his neck. But looking in his eyes, I knew immediately it was him.

"Father, you're alive!" I threw my arms around his neck and heard a muffled groan. Stepping back, I said, "I'm sorry. I didn't mean to hurt you. I just ... I can't believe it. I'd given up hope that we'd find you. I'm so ..."

And that's when I realized he hadn't said anything else. That he was just standing there. Staring at me. And that his eyes were filled with confusion.

An older man standing next to him noticed me. "Do you know this man? He wandered onto our farm a couple of weeks ago. We've been waiting for him to heal up enough to bring him back to the city in hopes that they could help him remember who he is. We've been calling him John."

For several seconds, I couldn't speak. My father was alive. My father was alive!

"His name is Kassius Brentwood. He's my father."

The two men looked at each other. "Does that sound familiar, John? I mean, Kassius? Does that trigger anything?"

Father looked back at me. "No, not the name. But I do know I know her. I can't remember how or why, but I know her." He still hadn't let go of my arm.

"Father, it's me, Calyssa. Your youngest daughter." I searched his face, but still no glimmer of recognition.

"Do I have other daughters? Or sons? Am I married? Do I work? What do I do?" The questions were pouring out of him. I pulled back a bit, but he jerked me back toward him. I tried to pull my arm free, but he wouldn't let go.

The older man placed his hand on Father's arm. "It's okay, Kassius. Let her go. You don't want to hurt your daughter."

"My daughter." He said it like he was tasting the word, trying to decide if he liked it or not. But he let go of my arm, and I took another step back.

Rubbing my wrist, I said, "You're Kassius Brentwood IV, CEO of Advanced Human Genetics Assessments. You have two daughters, me and Livvy." Then I realized what I'd said, and I closed my eyes.

"What is it?" the other man asked.

I opened my eyes and looked into Father's eyes. "You *had* two daughters. Livvy was killed in the bombing. Her body has already been identified."

Father shook his head. "Two daughters? But one is dead?" He looked at the other man. "Why can't I remember them?" And then back at me, "Why can't I remember you?" He looked bewildered, his eyes darting around, his good hand rubbing the one sticking out of the end of the cast.

"I'm not sure, Kassius. You just have to give it time. Calyssa, my name is Jayce Mills. This is my daughter, Creta," he said as he turned to the beautiful redhead standing next to him. "Your father has been a guest in our home, and we'll do anything we can to help both of you out." Looking back toward the stage, he continued, "I know Andrew Stayton. Not well, but we've done some business together. I agree with what he said today. He made more sense than most of the others up there."

I looked toward the stage, too. I guessed that the meeting had ended, because no one else was at the podium. Andrew stood in front of the stage with Nana Jane, talking to people and shaking hands. "That's who I've been living with since the bombing. With the Staytons. I went to school with their kids."

Jayce looked back at me. "Well, let's go see Andrew. He'll probably want to know that your dad is alive."

344

Father had never stopped staring at me. "It's Calyssa, right?"

I nodded.

"I'm sorry I can't remember more." He reached up and touched the jagged, stitched line on his forehead. "But I'm happy I found you. Being with you makes me feel ... better about things. The doctor said he thinks my memory will come back. Maybe seeing you ... recognizing you ... is the first step."

"I'm sure it is, Kassius," said Jayce. "Let's take you and Calyssa to see Andrew Stayton. We'd said we wanted to talk to him anyway at the end of the meeting. Remember that?" Jayce reached down and picked up a crutch that he handed to Father.

Father nodded. Taking the crutch with his good arm, I saw that his leg was casted, too. I stepped forward to help him, but Creta stepped in beside him and wrapped her arm around his waist, careful not to bump his casted arm. Smiling, she said, "So it's Kassius, is it? I like that name. It suits you better than John anyway." He smiled back at her and I noticed that he relaxed at her touch, leaning into her. "Why don't you lead the way, Calyssa? Your dad needs a little extra room to navigate."

And I realized I felt jealous. *That's ridiculous*, I thought. *He just doesn't remember me yet. And she's probably been there helping him recover.*

I took the lead and headed back toward the stage. The crowd was thinner now. I saw Nana Jane notice us before Andrew. She touched his arm, then leaned over and said something in his ear. He immediately looked in our direction.

"Kassius?" Andrew asked, his voice unsure.

"That's what I've been told," Father answered.

"He suffered some head injuries and doesn't remember anything yet. But he did know that he knew me." I looked back and forth between the two men. "Andrew, Nana Jane, do you remember Jayce Mills and his daughter, Creta? I think you've had some previous business deals together."

Everyone nodded, murmuring polite hello's and shaking hands. We talked for the next half hour, Jayce explaining how he'd found Father and how we'd just discovered each other. Father was silent for most of the conversation. By the end, it was decided that Father would come back to the Stayton farm with us. Jayce and Creta left, saying they would be by within the next couple of days to check in on him.

Back at the farm, Father continued his silence. As the sun set, I asked him if he'd like to sit outside on the porch for a bit. He agreed, and I helped him out to the swing that overlooked the farm's fields.

"Can you tell me some things about our lives, Calyssa? Anything. I'm just hoping that something you say might trigger memories." Father looked tired and frail. It worried me to see him like that.

"Hold on a minute. I can do even better than that." I ran back inside.

A few minutes later I returned with my memory bracelet. Setting it on the enlarged, three-dimensional holographic viewing mode, I began to flip through digital images. With each one, I explained who it was, how we knew them, where it was, and anything else I could think of. Livvy and me. Lena. Lulu. Ayva. AHGA. Our home. He listened intently and asked questions.

Suddenly, Father sat up and leaned forward. "Stop. There. Go back to the one before this one."

I flipped back to a picture of Lulu in my room. "That's just Lulu. She's our mini-cow, the same one in the last few pictures," I said gently, thinking that maybe he was tired and we'd been at this for too long.

"No. The frame on the dresser in the background. Can you zoom in on it?"

"Sure." I selected the portion on the image he was talking about. It was a digital clip frame. The image captured on it was one of Livvy and me playing in a park when we were little. "That's Livvy and me, Father. I think I was four or five there, which means Livvy would have been six or seven."

"Can you enlarge it more?"

"I think so." The frame now was projected life size in front of us.

Father sat silently studying the image, slowly tilting his head, his eyebrows furrowed. "That's her hand, isn't it?" he asked, pointing to the very edge of the image.

I looked closely. A partial hand was there. I hadn't noticed it before. "Whose hand–"

He interrupted me. "It's her … wedding ring … I gave that to her … to … Evalayne … Layney. She's … my … wife." He looked up at me, startled. "I remember Layney. Where is she?"

I thought about telling him she'd died when I was little. The story he'd told me. It would have been much simpler. But I'd learned over the last couple of months about what happens when people aren't honest, or when the truth is kept hidden.

So instead, for the next several hours, we sat outside and I told him everything I knew, about Mom "dying" when we were little, and what I learned about Eve from Jaxx. When he asked why I'd been in trouble with Jaxx, I told him about the file, about Livvy's involvement with Gunner and the rebels, and then about how I knew Gunner. Over the course of the night, my father learned more about me than he'd ever known in the eighteen years we'd lived together.

He asked questions, and I answered them honestly. We talked about Ana, and Nock, and Maddax, and Livvy. We talked about college, and AHGA, and our previous relationship. At several points, he had tears in his eyes.

But for some reason, I never brought up Gabe. I didn't share how I fell in love with him or how I left him. Nothing about my coming back to the farm, Gabe's rejection, my anger, or me blaming Gabe for Livvy's death – something stopped me. That part of my life wasn't a part I was ready to share yet.

As the sunrise began to cast beautiful pinks and reds across the sky, Father stood up shakily. "I think it's time to get some sleep." I stood and walked over to help him.

We went back inside, and slowly made our way up the stairs to the bedroom where Father would be staying. At the doorway, he paused, "Calyssa, thank you for tonight." His eyes held tears again.

"You're welcome. It's been good to talk to you."

"We didn't do that much before, did we?"

"No, not really. But you were very busy with work. A lot of people depended on you." I smiled weakly.

"I'm ... I'm so, so sorry, Calyssa. I haven't been a good father."

"I'm sorry if I gave you that impression," I rushed to say. "I didn't mean to. I know–"

"It's not what you said. It's ... well ... I don't exactly know. Not really memories, but feelings that I got as you were talking." He looked down.

"Really, Father, we had a good life. We–"

When he looked up, he had tears running down his cheeks. "Please give me another chance, Calyssa. To be a better father. A better man. I ... I ... I love you, Calyssa."

And for a second, I couldn't say anything.

Then, I put my arms around him, and melted against him, my own tears now streaming down my cheeks, too.

"I love you, too, Father. I love you, too."

Chapter 49

Each day Father grew stronger. Within a month, he was working with Andrew and Nana Jane on projects for the city. Little by little, his memory seemed to be coming back. And as it did, he became more and more like his old self. Focused. Confident. Driven.

Andrew was appointed temporary mayor of SciCity, a position that in the past had always been held by a Green citizen. He selected men and women, Greens and non-Greens, to sit on a council for growth, development, and reconstruction.

Specialists were flying in from around the world to help. The dam was going to be repaired, and rebuilding was already happening. Tech was going back up, and new researchers were joining the fight against PKPH. There was even talk that, in the fall, university classes might be able to start up again.

But not everyone was happy. Rebel outbursts continued, more sporadic than the attacks in the past, but enough to keep people on edge. Cases of the PKPH virus seemed to be on the rise again. Father went back to work at a medical facility that was temporarily housing AHGA so he could help try to find a way to stop the virus. We spent less time together as he got more involved with his work again.

With spring coming, Gabe and I used most of our time helping the farmhands. Gabe spent his days out in the fields, and I spent mine working with the animals and with Ben. Nana Jane was still only back a few times a week, so I'd taken over Ben's schooling, too.

One morning, a message chimed on my iBud. I must have missed the call when I was in the shower. Play message, I thought.

Hello, Calyssa. A voice I didn't recognize. You seem to be quite comfortable in your new life. Just remember that things are not always as they seem. Not everyone has good intentions. Oh, and Calyssa, just a heads up - Eve is still out there. And she's watching you. You hold the key to the Viridis Eugenics Project. She's not going to let that go.

That was it.

I immediately went to replay the message, but I received an iBud notification that the message was no longer available. I tried several more times, but it was gone.

All I had now were questions. Who had sent the message? What did they want from me? Was Eve alive? If she was, what was she doing? And, what did this Viridis Eugenics Project have to do with me?

I thought about going to Father, or Nana Jane, or Andrew, but what would I tell them? The message was gone, and there wasn't really a specific threat anyway. Everyone was busy with their jobs. They had enough on their plates right now. This was something I needed to do – to find out about the Viridis Eugenics Project and why I was the key. I found myself wishing that Livvy was here. But she wasn't. This was on me.

One day I'll allow myself to be less strong. But not today. Today I hunt for the truth.

About the Author

Heather S. Ransom is a middle school science, careers, and creative writing teacher in Grants Pass, Oregon, where she lives with the man of her dreams, Marv. When Heather isn't teaching or writing, she and Marv run a pizza pub and cigar shop. You can follow her on Facebook and Twitter (@heathersransom), or learn more about her life and check out her upcoming books on her website, www.HeatherSRansom.ink. She'd love to hear from you!

Special Thanks

Many contributors helped bring life to this novel. Each of you has been invaluable in the light and the dark of the writing process. First, my family:

- Marv, you continually surprise me – I delight in the knowledge that every day will be an adventure with you. I love you.
- Marvin, Danielle, and Jason, I couldn't ask any more of three truly exceptional individuals. You make your mom proud every day.
- Barb and Ron, or, as I like to call you, Mom and Dad, your strength, love, and commitment have meant the world to me.

Next, my supporters, those who read, corrected, challenged, cried, squealed, yelled, demanded, and then reread, only to start the process over:

- Eva, Cyndy, and Virginia, once again, I couldn't have done it without you. There's a special place in heaven for people who edit their friends' books. Yours will be among the best of the best since you just keep coming back to give me more and more.
- My Super-Secret YA Writing Group – Sarah, Laura, Casey, Murakami, and Tracy, thank you for making me look, listen, question, and smile. I can't wait to read the published copies of your stories.
- Sydney Culpepper and Rachel Warren, you brought valued insight that made *Greener* the story it is today. I

appreciate your time, dedication, and help.
- Benjamin and Paige Gorman, my publishers, without you, there would be no *Green* series. Your belief in me has awakened a need to tell the stories I love to the world.

And, finally, my readers. To those of you who read *Going Green* and wanted to know more about Calyssa's story, thank you for your emails, letters, notes, and conversations – your words and pictures are sunshine. The little things you notice make my heart sing.

To each of you –
I'd run with you in the rain.

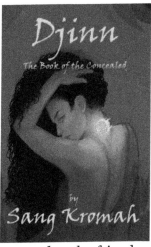